THE LAST MATRYOSHKA

A JO EPSTEIN MYSTERY

THE LAST MATRYOSHKA

JOYCE YARROW

FIVE STAR
A part of Gale, Cengage Learning

GALE
CENGAGE Learning

Detroit • New York • San Francisco • New Haven, Conn • Waterville, Maine • London

This novel is a work of fiction. Names, characters, places, and incidents are either the product of the author's imagination, or, if real, used fictitiously.

The publisher bears no responsibility for the quality of information provided through author or third-party websites and does not have any control over, nor assume any responsibility for, information contained in these sites. Providing these sites should not be construed as an endorsement or approval by the publisher of these organizations or of the positions they may take on various issues.

Set in 11 pt. Plantin.

LIBRARY OF CONGRESS CATALOGING-IN-PUBLICATION DATA

Yarrow, Joyce.
    The last matryoshka : a Jo Epstein mystery / Joyce Yarrow. —
1st ed.
        p. cm.
    ISBN-13: 978-1-59414-887-3
    ISBN-10: 1-59414-887-2
    1. Private investigators—Fiction. 2. Americans—Russia—Fiction. 3. Organized crime—Russia (Federation)—Fiction. I. Title.
PS3625.A7385L37 2010
813'.6—dc22   2010030141

First Edition. First Printing: November 2010.
Published in 2010 in conjunction with Tekno Books and Ed Gorman.

Printed in the United States of America
1 2 3 4 5 6 7 14 13 12 11 10

For Gary—and the "myriads of possibilities"

ACKNOWLEDGMENTS

I received invaluable help in researching and writing this book from Nancy Luther, Yuri Luther, Ilya Eshai of the Moscow Criminal Police, Moreen Littrell, Lyuda West, Jane Isenberg, Pete MacDonald, my editor Libby Malin Sternberg, and, as always, my brother Rick Smith.

the detective runs down digs up
uncovers exposes and brings to light
what we refuse to touch but can safely see
from the other side of the TV screen
munching genetically modified food
to put us in the mood

the detective seizes embraces squeezes
the shadow side
her pain is un-a-nesta-sized
staggering under the weight
of what we're not prepared to know
preferring spectator sports
and bottles of pills that kill
the impulse to go

the poet stares with bright hot eyes
investigates and penetrates the ring of lies
floating like a halo over the prize
that no one can win
the poet steadies the arrhythmic heartbeat
turning and tapping in time to the sweet street
scaring away with words that flare
tearing up the day
laying down the dare

the poet waits, hibernates and then relates
images from dream to dream
connecting the dots in an unconscious stream
trusting in the end they'll reveal what they mean

the detective collides—the poet rides

PROLOGUE:
VLADIMIR CENTRAL PRISON
1957

Ishkhan estimated four seconds before the boy passed out. He couldn't help but admire the nerve of the *fraier*, or "stuffed deer," as newcomers to the zone were called. To accuse a thief of being an informer in front of his cellmates was nothing short of suicidal.

"Enough!" he commanded, and the would-be strangler, an emaciated but ferocious Ukrainian known as Wolf, reluctantly loosened his hands on the boy's throat.

"I want to talk to him, alone." Within moments Ishkhan's authoritative whisper had emptied the cell.

"Can you give me one reason you are worthy of my protection?"

The boy, whose soft face belied the wiry strength of his body, spat on the floor before answering. "I don't need anyone to look after me."

"So you prefer strangulation to serving your sentence?"

The boy glared at him defiantly. "It's all the same to me."

"Since you're so resigned to your fate, why not tell me about it?"

"Give me a Sobranie and I will."

Amused by his insolence and wondering how the boy knew he had access to such luxuries, the *vor-v-zakonye* (thief-with-a-code-of-honor) complied, handing him a cigarette. They inhaled the pungent smoke, which curled into a hangman's noose above them, as the boy related his story—one more sad tale among the hundreds of thousands told every day in the Russian gulag.

"My father was a general. He was a Red commissar in the civil war and then a hero resisting the Nazis. I never found out why he was arrested. Maybe there were too many medals on his chest and Koba was jealous."

Ishkhan was impressed to hear Stalin's name spoken aloud. All the thieves hated Koba—many of their elaborate tattoos showed him in obscene poses—but in spite of his death four years ago, his apparatus of terror lived on.

"What happened to your mother?"

The boy looked away for a moment, and when he looked back his lips no longer trembled. "She was a foreigner—from France—so she knew they would come for her eventually. On the day she was arrested I was picked up at school by two men. I thought they were taking me to prison, until one of the Cheka agents said, 'Don't be afraid. You're lucky. No labor camp for you.'

"What he meant was that they were taking me to the Home for Children of Enemies of the People, and after I'd been there a while, I thought he might be right—at the Home we ate well, compared to most people, and sometimes I felt strangely happy. But that was because of the drugs they put in our food. I saw a psychiatrist every day. He said that he wanted to help me, that I was confused and wasn't myself. He said I needed to erase all the false memories of my family to make room for my real identity as a good communist.

"When I had had enough, I set fire to my bed in the dormitory, and in the confusion I climbed over the wall. I had a relative—a cousin in Novgorod, and I used the last of my money to pay a truck driver to take me there. I thought I was one of the clever ones until I saw the phony smile on my cousin's face. I knew I couldn't stay."

The boy told Ishkhan how, on the outskirts of Novgorod, he'd fallen in with a band of nomadic train thieves. They taught him to ride in the "dog box"—a contraption fastened to the undercarriage and used to transport tools—his head perilously close to the speeding ground. He and his partner, whose nickname was Tarzan, would stuff themselves so tightly into the small space that they could hardly breathe. Riding this way for hours, they waited for nightfall before pulling themselves up to enter the railcar and relieve the sleeping passengers of their valuables. Then, facing the true test of their profession, they jumped from the hurtling train into the darkness.

The teenager survived the perils of train larceny, but, as he told Ishkhan, "I missed playing music and that was my undoing. One day Tarzan and I were in Leningrad, and as we walked past the conservatory, I told him about my training on the violin and my boyhood dream of becoming an orchestra conductor. On impulse, Tarzan decided to steal me a violin and dragged me inside. We waited outside the practice rooms and the first unfortunate student to take a break had his instrument liberated. It was a student model but to my ears sounded like a Stradivari.

"That same afternoon, we were spotted on top of a train and Tarzan took a flying leap to freedom. I should have followed, but I couldn't bring myself to damage the violin. Instead, I climbed down the ladder, right into the arms of the militia."

As he listened, Ishkhan thought fondly of his own seven-year-old son, Feydor. "If your fellow thieves find out your father was a general, they'll make you so miserable you'll wish you had died under the train wheels," he told the youngster.

"Why? We all have the same Motherland."

"You should know by now that the only people thieves hate more than stoolies are 'sukas,' those of us who break the code and serve in the military. Collaboration with society is forbidden. Even *I* have to send my son to school in secret."

The *vor* paced the cell, searching for a solution. "You will need a *klichka* to hide your identity. Since your claim to fame is riding in the dog box under the trains and you are the youngest thief here, an underling, your nickname will be *Pesik*—Little Dog."

★ ★ ★ ★ ★

PART ONE:
NEW YORK CITY
THE PRESENT

★ ★ ★ ★ ★

Feydor surveyed his work. The body was positioned en situ, exactly as it had fallen. He pressed the button for the sixth floor, and the aging elevator jolted, then climbed slowly upward, passing four floors before coming to a stop. Holding the door open with one hand, he reached back with the other to push the button for the second floor and then stepped out. He checked his shoes for blood before climbing the wide stairs leading to the roof. Behind him he could hear the cables creak, as the elevator descended with its unholy burden. Outside, the air smelled of smog mixed with rain. He leaned back on the heavy metal door that had swung shut behind him. Taking his first deep breath since his work began, he peeled off the rubber gloves, freeing his hands to unbutton the blood-spattered shirt and exchange it for the one he'd brought from home. Then, fearful that some insomniac might spot his profile against the skyline, he ran in a low crouch toward the edge of the roof.

At last his design was in motion and it was a thing of beauty, not at all like what *they* had done. He had been merciful and quick. He was far above their level. There was no getting around the fact that he'd sacrificed a life, but he had chosen carefully, not at random like Raskolnikov or out of sadism like Stalin. Some might even say the victim had chosen him.

He found the ladder and climbed over the parapet wall, stepping as lightly and silently as he could on the metal rungs as he descended backward, his heart rate increasing as he passed each window overlooking the fire escape, his eyes averted from any light shining within.

n bathtub to put a permanent chill on the bathing
ce.

my pulse rate approaching normal, I stepped out of the
oted tub and donned the bulky robe that my mother had
me, the one that made me look and feel like a Siberian
y. Although I hated sleeping on a wet pillow, I resisted the
to towel-dry my hair. Unless I wanted my red curls to fizz
ke a head on a hastily poured glass of beer, I would have to
them be. In the living room, I pressed the button on the
ne cradle and, following the beeping tone like a blind person
ossing the street, found the receiver under the couch cushions.

I deleted an obnoxious prerecorded sales pitch from my voice
ail and then listened to the cryptic message that followed it.
"Jo, you come now. No hesitation." There was only one person I
knew with a Russian accent and no manners. No use calling
back. He hated talking on the phone and would only repeat
himself. It must have cost Nikolai a lot to make that phone call
to me of all people. So, in spite of my certainty that he would
never do the same for me, I was dressed and out the door in
five minutes.

The breeze off the Hudson chilled my pores, still open from
the bath. With difficulty, I wiggled the Protégé out of a prize
parking spot on the even side of the street—what a waste. Cutting east through Central Park, I turned right on Second Avenue
and followed it all the way to Houston—then over to Bowery
and south to the Manhattan Bridge, almost halfway to my
destination. The rolling tires of the Protégé pulled a high-pitched
complaint from the bridge's metal deck.

When my mother remarried, seemingly out of the blue, she
had picked a dour but musically gifted Russian from her slew of
boyfriends, for no apparent reason other than his dogged
determination to win her. Plus the fact that he was six years her
junior and—as she confided with total disregard for my im-

CHAPTER ONE

I had been soaking for an hour, inhaling lavende.
in a vain attempt to dissolve the sting of defe.
tough to lose, even when your opponent is someon.
But to relinquish a seven-point lead in the third r.
slam to a semi-literate wannabe, a phony whose on
for stringing together profanities and packing overble
tion into his so-called *poems*, that was unbearable.

I slipped beneath the water to wet my hair in prepara.
applying the green tea shampoo. Gripping the sides of the
was about to pull myself up when those familiar strong fir.
wrapped themselves around my throat. I pushed upward
hard as I could, my palms braced on the bottom of the tub, b
his grip was too strong. Dizzy from lack of oxygen, I struggled
to remain conscious as the pressure on my windpipe grew. Blue
and green phosphenes sparkled in the suffocating darkness. A
persistent voice in my head kept telling me *this isn't real*, but my
pounding heart disagreed and the sense-memory threatened to
engulf me completely. Forcing myself to open my eyes, I gradually gained control of my breath, focused on thinking those
calm thoughts.

I had worked hard to rid my consciousness of the fallout
from last year's attack. A murder suspect in a case I was working on had come close to killing me, and it wasn't with his good
looks. There's nothing like having someone try to drown you in

your own bathtub to put a permanent chill on the bathing experience.

With my pulse rate approaching normal, I stepped out of the claw-footed tub and donned the bulky robe that my mother had given me, the one that made me look and feel like a Siberian Husky. Although I hated sleeping on a wet pillow, I resisted the urge to towel-dry my hair. Unless I wanted my red curls to fizz up like a head on a hastily poured glass of beer, I would have to let them be. In the living room, I pressed the button on the phone cradle and, following the beeping tone like a blind person crossing the street, found the receiver under the couch cushions.

I deleted an obnoxious prerecorded sales pitch from my voice mail and then listened to the cryptic message that followed it. "Jo, you come now. No hesitation." There was only one person I knew with a Russian accent and no manners. No use calling back. He hated talking on the phone and would only repeat himself. It must have cost Nikolai a lot to make that phone call to me of all people. So, in spite of my certainty that he would never do the same for me, I was dressed and out the door in five minutes.

The breeze off the Hudson chilled my pores, still open from the bath. With difficulty, I wiggled the Protégé out of a prize parking spot on the even side of the street—what a waste. Cutting east through Central Park, I turned right on Second Avenue and followed it all the way to Houston—then over to Bowery and south to the Manhattan Bridge, almost halfway to my destination. The rolling tires of the Protégé pulled a high-pitched complaint from the bridge's metal deck.

When my mother remarried, seemingly out of the blue, she had picked a dour but musically gifted Russian from her slew of boyfriends, for no apparent reason other than his dogged determination to win her. Plus the fact that he was six years her junior and—as she confided with total disregard for my im-

Chapter One

I had been soaking for an hour, inhaling lavender-scented steam in a vain attempt to dissolve the sting of defeat. It's always tough to lose, even when your opponent is someone you admire. But to relinquish a seven-point lead in the third round of the slam to a semi-literate wannabe, a phony whose only gift was for stringing together profanities and packing overblown emotion into his so-called *poems,* that was unbearable.

I slipped beneath the water to wet my hair in preparation for applying the green tea shampoo. Gripping the sides of the tub, I was about to pull myself up when those familiar strong fingers wrapped themselves around my throat. I pushed upward as hard as I could, my palms braced on the bottom of the tub, but his grip was too strong. Dizzy from lack of oxygen, I struggled to remain conscious as the pressure on my windpipe grew. Blue and green phosphenes sparkled in the suffocating darkness. A persistent voice in my head kept telling me *this isn't real,* but my pounding heart disagreed and the sense-memory threatened to engulf me completely. Forcing myself to open my eyes, I gradually gained control of my breath, focused on thinking those calm thoughts.

I had worked hard to rid my consciousness of the fallout from last year's attack. A murder suspect in a case I was working on had come close to killing me, and it wasn't with his good looks. There's nothing like having someone try to drown you in mense embarrassment—was the only one virile enough to keep pace with her. After their wedding, Nikolai's attitude toward me grew increasingly hostile. He tolerated my visits but refused to recognize any family ties between himself and the daughter of another man. Which was fine by me. And since the man would rather be eaten by wolves than ask me for a favor, there was no doubt in my mind that tonight's would be a big one.

A few minutes after merging onto Ocean Parkway from the Prospect Expressway, I turned left on East 15th and spotted the blue and whites, their red lights flashing in front of Mom's apartment building. As far as I knew, she was still out of town, visiting a friend in Connecticut. I parked and, working on my story as I went, made my way down the one-way street, past well-kept, redbrick apartment buildings punctuated by dilapidated single-family homes. Halfway down the block I came up with a plan that required me to backtrack and retrieve a small paper bag from the glove box of my car.

At the crime scene perimeter a uniformed officer motioned for me to stop, bloodshot eyes saying *what now?* "Sorry ma'am, no one's allowed in or out." Two other cops, stamping their feet to keep warm, gave me the curious eye.

"I'm staying with my mother. She lives in 5J." Pulling out the paper bag from my purse, I held up the vial of Hydrocodone. "My mom needs these. I promised I'd get them to her by dinnertime, but I got held up at work, had to work an extra shift, so I'm late as it is. If she doesn't get these right away she'll—"

"What's your name?" The patrolman interrupted before I could provide more unwelcome details about my mother's health.

"Epstein. Jo Epstein." I handed him my driver's ID before he could ask, but there was no way I was going to complicate things by showing him my PI license. While he checked out the name on the bottle, I gave thanks that after signing hundreds of watercolors as RLE—Ruth Lynn Epstein—my mother had chosen to keep my father's name when she remarried.

"Wait here," commanded the officer, striding into the vestibule. Through the glass doors I could see him checking the building directory; then he waved me inside. "I'll walk you up. The elevator is, uh, occupied."

On the second floor, where crime scene tape blocked off half the hallway, he got jumpy, anxious about what I might see.

"Is this where it happened?" I asked, not because I expected an answer but because I knew he'd wonder later why I'd failed to pose the question.

"Lady, you're lucky I let you in the building. Wanna get snoopy, you can read all about it in tomorrow's paper."

As we climbed the stairs, indestructible marble steep and wide in memory of another time, I wondered how Nikolai, given the level of anxiety conveyed by his voice message, might react if this cop decided to accompany me to his front door—or worse yet, invite himself inside. I slowed my pace to a crawl, forcing my escort to halt on each landing and wait for me to catch up. At the fifth floor, I made a show of catching my breath, and by that time he was so anxious to get back to his post that he said a quick, "Take care, lady," and dashed down the steps.

I let myself in, turning a different key in each of the two locks. In the kitchen, starkly lit by a round fluorescent bulb on the ceiling, Nikolai slumped at the table, contemplating a full glass of wine and an untouched tin of sardines. He had those ugly good looks that European men seem to get away with, mouth askew and nose crooked, a shock of hair that was thick and brush-like when he wore it short, as he did now, and a little greasy when he let it grow. I didn't know how many years Nikolai had lived in the U.S., just that he'd been married to my mother for nine of them.

"Have a drink." There was a bottle of Merlot on the table

and Nikolai pointed to a cabinet full of upside-down glasses. His hand shook, but that might have been due to age. After a few sips, I asked, "What happened?"

"I went to rehearsal—a string quartet. They invited me to join two weeks ago." He paused, as if wondering how much he should say. "I had a drink with the cellist, that is why I was so late to come home." Another pause, this time extended.

"What happened?" I asked again.

"There are two men waiting by the elevator. One of them holds the door open for me to enter. Up we go, and then, in between the second and third floor, he pushes the red button. A second later he has a knife in his hand. I am going to give him my money, my ring, whatever, when the other man yells, 'He's going to kill us!' So instead of my wallet, I pull out my gun." Although his stress level had pushed the story into the present tense, Nikolai referred to drawing a handgun as if it were the equivalent of pulling out an iPod and headphones. Given the neighborhood crime rate, maybe it was.

"The robber, he sees the gun, so he drops the knife and—very quick he was—the other man, he grabs it off the floor. I'm thinking, 'Now it's over,' but he surprises me—he throws his arm around my chest and holds the knife at my throat. 'Give me your gun,' he says. I had no choice. And just like that he shoots the robber—in the head—it was so loud in there I thought I'd be a deaf person for the rest of my life."

A man was dead. Nikolai's ears were ringing. Which was worse? He drained his wineglass and held it up, toying with the stem. I could sense anger and frustration building inside of him, and for a moment I thought he was going to hurl my mom's single crystal goblet into the sink. "He was wearing gloves—the kind that doctors wear."

"Latex?"

"Yes, latex. After he shoots the man, he shoves the gun in my ear, and my mind goes blank. I remember to say a prayer to your mother to remember me. But he does not shoot me. Instead, he grabs my hand and makes me take the gun. 'Shoot him. Shoot him or you die.' "

Nikolai's face twitched as he spoke, like an inflated balloon being pulled upward and then let go. "The man was already dead. Why do you think he made me do this?"

"Were you wearing gloves?"

"No." He considered this for a moment. "He wanted my fingerprints." He pushed on the tabletop to leverage himself up.

"You hurt your back?"

"I'm fine," he grumbled, but I wondered. He prided himself on keeping fit.

"I want to hire you, Josephine."

"You can't hire me. I'm family."

He pulled a checkbook out of his back pants pocket, waving it like a baton. "If you won't let me pay you, then recommend someone else who can do the job."

I accepted the check—a $500 retainer that would barely cover a day's work—knowing that if I didn't, and someone else took the case and botched it, my mom would be the one to suffer. Always independent, Ruth put up a good front most of the time, but she was not herself lately, as was made clear by the story Nikolai had told me during my last visit. How he'd gone to fetch her at the senior center at one o'clock like he always did and found her wandering on the wrong side of King's Highway, insisting that she knew the way home.

"Let's start with the victim," I said, retrieving a notebook and pen from my purse. "What did he look like?"

Nikolai closed his eyes, forcing himself to focus on the details of a grisly scene that I imagined would soon be replaying itself ad nauseam in his mind. "He looked familiar. Like someone I might see around the neighborhood. He wore a cheap nylon windbreaker, the kind they sell at the dollar store."

"What about his face?"

"Pale, but his hair was dark, curly like a lamb's. His eyes were brown, I think. Afterward, all I could bear to look at were his feet. I was thinking, when I die please may I not be wearing dirty running shoes."

"Tell me about the other man."

Nikolai walked to the window and looked out at the street. Perhaps he was constructing a face to sell me—maybe borrowing features from his neighbors, many of whom by now had been pulled from their beds by the flashing lights on the street, the universally hypnotic force of calamity.

"Not so easy to describe," he said, his back stiff, one arm twitching. "Russian, but almost no accent when he spoke."

"Then how could you tell?"

"The same way you Americans recognize each other in a foreign country—it is the way we are. I could not see the color of his hair because of the hat—it looked like felt, old-fashioned, maybe a Fedora—and beneath it he wore dark glasses, like mirrors, and a thick scarf, covering half his face."

"That's helpful," I said, although his description brought to mind a 1930s crime boss who doubled as a ski instructor. "You have no idea who this man is or why he would have done this?"

He turned around, his back to the window, and shook his head no.

"What happened after you fired the gun?"

"He took the gun away from me and tightened the knife against my throat. I closed my eyes, getting ready to die if one can do such a thing. Then I felt the elevator moving. It stopped at the third floor, and he pushed me out. Somehow I got upstairs and inside the apartment. I don't remember that part very well."

"Do you know if you tracked any blood on the stairs?"

"I took off my shoes." There was something in his face when he said this, a sly knowingness rooted in a past I knew nothing about. He looked around the kitchen as if to make sure the table and chair, the walls, were still there. "Thank you for coming, Jo. You had better go now."

Like it or not, he was now a client, so I swallowed my resentment at his preemptive tone and said, "The surest way to bring the police to your door is for me to leave your apartment at four A.M."

"You know where your mother keeps the bedding."

I grabbed some sheets out of the hall closet. Then I pulled the lime green slipcover—adorned with white and pink roses climbing trellises toward eternity—off the single bed in the living room that did double duty as a couch. The early morning rush of steam was reaching its peak and the atmosphere in the apartment was stifling. I asked Nikolai to let in some air. It was a complicated procedure, involving a long metal pole with a hook at the end. He poked this apparatus upward through a gap in the security gate, catching the latch at the top of the frame and pulling the window down a few inches.

It was awkward, the two of us getting ready for bed without my mother's chatter as a buffer zone. Five years ago I had stayed with the two of them while I waited for my newly rented apartment to be repainted, growing increasingly nervous about moving into a place where the previous tenant had committed suicide. During those endless two weeks I had learned to tiptoe around Nikolai's obsessions. If so much as a pencil was moved from its accustomed place, he would go on the hunt like a dope fiend looking for the last fix on Earth. Consequently, I'd spent as little time in 5J as possible, and as much as I could on the floor below, with Ludmilla and Sasha and the crowd of Russian music fans who flocked to their house for the concerts they held in their living room on Friday and Saturday nights.

I was half-dressed when the doorbell rang at eight A.M. All I could see through the peephole was the top half of a fidgety woman in a uniform. I slipped on my jeans and opened the door to a thin, bleached-blonde Hispanic, who introduced herself as Detective Ortiz. Nikolai appeared and invited her into the kitchen, where the detective seemed to enjoy his chicory-flavored coffee as much as I detested it.

"This is a routine procedure. We're interviewing everyone in the building to ask where they were between midnight and three A.M."

"Did something happen?" asked Nikolai, his cool demeanor speaking to years of experience perpetrating the everyday deceptions so necessary for survival in what was once known as the Soviet Union.

The Sergeant's answer had a scripted quality. "I'm not at liberty to provide the details, but a crime has been committed. I need to confirm your identity, a driver's license or a birth certificate, and to ask you a few questions."

I went first. Assuming that Ortiz had read the activity report from last night, I stuck to my story and described the officer who had let me cross the police line to deliver medicine to my mom.

"That would be Officer James," Ortiz said. "Is your mother at home now?"

"She went out early. She helps serve breakfast at the senior center," I ad-libbed, the truth being that Ruth was out of town and it was me, not her, who needed the Hydrocodone for back pain. Fool that I was, I'd put a kink in my back by working out on that new side-to-side machine at the gym.

The soft-spoken detective seemed satisfied and turned her attention to Nikolai. He answered her questions like a celebrity dealing with an up-and-coming reporter. "I was home all evening. I remember I had reached the last page of *The Russian Passenger* when Jo arrived. Have you read it? If not, you should. So much suspense—I couldn't put it down."

I knew he was overdoing it, but the Sergeant made a few more notes on her clipboard and stood up briskly. "Thanks for your cooperation, Mr. Kharpov," she said, as Nikolai saw her to the door.

Back in the kitchen, he cleared the breakfast dishes off the table and carried them to the sink, as if this would make it all go away.

"You told me you were at a rehearsal last night. Which one of us did you lie to?"

"It's complicated."

"I'm not asking you to triangulate Neptune and a speeding comet. Tell me where you were."

"I was driving, that's all."

"You mean home from rehearsal?"

"No, I mean driving." He was wiping the silverware dry with a dishcloth, polishing each piece with agonizing slowness before placing it carefully in its designated compartment in the drawer. The kind of behavior that drove me crazy.

"So you didn't tell the officer about the rehearsal because she would have checked it out and that's not where you were?"

He ran out of utensils and started in on the cups. "On Tuesday nights I drive for Avenue L Car Service. The rent never stops rising—I've got to do *something*." He waved his arm at the doorway, as if someone were standing there. "Your mother doesn't know. I tell her I practice and go out with friends afterward. That way she is not worrying the whole time, the way she does, that I've been robbed, or worse."

I was tempted to say that worse had already happened. He disappeared into the other room and came back with a plastic bag. "If you would dispose of these I'd be grateful."

I thought of a million reasons not to, but I took the bag. "What's in it?"

"You're the detective. You work it out." He walked out of the kitchen, a wobble in his gait I hadn't noticed before.

CHAPTER TWO

"Jo! What a nice surprise. To see you is most pleasurable." It was Ludmilla with her husband Sasha at her side. We were in the lobby, which they had entered from the street just as I came down the stairs. I was in no mood for chitchat, but I surrendered gracefully. To be rude to Ludmilla would be tantamount to punching out a puppy for wagging its tail.

"Did you hear the commotions last night?" she asked.

"Not a thing. I sleep with earplugs when I stay over—otherwise, the sirens from the firehouse . . ." The station was only two blocks away and one of the busiest in Brooklyn.

Sasha put his arm around Ludmilla's shoulders protectively. "They are saying something happened in the elevator."

"That's terrible. The tenants should get together and hire a doorman," I said. They would learn the truth soon enough. Having to lie to your friends is but one of the unpleasant job requirements that should be printed on the flip side of every private investigator's license.

Ludmilla obligingly changed the subject. "We are to present a concert on Sunday night at Dimitri's Palace in Sheepshead Bay. Maybe you can come? Pavel will come and sing for us, the baritone I told you about."

"Join us for dinner before the music," Sasha added, digging into his jacket and pulling out a postcard. A headshot of Nikolai, looking at least ten years younger than his full sixty-five, was artfully blended into a montage of musicians, all Russian I as-

28

sumed, staring out at me from under the Cyrillic text.

"He is going to play a medley—" said Ludmilla.

"Of folk songs arranged by Kutuzov," finished Sasha. These two coauthored their sentences in a way that only old friends, who happened to be married, could.

Last year Ludmilla had translated a poem of mine into Russian and set it to music. One of her protégés, a soprano from Poland, premiered the piece at a Sunday afternoon house concert at the Volodya's. When Sasha "retranslated" the lyrics back into English for me, I discovered that *to understand* had become *to break your head over* and *don't fool me* was now *don't hang noodles on my ears*. No wonder our countries had so much trouble understanding each other.

Sasha bent down to tie his shoe, and Ludmilla, who was holding his arm, struggled to stay balanced on her high heels, her favorite black shawl with gold embroidery slipping down off her shoulders. This short but big-breasted five-foot-one dynamo with chestnut hair cascading down her back was no prude. I'd seen her flirting outrageously with the male artistes she featured at her soirées. This invariably happened after she'd consumed enough Ikon or Stolichnaya to paralyze a normal person. Sasha kept a sharp eye on her, masked as tolerant amusement but fooling no one. Now I saw him give her hand an almost imperceptible tug.

They took turns giving me hugs, followed by traditional kisses on both cheeks. "Remember, do not forget the concert," Ludmilla said, the shine of her burgundy lipstick augmented by a flash of sunlight bouncing off the lobby mirror.

Trapped in rush hour traffic creeping toward Manhattan like a giant segmented worm, I had plenty of time to fume at Nikolai. Inch by inch on Prospect Parkway I relived my dutiful visits to Brooklyn over the past six years, each one ruined by innuendos about my latest reversion to being single or sarcastic remarks about my inappropriate profession (for a woman, that is). The man never had an unpleasant thought he didn't share. He had brought these troubles on himself, I was sure of that. And now I had a bag of his bloody clothes in my trunk.

Never let them pin one on you. By *them,* Stan Reese had meant our clients. Although my memories of Los Angeles were becoming as faded as the leaves of the sun-drenched palm trees that struggled for survival in front of Stan's detective agency in Torrance, his words of advice had a way of echoing in my ear.

Stan had supervised my apprenticeship, first burying me in paperwork and then, when I'd earned his trust, saddling me with all the humdrum tasks that filled the boring life of a fledgling private investigator. I was the one who Stan sent out when garbage needed to be sorted in search of important evidence. It was me who shot all the pre–digital age tapes of insurance fraud perpetrators mowing their lawns and painting their houses in spite of their "injuries."

I stayed with Stan for two years after qualifying for my license, and then set up on my own, enjoying some success as a class-A insurance investigator and "divorce consultant." Until one of my clients pushed her lawyer husband out of his penthouse office window, using evidence I'd provided as an excuse for her crime. The repercussions from this episode put the kibosh on my marriage to my profession as well as the one to my second husband. Goodbye L.A., hello Manhattan.

An hour later, I beat out an uppity Prius for a parking spot and walked back three blocks to West 23rd. Unbolting the downstairs door to Scandal's, which was locked up tight during the day, I climbed the stairs to the second floor. I could tell, from the number of cigarette butts and gum wrappers littering the landing, that last night had been a lucrative one for the club. I keyed

—anything?"

[...]e got a name for you, but that's it. Micah Goldman. Don't [...] for details; there's a lid on this one, at least for a day or [...]ut I can give you a contact in Brooklyn—Lenny Grimes. [...]ansferred out of here a few months ago, when one of the [...]tives at the 70th retired. I told Lenny only a fool would [...]e Brooklyn over the Bronx, but this was his big chance to [...] undercover. Lenny isn't one for the rule book, so if you [...] him up he might talk to you."

[...]his was all good. The 70th had jurisdiction over East 15th [...]et. The background noise on Hasim's end of the line was [...]ding. "Gotta go," he said. The Lieutenant's open door policy [...]y have been great for precinct morale, but it was a wonder he [...] any work done.

"Thanks, Hasim. Let me know if I can return the favor."

"Forget it, Jo. But if you should happen to bump into Grimes, [...]k him to call me."

There were seventeen Goldmans listed in the Brooklyn phone [...]ook, and to flush out the one I wanted, I became Serina Del-[...]onte, representative of Ballinger's Funeral Home, calling to [...]ee if she could be of service. After six highly annoyed hang-ups, one lonely soul who kept me on the phone by pretending to know Micah, and one Goldman who spoke only Hebrew, on the eighth call I finally got the reaction I was seeking. "You people are vultures! I wouldn't be surprised if you killed him yourself to get the business. I should report you to—"

"Mrs. Goldman, I apologize for the insensitivity but I've got no choice—if I didn't do this I'd lose my job."

"Try losing a son."

"It must have been terrible when you got the news." It was the first truthful thing I'd said to her, and it didn't make me feel any better.

in the alarm code and tugged hard on the handle of the metal door. My footsteps boomed on the newly stained wood floor and I was greeted by the lingering odor of stale beer, which had combined with perspiration to create whatever the opposite of nostalgia is. Dancing shadows, drawn by streaks of sunlight that had penetrated the dirty windows, gyrated on the pink tablecloths and the tin ceiling

I pulled a can of Medalia d'Oro out of the fridge behind the bar and dumped three scoops into the coffeemaker. Back in my office, I wrote a few checks that would be covered when I deposited Nikolai's retainer. Then I placed a call to Chris Leeds, a reporter who worked the police beat for the *Post*—a paper that left no bloodbath uncovered. I counted Chris as a friend because she didn't keep score and shared information even when she got nothing—or almost nothing—in return.

"It was a slow night, no fatalities," Chris complained, not bothering to hide her disappointment. She was an unabashed ambulance chaser. "We got a stabbing in Brooklyn Heights, three medical emergencies in Brighton Beach—lots of old folks out there—but no shooting on East 15th. I'm sure I would have heard." When it came to violence in New York, Chris was tuned in tighter than an offshore DJ.

It looked like getting an ID on last night's victim wasn't going to be easy. I considered my next move while staring out the window at an Amazon of a woman with writhing snakes for a hairdo and a budding tree branch poised in her grip in midair like a javelin—her target, a mythic male in blue jeans striding through a chrome-walled canyon.

The first thing I did after moving into the office—a cramped space smaller than Idi Amin's conscience, opposite the emergency door and a few steps from the men's room—was to ask Marilyn Searl to paint me a view on the wall opposite my office window. In return, I helped her obtain a peddler's license, which allowed her to sell her paintings on Sixth Avenue free from harassment. Being a big fan of artistic independence, I had left Marilyn to her own devices and now, every day, I took a few moments to enjoy a cityscape that was a cross between Picasso's Guernica and a Ralph Lauren perfume ad.

Chris called back. "You got my curiosity up, so I contacted a Sergeant I know at the 70th. He said they're not going public with the vic's name until the family identifies the body. Actually he gave me a hard time, wanted to know where I got the lead, since the police stayed off the air last night. When I said my source was confidential, he said I should know better, that journalists were not priests and he was happy to see at least some of us doing time."

"Maybe he'll give you a tip so you can apply for a vacancy at the *Times* when the next one of your colleagues goes to jail."

"I'll let that remark go, since you've handed me a scoop. My editor's gonna love this." Chris promised to call me back if she got an ID on the corpse, but from what she'd told me, it didn't seem likely.

I collected a few files and headed down the stairs. After shooting the deadbolt on the downstairs door, I dodged through the 6th Avenue traffic, accompanied by a symphony of angry car horns, determined to reach the Protégé before the parking enforcer could ruin my day.

I was craving a shower but not the one dumped on me as I walked home from my parking spot at 98th and Amsterdam. Unpleasant images of what might happen if Nikolai's bloodstained garments got wet began playing in my head, and I furtively tucked the plastic bag under my denim jacket. I told myself I would dispose of Nikolai's gift as soon as possible, but I had some thinking to do first.

On Broadway, the storeowners were scurrying to pull their

---

racks of cheap clothing and other
downpour. Too tired to go food shopp
there was something at home in the fridg
be eaten.

By the time I walked into the washed-o
ing on West End, I was totally drenched. I i
off the lobby and took a shivering ride in th
elevator, a rundown amenity that failed to
rent. Once inside 9G, I found a place to hide
before stripping off my own and stepping int
hot water revived my spirits, if not my body, b
seed muffin I ate afterward caused a relapse. W
this?

I put a call in to Lieutenant Saleh. "Jo! Where
The last time we spoke you told me you were bus
own agency."

Actually, when last we spoke, it had been my un
to inform him that his nephew Khurram had d
spring avalanche in California. I didn't bring it up.
keep their painful memories close by, ready to tortur
at the first opportunity; others bury the past afte
amount of time. Hopefully Hasim had done the latte

"I'm sorry I haven't been in touch, it's just that—"

"A virus ate your address book," he finished for m
do you need?"

"Some information on a murder victim, last night, B
East 15th Street, male Caucasian."

"Stay on the line and I'll see what I can do."

I switched to the speaker phone and leaned back in the
leather chair, fatigue pressing down on my eyelids. I was
to need a nap if I was going to cover my usual security duti
Scandals without a screw-up.

"Jo—you still there?"

There was a pause while Muriel Goldman made up her mind. Then she told me they had sent a policewoman to her house. "She was so young—I think it was her first time having to tell someone that their—"

I waited, afraid to break our tenuous connection along with the silence.

"My daughter Rebecca is the one who had the courage to go into that place and identify him. She said there was no face left to see." Mrs. Goldman's voice cracked, and I visualized *her* face, distorted by grief, blank eyes staring inward at the terrible image her words had conjured. "If it weren't for the jacket and the wallet, Rebecca told me she would never have signed the papers," she finally said. "Look, you sound like a nice girl but we've already made arrangements with Gladnik's Memorial. We're Orthodox and there are certain rules we have to follow. You probably don't know anything about that, not being Jewish."

I wanted to correct her assumption, but as a secular Jew, I was afraid of losing what little rapport we had. "I do know that burial needs to take place within forty-eight hours."

"That's right, miss. I've got a lot to do, so if you don't mind, I'll say goodbye."

"Thanks for talking with me, Mrs. Goldman." I meant it— I'd been given a lot to go on.

Next I called Gladnik's and a man with crocodile tears in his voice told me that the Goldmans had scheduled a memorial for two P.M. tomorrow, to be followed by a graveside service. And did I have any plans for a final resting place of my own?

With that disquieting question echoing in my brain, I closed the window shades, set the alarm for eight, and fluffed up my pillow. Drifting toward sleep, I made a mental note to water the poor geraniums.

CHAPTER THREE

At nine P.M. I was double-parked on East 15th, across the street and about thirty feet back from the entrance to Mom's apartment building. A creepy feeling, staking out a family member, but Nikolai's reticence had given me no choice.

Within a half hour, he came out—walking fast toward Avenue O, which he crossed, and continued north. I followed as slowly as I could, fairly sure that his body language indicated no awareness of automotive company. Two blocks down he turned left and then ducked into a small building that I recognized as home to the Avenue L Car Service—which, with typical Brooklyn logic, was located on Avenue M.

The white limo that zoomed out of the driveway with Nikolai at the wheel was a surprise. But that was nothing compared to the shock of seeing the three hookers he loaded into the car in front of the Duane Reade on Kings Highway. My mom sure knew how to pick 'em.

Staying two cars back, I followed the limo into Manhattan, where I watched Nikolai drop each girl off at a different address on the Upper East Side. He then killed more than two hours at Bill's Bar and Grill, while I waited in the car.

He left the bar at ten-fifty and at exactly eleven the same three girls were waiting for him on the corner of Lexington and 88th. They were also visible on the display screen of my camera, bare-midriffed and barely out of their teens, arms held across their chests to ward off the cold.

I tailed him for a few blocks, until I was sure he was zigzagging his way to the East River Drive on-ramp, chauffeuring his working girls back to Brooklyn. Since I was late for my own job already, I didn't follow. He'd be hearing from me soon enough.

A wall of noise rebounded off the tin ceiling and hit me as soon as I entered the club. Scandal's was packed, and the Slam was in full swing. The prelim finals tended to attract an enthusiastic crowd, which translated into more booze consumed and more frustration with the judges over controversial calls. It had been a while since I'd actually bounced someone out of the club, but when inebriated people experience disappointment, the potential for trouble is always there. Linda ran a zero-tolerance club, hence my guaranteed employment and office space.

A wraith-like poet occupied the stage like it was a foreign country, her mouth set in a firm line below kohl-outlined, bloodshot eyes. Rocking back and forth on the soles of her feet, she gripped the mic stand with both hands as the words burst out, starting the three-minute timer:

> This broken bottle-edge
> held at your throat
> is no joke
> you should've known I'd reclaim
> what you stole
> I'll tear open your vein
> if you touch my main
> lover man

Trying hard to tune out the rest of this embarrassing performance, I came close to missing the remark that Linda Cammarano tossed at me from her seat at the bar. "Sometimes the judges prefer ghoulishness to talent." Linda patted the stool next to her, and I accepted the invitation.

"You should be grateful you're sitting this one out." She was referring to the fact that my name was not on tonight's sign-up sheet.

An expectant silence filled the room, as Marty Elias took the stage and polled the judges—five audience members, deliberately chosen for their lack of affiliation with any of the poets on stage. They held up their score cards and Marty tallied the results (dropping the highest and lowest scores). "Twenty-seven points for Violet Vane," she announced, her voice crammed with false enthusiasm. Loud booing erupted from a table up front, the regulars voicing their displeasure with the high score. Slam audiences are encouraged to share their feelings, so if you sign up to be a judge you're guaranteed some incoming fire.

Linda ordered me a Steamer, a signal that she wanted to talk. For several years I had known her only as "the giraffe," a tall, thin poet who had to stoop when performing in order to avoid scraping her teased chestnut hair on the low ceiling above the stage. She started competing in the Slam right after dropping out of Sarah Lawrence. And although her satirical piece about Heidegger flew right over their heads, even the randomly picked judges could see she was something special. It was like observing a debutante at a poker game or a soccer mom at a heavy metal concert. The torn jeans and tie-dyed t-shirts didn't fool anyone. Which didn't make a damn bit of difference, since every time this woman opened her mouth, she pulled her audience into a world of suburban angst that was every bit as tough and hazardous as the fabled streets of hip-hop.

The rumors about Linda buying the club from Phat Francis had seemed unlikely to me because she was always running low on cash, bumming cigarettes and drinks, creating the impression that she'd put a lot of distance between herself and the money she obviously came from. I didn't see her for a while, racks of cheap clothing and other sale items out of the downpour. Too tired to go food shopping, I could only hope there was something at home in the fridge still young enough to be eaten.

By the time I walked into the washed-out yellow brick building on West End, I was totally drenched. I ignored the mailboxes off the lobby and took a shivering ride in the mahogany-paneled elevator, a rundown amenity that failed to justify the inflated rent. Once inside 9G, I found a place to hide Nikolai's clothing before stripping off my own and stepping into the shower. The hot water revived my spirits, if not my body, but the stale poppy seed muffin I ate afterward caused a relapse. Why did I live like this?

I put a call in to Lieutenant Saleh. "Jo! Where have you been? The last time we spoke you told me you were busy starting your own agency."

Actually, when last we spoke, it had been my unpleasant duty to inform him that his nephew Khurram had died in a late spring avalanche in California. I didn't bring it up. Some people keep their painful memories close by, ready to torture themselves at the first opportunity; others bury the past after a decent amount of time. Hopefully Hasim had done the latter.

"I'm sorry I haven't been in touch, it's just that—"

"A virus ate your address book," he finished for me. "What do you need?"

"Some information on a murder victim, last night, Brooklyn, East 15th Street, male Caucasian."

"Stay on the line and I'll see what I can do."

I switched to the speaker phone and leaned back in the creaky leather chair, fatigue pressing down on my eyelids. I was going to need a nap if I was going to cover my usual security duties at Scandals without a screw-up.

"Jo—you still there?"

"Yes—anything?"

"I've got a name for you, but that's it. Micah Goldman. Don't ask me for details; there's a lid on this one, at least for a day or two. But I can give you a contact in Brooklyn—Lenny Grimes. He transferred out of here a few months ago, when one of the detectives at the 70th retired. I told Lenny only a fool would choose Brooklyn over the Bronx, but this was his big chance to work undercover. Lenny isn't one for the rule book, so if you look him up he might talk to you."

This was all good. The 70th had jurisdiction over East 15th Street. The background noise on Hasim's end of the line was building. "Gotta go," he said. The Lieutenant's open door policy may have been great for precinct morale, but it was a wonder he got any work done.

"Thanks, Hasim. Let me know if I can return the favor."

"Forget it, Jo. But if you should happen to bump into Grimes, ask him to call me."

There were seventeen Goldmans listed in the Brooklyn phone book, and to flush out the one I wanted, I became Serina Delmonte, representative of Ballinger's Funeral Home, calling to see if she could be of service. After six highly annoyed hangups, one lonely soul who kept me on the phone by pretending to know Micah, and one Goldman who spoke only Hebrew, on the eighth call I finally got the reaction I was seeking. "You people are vultures! I wouldn't be surprised if you killed him yourself to get the business. I should report you to—"

"Mrs. Goldman, I apologize for the insensitivity but I've got no choice—if I didn't do this I'd lose my job."

"Try losing a son."

"It must have been terrible when you got the news." It was the first truthful thing I'd said to her, and it didn't make me feel any better.

in the alarm code and tugged hard on the handle of the metal door. My footsteps boomed on the newly stained wood floor and I was greeted by the lingering odor of stale beer, which had combined with perspiration to create whatever the opposite of nostalgia is. Dancing shadows, drawn by streaks of sunlight that had penetrated the dirty windows, gyrated on the pink tablecloths and the tin ceiling

I pulled a can of Medalia d'Oro out of the fridge behind the bar and dumped three scoops into the coffeemaker. Back in my office, I wrote a few checks that would be covered when I deposited Nikolai's retainer. Then I placed a call to Chris Leeds, a reporter who worked the police beat for the *Post*—a paper that left no bloodbath uncovered. I counted Chris as a friend because she didn't keep score and shared information even when she got nothing—or almost nothing—in return.

"It was a slow night, no fatalities," Chris complained, not bothering to hide her disappointment. She was an unabashed ambulance chaser. "We got a stabbing in Brooklyn Heights, three medical emergencies in Brighton Beach—lots of old folks out there—but no shooting on East 15th. I'm sure I would have heard." When it came to violence in New York, Chris was tuned in tighter than an offshore DJ.

It looked like getting an ID on last night's victim wasn't going to be easy. I considered my next move while staring out the window at an Amazon of a woman with writhing snakes for a hairdo and a budding tree branch poised in her grip in midair like a javelin—her target, a mythic male in blue jeans striding through a chrome-walled canyon.

The first thing I did after moving into the office—a cramped space smaller than Idi Amin's conscience, opposite the emergency door and a few steps from the men's room—was to ask Marilyn Searl to paint me a view on the wall opposite my office window. In return, I helped her obtain a peddler's license, which allowed her to sell her paintings on Sixth Avenue free from harassment. Being a big fan of artistic independence, I had left Marilyn to her own devices and now, every day, I took a few moments to enjoy a cityscape that was a cross between Picasso's Guernica and a Ralph Lauren perfume ad.

Chris called back. "You got my curiosity up, so I contacted a Sergeant I know at the 70th. He said they're not going public with the vic's name until the family identifies the body. Actually he gave me a hard time, wanted to know where I got the lead, since the police stayed off the air last night. When I said my source was confidential, he said I should know better, that journalists were not priests and he was happy to see at least some of us doing time."

"Maybe he'll give you a tip so you can apply for a vacancy at the *Times* when the next one of your colleagues goes to jail."

"I'll let that remark go, since you've handed me a scoop. My editor's gonna love this." Chris promised to call me back if she got an ID on the corpse, but from what she'd told me, it didn't seem likely.

I collected a few files and headed down the stairs. After shooting the deadbolt on the downstairs door, I dodged through the 6th Avenue traffic, accompanied by a symphony of angry car horns, determined to reach the Protégé before the parking enforcer could ruin my day.

I was craving a shower but not the one dumped on me as I walked home from my parking spot at 98th and Amsterdam. Unpleasant images of what might happen if Nikolai's bloodstained garments got wet began playing in my head, and I furtively tucked the plastic bag under my denim jacket. I told myself I would dispose of Nikolai's gift as soon as possible, but I had some thinking to do first.

On Broadway, the storeowners were scurrying to pull their

and then, one Wednesday night when I'd come in early to sign up, there she was. But instead of sitting at her usual place in front of the bar, she was behind it, and in place of her usual grubby outfit, the giraffe was wearing a designer dress, pearls, high heels and, incredibly, pantyhose. I didn't bother to hide my amazement. "What's wrong with acting the part?" she asked. The expression on her face was so consistently ironic that I couldn't tell if she was offended or amused.

Lots of poets thought it was a shame when she quit slamming, but Linda insisted that if she competed—even for a symbolic twenty-five-dollar prize—it would look too much like conflict of interest, or worse yet, like she was using the club as a "vanity stage." Her takeover of Scandal's was also a difficult adjustment for the regulars, who hated her for cutting off their credit. No surprise, since some of them had tabs running longer than a Broadway smash.

Tonight she was wearing a dark green t-shirt dress, cinched at the waist with a yellow cloth belt.

"Jo, I hate to say it, but you're bringing some bad juju into the club."

"You want me to bring in a shaman to purify the space?"

"It's not a joke. The police were here an hour ago."

"How many?" I envisioned a raid, a charge of serving minors. Although Linda had a strict policy, there were always a few youngsters who slipped by. It was my responsibility to catch them. Any mess-up belonged to me.

"There was only one officer, but he had a warrant to search your office."

I felt the muscles between my shoulder blades seize up. "Did you get his name?"

"He flashed a badge and let me take a quick look at the warrant, but then, when I followed him into your office and asked for his name, he threatened to charge me with impeding an investigation and threw me out. Some customers heard him yelling and left. You know how paranoid people get."

"What did the warrant say?"

"Frankly, I was so relieved that the search would be restricted to your office that I didn't pay much attention after that."

"Great. So you've got no idea what the probable cause was?"

"No Jo, I don't."

"What did the cop look like? Was he in uniform?"

Linda stiffened. "You don't get it, do you? Our arrangement does not cover my providing descriptions of law enforcement officers. If this happens again, you'll need to relocate."

"Go ahead. Knock yourself out. Hire a cheap rent-a-cop to intimidate your clientele and drive away business. Who am I to stop you?" As I shoved my way through the crowd, I chided myself for having put so much effort into tracking down the itinerant poet Linda had invited to stay at her apartment during the poetry festival last year. Artistically bankrupt but richly talented when it came to larceny, the woman had stolen Linda's identity and charged more than $15,000 worth of goods on her credit card by the time I cornered her in a motel room in Atlantic City. Evidently the giraffe's gratitude finished second when competing with self-interest.

The cop, if that's what he was, had closed my office door but left it unlocked. The mess wasn't the worst I'd seen, but the feeling of invasion infuriated me so much that my hands shook as I picked up the file folders the intruder had dumped all over the floor.

When I moved my office from the walk-in closet in my apartment to Scandal's, it never occurred to me that having a more public face on the business could mean trouble. I had only considered the advantages: the steep discount on meals and the prospect of picking up some work from customers who were sober enough to read the gilt letters etched on my opaque glass door on their way to the john. As it turned out, I did take on some new clients for whom I handled lightweight assignments, mostly troubles they'd put off dealing with, like collecting gambling debts (I referred them to my more Hulk-like colleagues) or locating lost relatives old enough to be milked for a place in the will. Now it looked like Scandal's clientele would have to look elsewhere for investigative services.

In a half hour I'd determined that nothing was missing, which meant that the invasion was either an exercise in intimidation or a search for something that wasn't there. I thought of Nikolai's plastic bag sitting on the floor of my bedroom closet. It was a lucky break, my choosing to hide his clothes in the apartment rather than somewhere in my office. Too bad I didn't feel confident enough in his story to dispose of the evidence entirely.

The rest of the night kept me too busy to speculate further on why a cop—or someone impersonating one—would rifle through my files. Two pickpockets were working the stairs and I didn't spot them until a group of tourists from Prague turned up with empty pockets when the time came to pay their bill. I barely escaped being barfed on by one of the regulars while I was coaxing her into a taxi. These events predictably happened in the early morning and were part of what I called "phase three."

Scandal's was like a woman who dressed down every night, progressively shedding her layers of respectability. For dinner she wore her business clothes—hosting those who were out to impress a client with trendy insider dining and phony "I bumped into so-and-so" stories. The poetry slam loosened things up— definitely casual—but some basic coherence was still required to deliver words from the stage. It was after hours when Scandal's jettisoned her inhibitions and stripped to her undies, sleek lingerie, thongs, whatever was handy. At that point it was my job to prevent bad things from happening—to keep an eye on what went on in the bathrooms that wasn't related to hygiene, to listen for voices that crossed the boundary from boisterous to confrontational, and to make sure it was the drinks, and not the police, that kept coming.

CHAPTER FOUR

Thirteen years ago, Lawrence Avenue was the scene of daily protests staged by the Haitian community. They had every reason to be upset. Abner Louima had been sodomized with a broomstick while in police custody, resulting in a punctured bladder and a severed colon. The case was brought to trial ten years ago and the officers responsible were serving their time. Still, the brickwork curving over the entrance to the 70th Precinct had served as the backdrop for so many TV broadcasts that today, walking up the steps, I felt like I was entering a movie set rather than a police station.

Having never believed in guilt by association, I tried to put these grim thoughts aside upon entering the building. The weekend duty officer—a bulldog of a man with tufts of thick white hair half covering his scalp and a name tag reading *Sergeant Kefauver*—was busy filling out some forms on a clipboard. He took his time acknowledging my presence.

"I'm here to see Detective Grimes."

Kefauver shook his head. "I got no one by that name," he said, not bothering to consult the roster.

I couldn't very well say "Lieutenant Saleh from the 42nd in the Bronx told me that Grimes is undercover, so won't you please tell me what alias he's using," so I tried a new strategy. "You look tired—had a busy night?"

"You a reporter?" he countered.

"I'm a concerned citizen. My uncle lives on East 15th."

"So? You got some information?"

"If I did—and I'm not saying I do—who would the officer of record be?"

"If you're not willing to state your business, I can't help you." The Sergeant pressed his lips together and returned to his paperwork.

"Alright, you win." I handed him a press pass and produced what I hoped was a convincing sigh of capitulation.

"Is this thing real?" Kefauver asked.

"Printed right off the Internet. Notice the smudge in the right-hand corner."

"I never heard of this rag, *Best of Brooklyn.*"

"You will soon. It's an online paper and I'm writing a piece on the great job you guys are doing keeping the streets safe. My uncle called me—said there were more blue and whites on his block last night than he'd seen since the Dodgers won the World Series in '55."

Kefauver grinned—he was old enough to remember the baseball riots, but probably not by much—and took a cursory glance at the press pass. "Detective Dino Spinelli is the officer you want to talk with. His shift doesn't start until three."

"Thanks, Sergeant, I'll give Detective Spinelli a call." I snatched the press pass off his desk on the way out. It had required calling in a favor from a friend who owned a Mitsubishi Diamond printer. Hi-res is the only way to go.

In the spotless lobby of Gladnik's Memorial, Micah Goldman's relatives perched uneasily on Queen Anne chairs that were artfully upholstered in purple velvet, sipping coffee and waiting for the rabbi. It was easy for me to understand why my mother hated this place. From the polished marble floors, designed to put you in the mood for eternity, to the disinfected air—a heady mixture of scented flowers and something unpleasant underneath, possibly fear—this mausoleum had little peace to offer a recently liberated soul.

Last year, on one of our snail-paced walks through the back streets of Brooklyn, Mom had pointed out Gladnik's, saying "That's where the Orthodox go, very expensive, not for me—I want something simple, Jo." This was not a conversation I wanted to have and I had said so.

"If not now, when?" Ruth responded, with uncustomary candor. "I want to be cremated, no fuss, no muss."

"Okay, okay. I hear you. Any particular place where you'd like your ashes sprinkled?"

"No sprinkling. I want a simple urn."

"Why tell me and not Nikolai?"

"He already knows, but I was afraid you wouldn't take his word for it."

"Why wouldn't I?"

Ruth pinned me with her *I'm wise to you* look and I capitulated.

A few weeks later Mom had hip surgery, followed by a pulmonary embolism that could have been avoided if the ambulance had been allowed to go to a different hospital—one that kept circulation boots in stock and knew when to use them. A month after getting home from rehab, she invited me to dinner and, along with dessert (a low-carb pudding that smelled and tasted like the paste I remembered making from flour and water in kindergarten) presented me with a small cast-iron box.

"What's this? Stalin's long lost confession, still under lock and key?" I liked to tease Ruth about her misplaced affection for my namesake, which dated back to her flirtation with communism in the 1940s and ended abruptly with Khrushchev's revelations about his pathological predecessor. But this had been no joke. It was Ruth's living will, and the little box was now collecting dust on the top shelf of my closet, where I hoped it would stay for a good long time.

A picture of Micah Goldman was displayed on an easel near the entrance to the chapel. His curly black hair matched Nikolai's description, but it was hard to imagine this upright young man either forgetting to shave or choosing to grow the beard stubble that Nikolai so vividly remembered. Two women had been photographed with Micah. The older I assumed was his mother Muriel, who I had talked with on the phone. The younger, most likely a sister, looked familiar. I got out my camera and flipped through the pictures I'd taken when I followed Nikolai on his late-night run. The comparison held. If Goldman knew that his sister was turning tricks and tried to interfere with her "handlers," that might have been what got him killed. How did Nikolai figure in all this? So far he'd told me more lies than truth. I had to ask myself—did my mother marry a pimp? The absurdity of this thought made me laugh out loud, at the same time cementing my resolve to pin Nikolai against the wall and get some answers.

Most of the females at the memorial service were wearing the customary Orthodox attire of ankle-length skirts or dresses, so the two bottled blondes, one in jeans and the other in a mini-skirt, stood out like neon tetras in a tank full of goldfish. They were dressed like tramps but exuded a self-possession and youthful defiance that telegraphed spoiled middle-class brat. When they disappeared into the ladies' room, I followed.

Mini-skirt was busy applying glittering green eye shadow above, around, and possibly in her eyes. Her friend kept busy tying and re-tying a gaudy silk scarf around the waistline of her stiff $250 Blue Cult jeans. Both of them were so absorbed they paid no notice when I entered one of the stalls.

"I can't believe Becky's not here," said Mini-skirt.

"I feel sorry for her mother," replied Blue Cult. "Her son is dead and her daughter might just as well be." There was enough false sympathy dripping from her voice to form a good-sized puddle around the magenta-painted toe nails protruding from the thin silver straps of her high-heeled sandals.

"I don't know what happened," opined Mini-skirt. "Rebecca dressed like an immigrant and I swear she never wore deodorant, but in high school the dumb asses would kill for a chance to sit next to her so they could look over her shoulder during a test. How she became a whore nobody knows."

The tail end of these appallingly insensitive words were drowned out by the clicking of stiletto heels on the tile floor as the girls exited the powder room. Talking trash at a funeral put them on a par with the British tabloids, but I couldn't help but feel grateful to them for providing the name of Goldman's sister and saving me from the unpleasant task of questioning his mother on this of all days.

The small crowd of mourners dumped their paper coffee cups and crumb-covered plates into the garbage as they moved into the chapel, signaling that the rabbi had arrived. I wished Micah Goldman's soul some belated luck and slipped out the front door.

"I hear you've been asking about me."

The street was deserted and the voice had come out of nowhere. I turned around slowly, controlling my instinctive flight response as my fingers searched inside my cluttered purse for the Lady Colt.

"Sorry to sneak up on you," he said. "Kefauver said you were asking for me, so I thought I'd meet the neighborhood reporter who was smart enough to break my cover in just two weeks." *Lenny Grimes.* His round face, fleshy but not fat, wore a sheepish grin, blue eyes set on friendly to disarm. I loosened my grip on the gun.

"Wish I could take the credit. Lieutenant Saleh is a friend of mine. He suggested I look you up. I'm working on the Gold-man homicide."

He took this in. "Private?"

"Yes." I gave him my card.

Grimes grabbed my elbow and pushed me into the entryway of what had been Money-in-Hand Records but was now a deserted storefront. "Detective Spinelli is the case officer. Let him handle this. There are players here who you don't want to tangle with."

"That's usually the case when someone is murdered."

"Suit yourself, Epstein. If you enjoy ducking bullets, that's up to you. But do me a favor. Don't spread my name around." He was already scanning the street, preparing to walk.

"What part of Russia are you from?" I asked.

He ran his fingers through his curly brown hair and surveyed me with new interest. "Far enough east that it's someplace you never heard of," he said.

"You must have some ideas about who killed Micah Gold-man."

"Give me one good reason I should share them with you."

"Did you know his sister was a hooker?" I asked.

Grimes laughed. "You're free to look in that direction. In fact, I would encourage it." He stepped out of the doorway and as he walked away, looked back briefly over his shoulder. "It will keep you out of the crossfire."

Parking on East 15th was always difficult, but on a Saturday morning it rivaled looking for a candle at the supermarket during a blackout. The narrow street was packed with cars that wouldn't be moved until well after sunset. I circled the block twice unsuccessfully, stopping both times to let strolling groups of men in black hats cross the street on their way to the synagogue. Four blocks away, on Ocean Parkway, I squeezed the Protégé into a tight spot behind an Audi with a Midwood Yeshiva window sticker. Walking back on East 15th, I passed two long-skirted women, each holding a toddler by the hand. One of them risked a sidelong glance at my jeans and pullover, which were in flagrant violation of the neighborhood dress code. The other woman entered Mom's apartment building directly behind me. I didn't bother to hold the elevator, which was now minus all signs of crime scene investigation. It being so close to the beginning of Sabbath and all, I knew she would take the stairs. On the ride up, the overpowering smell of disinfectant triggered images of carnage in my head that made me wish I had joined her on the climb.

As soon as I rang the bell, Nikolai opened the door and joined me in the hallway, his voice a raspy whisper. "Your mother's home from Connecticut. You and I need to find an excuse to go outside so we can talk." I told him I'd take care of it, but I wasn't sure I could. Mom was well aware that her husband and daughter were far from buddies.

"Look at you. Coming to Brooklyn twice in one month. I'm not sick, am I?" Ruth joked. She was looking well, in spite of the way that her white hair—which she had stopped dying the color of burnt leaves a few years before—accentuated her natural pallor.

"I need Nikolai's help," I told her. "The woman who owns the club where I work wants to buy a piano." This explanation was not only plausible, it was brilliant, because it brought a smile to Mom's face. Her two favorite people had stopped butting heads, at least for the moment. Nikolai completed the subterfuge by telling her that he was taking me over to Fredrick's to look at some pianos that were a real bargain.

He put on the tan jacket he wore all year round, except for July and August, and as we left the apartment, I noticed he was carrying a parcel wrapped in brown paper, about the size of a shoe box. Bypassing the elevator with a shudder, he paused to wait for me at the top of the stairs. "A good way to keep fit," he said as we descended. We both knew what he meant.

On the street, we were greeted by a thin drizzle.

"Do you know someone named Micah Goldman?"

After the briefest of pauses he answered. "Not that I recall. Should I?"

"You met in the elevator last night—apparently he's the one who didn't get off."

"All you found out was his name?" whined Nikolai, making me wish I'd been less tactful and said something like, "he's the man whose head you disintegrated."

By the time we arrived at the playground off East 18th Street, where the screams of children jumping off the go-round prevented their mothers from overhearing our tense conversation, the rain had stopped.

"I know about your taxi service," I said as we sat down on a reasonably dry bench.

"You know nothing," responded Nikolai. He opened the parcel gingerly, as if it contained something fragile—or explosive. From beneath a wad of tissue paper, he pulled out a painted wooden doll, seven or eight inches high.

"This came in the mail last week."

"It's a Matryoshka," I said, showing off one of the ten Russian words I knew.

"It's pronounced ma-troo-shka," said Nikolai, not one to miss an opportunity to point out my failings.

The doll he handed over was about eight inches high and large enough to hold five or six smaller versions of itself. Somewhere in Russia, a factory worker had shaped this Matryoshka on a lathe, and then an artist painted the stern face of a judge, framed by an ornate white wig flowing down the front of his black robe. This wasn't a typical Matryoshka, like the peasant dolls I'd seen in store windows in Brighton Beach, painted en mass in colorful peasant costumes to please the tourists. For one thing, it was shaped like a rounded bullet, with no neck. Although the colors weren't faded and the lacquer finish had been polished to a high gloss, my guess was that it was very old.

"Look inside," Nikolai said.

Carefully I pulled off the judge's head, expecting to see an exact replica inside. Instead, a piece of paper was neatly curled around the empty nest. "I know I should have put this in plastic as soon as it arrived," said Nikolai, always on the defensive, "but someone who went to all this trouble to be anonymous isn't going to leave fingerprints."

I didn't bother to voice my displeasure—choosing instead to let the rubber gloves and evidence bag I pulled out of my purse speak for themselves.

It was a Xerox copy, readable but hastily assembled—letters and blocks of words cut from magazines and newspapers and pasted together. Oddly antiquated yet chillingly anonymous.

YOU RUINED MY SISTER AND NOW YOU WILL SUFFER!

"He—or maybe it's a she—was smart not to send the original," Nikolai said. "They must know how glue can leave traces, that kind of thing."

"So you've no idea who sent this?"

He shook his head emphatically. "There's no return address, but it was mailed from Manhattan. And in case you're wondering, I haven't been playing around with anybody's sister."

I tried to repress my smirk, but Nikolai had a quick eye. "I know what you're thinking. I'm an old man. But in my day . . ." For a moment I glimpsed him resplendent in tux and tails, conducting the Kirov Ballet orchestra, scanning the audience, picking out a beauty, making eye contact, already sure she'll be waiting at the stage door to go home with him.

"Maybe this 'ruined sister' is one of your Wednesday night passengers." This was more than an educated guess, but Nikolai had no way of knowing this. For the first time he looked at me as if I might be smart enough to turn the pages at one of his recitals. I thought he was going to say something, but instead he jumped up from the bench, smashing his foot down on a wind-blown candy wrapper, as if it were a small child about to step off the curb and be annihilated by oncoming traffic.

"When did you start driving for Avenue L?"

Nikolai picked up the wrapper and threw it in the trash can. When he spoke he avoided my eyes. "It's not what you think. I drove for them only one night a week for a year. Then, two weeks ago the dispatcher calls and says that a regular customer is requesting me as his driver, that he wants me for Tuesday and Wednesday nights. The pay was five hundred dollars round trip. I wasn't in a position to refuse, with the rent being raised every six months and your mother's blood pressure medication costing more than pure cut heroin. At least in Russia you could always get what you needed on the black market."

I considered offering to help him pay for Mom's drugs, but I could see this small confession had cost him a lot, and there's a limit to what a man's pride can swallow in one day.

Nikolai watched as I inserted the doll into the evidence bag, along with the crudely threatening letter, and put it in my purse. "I can't stay here," he said. I thought he meant the park, until he added, "You'll have to tell your mother."

"Nikolai, listen to me. I've had it with your cryptic messages and half-truths. You're driving hookers into the city, someone is blackmailing you for murdering the brother of one of your passengers, and even though you've told more lies than a tobacco executive at a Congressional hearing, you expect me to believe that you are innocent. Do I have it right so far?"

He sat down again, slumped over, hands on his knees, studying the ground intently. "I know what you must think of me, Jo. I was crazy to think you would help me and even if you wanted to . . . I won't continue to put your mother in danger."

"If you're thinking of pulling a disappearing act, you'd better consider what it would do to her. Last year, when you were sick, she told me that she didn't think she could live in a world without you."

Nikolai straightened up on his side of the bench and looked at me. "Did she say those exact words?"

"Would I make up something like that?"

"What choice do I have—whatever I do, she suffers." I had seen this before, the eternal pessimism that only those born and raised under a totalitarian regime seemed to have a right to. Still, I couldn't help saying, "This is America. There are options."

Nikolai's dry laugh said otherwise, but at least he was listening.

"She can stay with Uncle Jake until we figure this out," I proposed. "I'll ask him to tell her that he's had a medical procedure or something, that he needs her to look after him. She'll hightail it to Flushing and that will buy us some time." The *us* came out with difficulty.

Nikolai squinted up at the overcast afternoon sky as if watching his previous life disappearing into the stratosphere. He pulled a small tin of cigars from his shirt pocket and lit one up. It filled me with rage that at this crucial time he had the power to shut me out, and by simply ignoring a perfectly good suggestion, ruin my mother's life. But like most recalcitrant people, Nikolai had a built-in sense of exactly how much stonewalling a person can take. "Okay, she can go," he said, standing up to indicate the conversation was over.

We walked back toward the apartment in mutually beneficial silence. There wasn't much to say. We both knew whoever sent the letter and the doll might decide to tip off the police at any moment, and that Nikolai's fingerprints on the gun would cinch the deal.

We stopped at Fruits-A-Plenty and Nikolai picked up some of Mom's favorites—sugar-coated dates from Lebanon and big green apples from upstate. While he was shopping, I consumed a half-melted chocolate bar and called Uncle Jake on my cell, explaining enough of the situation to get him to agree to call Ruth.

When we arrived, breathless from climbing the stairs to 5J, she was already packing. "Your Uncle Jake had no problems flying spy missions over China, but a chest cold and suddenly he's revising his will."

Nikolai wanted her to leave right away, but Ruth insisted we have an early dinner first. "You've got to stay, Jo. You came all this way." You'd think they lived in Nebraska or something.

Uneasily, I accepted the invitation. In spite of her deteriorating sense of direction and sporadic symptoms of blurry thinking—last month she had woken from an afternoon nap during one of my visits and insisted that it was morning—my mother was still pretty sharp. I shouldn't have worried. Her desire for at least the appearance of family unity was stronger than any suspicions she might have had. All through the meal, she entertained us with her stories about the women in her watercolor class at the senior center. She was the most accomplished painter in the class and tended to look down on those eighty-year-old upstarts. "Helen draws great noses but her lips look like zucchinis."

"Maybe she should sell her work at the farmer's market," said Nikolai, taking a second helping of fried kasha with eggs and onions. Ruth's cooking skills, although sporadic, remained intact.

"Stella forgot her hearing aid last week and when Evelyn—

she's our new teacher, so young and pretty and creative—said to 'paint your own private thoughts,' Stella thought she said 'paint your own private parts.' " On her good days, and this was one of them, my mother cracked me up. She was an expert at turning tension into farce. Lord knows she had a husband who had given her plenty of practice.

Nikolai wasn't smiling. "You're a bunch of crazy old ladies wasting your time. You throw some polka dots on a canvas and presto, you're a painter. Art isn't a joke. In Russia, even a schoolgirl learns to imitate the masters."

Ruth looked as devastated as if he'd slapped her. Although she had chosen to put up with the wannabes at the Senior Center, my mother was no amateur and took her painting seriously. She pushed back her chair and stood, keeping one hand on the table to steady herself. "I'll get my things," she said. A year ago, before the bouts of dementia set in, she would have countered his ridiculous remarks with some cutting witticisms of her own.

I held my anger in check, knowing that if I let a single word escape, a torrent would follow and that seeing Nikolai and me go at it would make her feel even worse.

Nikolai called King's Highway Car Service—he wasn't about to use Avenue L—and carried Mom's suitcase out to the elevator. I vowed to deal with him later.

On the ride down, a young couple from the third floor joined us. I wondered—were they blissfully ignorant of the horror recently perpetrated in this claustrophobic space or merely callously indifferent?

An ancient Lincoln town car pulled up to the curb, driven by an even older Bulgarian. I had my doubts about Mom riding with him in view of the hair-raising ride to Park Slope he'd subjected me to a few months ago. But before I could protest, she was in the car. Nikolai leaned in to give her a kiss, and I saw her face lighten as she smiled at him. It wasn't much, but that's all it took these days to put everything right in Mom's world.

Leaning out the window, she pressed a twenty-dollar bill into my hand. "Get yourself a new blouse, the one you're wearing has seen better days."

We've all seen better days, I thought, and the chances for their return are slim. But it wasn't my job to bet on the odds—it was my job to change them. I added a ten to the twenty and handed both bills to the driver. "Two-twenty-one Main Street in Flushing, and there's no need to hurry."

CHAPTER FIVE

I'd always figured that Avenue L Car Service operated out of a storefront on Avenue M because they were not anxious to publicize their location. This made sense, given their habit of telling prospective riders, "We're around the corner and will be there in two minutes," and then showing up at the last possible moment—by which time the caller was ready to settle for not having a heart attack on the mad dash to the airport. After last night, I knew better. The place was a front and most likely for more than just prostitution.

In the small waiting room, where BO and cigarette smoke aggressively competed for dominance, two overweight, sleepy-looking men fulsomely occupied two small chairs, presumably drivers on a break.

"I'd like to speak to the dispatcher."

The un-dynamic duo nodded in tandem toward the back room before returning to their semi-vegetative states. Following the sound of a crackling radio, I found the dispatcher seated at an ugly metal desk. Veton, as the dark blue embroidered letters on his not-so-clean white shirt identified him, raised his head from the microphone clutched in his hand, giving me a clear view of a pointy chin and two puffy bloodshot eyes of indeterminate color. His hair was dyed an awful shade of yellow verging on green.

"What can I do you for?" The accent was Eastern European but that didn't tell me much.

"I'm looking for a part-time job and I heard you might have an opening for a driver."

"Who told you this?" He seemed amused, probably at the idea of a woman having the balls to work with his all-male crew.

"One of your drivers, the other night on the way to—"

Before I could complete this fabrication, the radio sizzled to life like a frying pan hit by a glob of lard. The only words audible to me were "pickup" and "Rockaway" but Veton didn't seem to have any trouble deciphering the transmission. He switched to the soft guttural sounds and singsong tones of what I assumed to be Russian.

While he was preoccupied, I inched toward the wall on my right, where someone had haphazardly Scotch-taped a business license as required by law. At forty-four, I wasn't the eagle-eyed youngster I used to be. Ten years ago I could have read the names from across the room: Na Khodu, Inc., dba Avenue L Car Service.

When Veton finished barking orders on the radio, he reached into a drawer, pulling out a piece of paper that he pushed over the desktop. "No job now, but maybe later. Women drivers not a problem here."

Yeah, right. We both knew what he was up to. I'd sooner douse all the cars in my garage with gasoline and light up a cigar than hire you, but since this form proves that I'm an equal opportunity employer, I'm going to insist that you fill it out.

While filling the blanks with fictitious information, I let it drop that I was available on Wednesday nights. A scowl crawled across his features. "No opportunity now. Maybe I call you, maybe not." The radio distracted him again. I'd obtained a lead on who owned the business and was tired of playing charades, so I made my exit.

The three-mile evening walk to Brighton Beach did me good. I wished I could say the same for my hair, which humidity turns into brillo.

Rows of single-family homes, some still wrapped like mummies in their original asphalt shingles, showed off last summer's wilted crop of impatiens and pansies in their tiny but well-tended front yards. The ambience could not have been more different than Manhattan's. Not a high-rise or a Starbucks in sight. Give it time.

I had passed by Russian Treasures many times before but never ventured inside. It was almost eight o'clock, but the heavily reinforced front door, located below street level, was still open, and a bell chimed when I entered. In keeping with the crowded display in the window, every shelf, counter, table, and chair was covered with knickknacks—porcelain figurines, gold-plated music boxes, ornate metal trays, wooden jewelry, "stone paintings" made out of gems and stones, religious icons, and thick, glazed pottery pieces that looked like they'd been made to last a thousand years. Embroidered napkins and scarves hung from the walls and, lined up in rows on the shelves of a bookcase in the corner, the Matryoshka dolls kept watch. The tallest one, about fifteen inches in height, was painted so that her hands appeared to be holding an icon of the Virgin Mary and baby Jesus.

"That one has fifteen pieces, each representing a different Russian saint," said the proprietress, who was dressed in basic black, probably as a way of making herself visible to customers amidst her store's riot of color. Blonde hair piled high on her head and held in place by an ornate mother of pearl barrette, she was seated on a stool behind a glass display case, polishing a painted lacquer box.

She held up the box for my inspection. Against a star-filled sky, an old peasant, a little girl, and a cat gazed upward in awe at a golden stag pawing the snow-covered roof of their hut. "See? He has five branches of antlers, the Silver Stag. It's from a folktale—very famous in Russia."

I introduced myself, and she told me her name was Marya. Then I showed her the *Judge*. Marya's sea-green eyes assumed the shrewd look of the appraiser. She put away the lacquer box and took the doll from me, pulling it open and miming a disappointed face when she saw there was nothing inside. "Only one? It looks like number three in a set of five or six, an unusual shape, very old."

She dipped behind the counter and came back up with a magnifying glass to use for a closer examination. "Someone has gone to a lot of trouble restoring this doll to original condition, but without all the pieces, I'm afraid I have no interest."

"That's too bad," I said, pretending disappointment. "Can you at least tell me where it was made?"

"Sergiev Posad."

"Was he the artist?"

She laughed at my ignorance. "Sergiev Posad is the name of a town, not a person. Most of the early dolls were made there, before the revolution. This one looks like early twentieth century. If you had all six pieces you could get a nice price."

"Is there some sort of registry—a way to keep track of when the more valuable dolls are bought and sold?"

Marya shook her head emphatically. "The collectors are spread out all over the world, and many of the older dolls are in museums. Matryoshki made before the Soviet period were unique and interesting, like yours. But when the Bolsheviks took over production, they standardized the designs and made the workers produce the same glorious peasant women over and over—bright colors but no imagination. Nowadays, the artists are free again to paint what they like—religious, political, humorous—there's no limit to what they can do."

She swiveled on the stool and opened a locked case on the wall behind her. Out of a cardboard box came a six-inch smiling Bill Clinton, an American flag in the background. Opening the doll, I pulled out first Monica, then Paula and Hilary (wearing a scowl) and finally, painted on the tiniest doll, a cigar. Marya chuckled. "It's a special order I'm holding for a customer: Bill Clinton and His Girls."

Seemed to me that Russians had plenty to be cynical about in their own country without picking on ours, but I stifled the urge to share this observation and took back the Judge from Marya. "Where do you think this might have been purchased?"

"You can find valuable dolls on e-Bay or one of the other internet stores, but that's unusual. Most people know what these older pieces are worth and don't try to sell them to the general public—they target collectors who are in the market for something unique. Of course it could be a family heirloom passed down through the generations. Impossible to tell. I wish I could be of more use."

"Actually, you've been very helpful." I looked around for an inexpensive way to show my gratitude and there, hanging on the wall, was a rectangular metal sign, its yellow letters glowing on a black background.

"A good choice," said Marya, ringing up the sale. "The Arbat is my favorite street in Moscow." She scribbled a few names and phone numbers on a pad next to the cash register, ripped off the page and handed it to me. "Maybe one of these collectors will know the provenance of your doll."

I knew I had a long night ahead of me, so I decided I might as well grab something to eat. The store windows on Brighton Avenue were crammed with everything from blue tins of imported black caviar to kielbasa (Russian salami), pickled mushrooms, and, my favorite, Russian chocolates. But it was the poppy seed honey cakes that I found irresistible, priced at a more than reasonable eighty cents each.

I stopped in at a figurine store to buy a tiny statue of a fiddler. After five years it was about time I put something on the mantle of my fake fireplace other than pictures taken in California.

When I heard the elevated tracks start to shake, I ran upstairs, reaching the platform in time to board the train and ride back one stop to collect my car. Five minutes later I was behind the wheel, directly across the street from the Three Minute Parking sign in front of the 24-hour Duane Reade where I had seen Nikolai make his pickup. Tonight, however, only one girl waited, standing to one side of the permanently open automatic door, indifferent to the river of late-night shoppers flowing past her. In contrast to the demure outfit she wore in the photo I'd seen at the funeral parlor, Rebecca Goldman wore a low-cut, turquoise mini-dress and high heels to match. Tall and slender, her black hair pulled back severely from her narrow, falcon-eyed face, she seemed so shy and fragile that it was hard to visualize her going through the motions with a john. When the light blue Mercedes arrived, it blocked my view but not before I saw her walk across the sidewalk in anticipation of entering the car. No white limo tonight.

It was late, not a good time for tailing a vehicle through narrow one-way streets. I drove as slowly as I could without losing sight of the subject. When the driver reached Ocean Parkway, I settled into position two cars back.

The Mercedes crossed the bridge and sped across Houston, turning left on Sullivan Street, into the heart of commercialized Soho, known as Little Italy in the days when I took the subway all the way from the Bronx to hang out with my poet friends in their tenement apartments with the bathrooms down the hall. Rebecca got out in front of The Mantle on Prince. I hustled to locate a parking spot and then walked back five blocks, passing at least ten recently opened eateries and several upscale clothing stores. On the corner of Thompson, the Tarot-reading emporium served as the sole relic of a more exotic but less ostentatious past. This formerly working-class neighborhood, where street festivals put on by the Catholic Church had been the most exciting yearly event, was now a stylish "place to be seen."

I had one hand on the brass door handle of the boutique when I saw the sign—*Closed for Private Showing.* "I'm sorry—this is by invitation only," said the prematurely sallow doorman, dressed for the part in a rock t-shirt and camouflage pants.

"I'll bet you score some big tips tonight. Worked here long?"

"Since two weeks ago. I'm a grad student at NYU," he volunteered, and I knew I had myself a talker. In a few minutes I learned that the lavish party and fashion show in progress at The Mantle was being thrown by Yuri Baranski to celebrate the birthday of his friend Serge Vasilev, owner of the newly opened Russian Banya in Tribeca.

"Banya means steam bath, doesn't it?" I asked to keep his mouth moving.

"It's the place to go when you need to recover from jet lag upon your arrival from Moscow or Paris—massages are only three-hundred dollars, a caviar wrap is one-hundred-fifty. These people know how to live."

Everyone in New York who kept up with such things knew that Baranski was a leading light among the New Russians. American born, he was an internationally known couturier with a knack for weaving mohair, Angora, and cashmere into plain denim to create garments that celebrities drooled over. His well-publicized donations to charity and sponsorship of art exhibits had done a lot to permanently put to rest the image of Russians—prevalent in the 1980s—as vicious gangsters murdering each other in Brighton Beach.

"If I give you a hundred bucks, can you get me in?"

"Forget it—a hundred won't cover the flowers at my funeral

if they catch me."

I could have shown him the phony press pass that the Desk Sergeant at the 70th Precinct failed to pick up on this morning, but there was a strong chance that the Fourth Estate wasn't welcome at the party. Upping the bribe offer might have aroused his suspicions. "The thing is, my girlfriend is in there with a guy who I found out has a rep for date rape. I've got to tell her. You can understand that, can't you?"

He looked doubtful—who wouldn't—but not completely disgusted, so I pressed on. "This is your chance to be a hero," I told him, slipping two fifties into his unresisting hand.

Crossing the threshold of The Mantle—which featured an open bar where customers who paid inflated prices for clothes earned the privilege of "free" drinks—was like entering a designer's conception of a future where all humans are genetically engineered and surrounded by objects as "perfect" as they are. The lighting was indirect, as were the glances thrown my way and immediately withdrawn. I might as well have worn a sign—*intruder, lacks style, shun at all costs.*

Feeling the doorman's eyes on my back, I assumed the walk of a woman on a mission—passing racks of men's clothing fashioned out of custom tweeds and cotton twills that no man I knew would ever be able to afford—moving straight toward Rebecca, who stood at the bar, her high-heeled, blue-green shoes abandoned on the floor beside her bare feet.

"I'm Jo Epstein. First let me say how sorry I am for your loss."

"How did you know about my brother? It hasn't been in the paper." Behind dark glasses, Rebecca's eyes were red and puffy. The sedated tone of her voice contradicted the challenge in her words.

Not wanting to lie during the first thirty seconds of our acquaintanceship, I avoided the question and asked one of my own. "Is it true he was upset about your working for the escort service?"

I'd never seen brown eyes freeze before. "I'm going to get Yuri," she said, gaining two inches in height by slipping into her shoes.

I waited with my back to the bar, gulping down a gin and tonic. Might as well quench my thirst before I was thrown out. But Yuri Baranski was all smiles, striding toward me in his gleaming loafers and light gray wool suit, probably of his own design, the cost of which would cover a year's worth of mortgage payments if my apartment ever went condo.

"I haven't had the pleasure," he said, shaking my hand vigorously. His thick raven hair, artfully disheveled and streaked with varying shades of purple and yellow, snaked over his ears, a style that, if anything, made him look older than the forty years I guesstimated.

"My name is Jo Epstein. I'm a private investigator looking into the murder of Micah Goldman."

Baranski's thin lips aligned themselves into a tense smile. "Not dressed for a party, are we?" he said, referring to my well-worn jeans and wrinkled white t-shirt. "May I see your credentials?"

He examined my investigator's license, holding it up to the light at various angles, as if checking for holograms. "How do we know you are for real, Ms. Epstein?"

"You can call the New York State Division of Licensing and give them my number."

He handed back the license. "I assume your employer is looking for whoever killed Rebecca's brother. I also assume that your professional ethics prohibit you from revealing this man's identity." I found it curious that he didn't refer to Micah by name and that he assumed my client's gender was male.

"What I *can* tell you is that my client and I would greatly appreciate your cooperation."

Baranski rewarded this tactful approach by picking up my drink and steering me to a small table at the end of the bar. Captured in motion in a photo on the wall, a sullen-faced, stringy-haired male model strutted toward us. Above black leather pants his six-pack abs showed off a fashionably grungy black mesh tank top, his forearms covered by prison tattoos, presumably fake. Gulag art as a fashion statement—how chic.

A waiter appeared and set down a drink in front of Baranski before disappearing with a flourish. "Ms. Epstein, I think we have some interests in common. But first there are some issues that we must air." You'd think we were at a G-8 summit, not a sleazy boutique.

"Mr. Baranski, I know that your company, Na Khodu, Inc., owns Avenue L Car Service."

His response was a shrug, but his expression conveyed grudging admiration. An impression that would be greatly diminished if he knew that I had not until that moment known that my hunch was correct. I finished my drink before continuing, hoping to strengthen the illusion of clairvoyance. "I'm also aware that Avenue L provides round-trip services to certain female passengers to Manhattan at very late hours of the evening."

"So that's why you've been looking at me that way, as if I were a *cherv*, a worm. I am not what you think, Ms. Epstein. I am no roof, or pimp as you call them here. These girls are being groomed to be supermodels, not hookers." He pronounced this last word as *who cares*. "Ask anyone. I'm a legitimate businessman," he added, having interpreted my amusement as disbelief.

"There are plenty of high-end modeling schools that hold classes during daylight hours and at one location."

"Yes, but what they teach is how to strike a pose on a runway or in front of a camera. There's so much more to learn if you're going to be accepted in the inner circles of society." Baranski picked up my empty glass, causing the waiter to repeat his magic act, before adding: "This may not be easy for you to grasp, since fashion is obviously of no interest to you."

Touché. I was crushed. I sipped my fresh drink and sat back in my chair. Let him think he'd won a round.

Baranski looked around to make sure that no one was within hearing distance of our isolated table. "I owe you no explanation, Ms. Epstein, but to get you off my back I will give you one. First, you must understand that I have many rich friends who are lonely. I introduce them to women with whom they can relax without fear of gold digging or extortion. These women are treated with respect and are given entrée to high-class clubs and restaurants. They rub elbows with the rich and famous and learn how to conduct themselves appropriately."

"And what do *you* get out of this?"

"Favors and good will, my dear—in business that's something you can't put a price on."

"So you expect me to believe that you're running some kind of old-fashioned escort service, with no sex involved?"

He didn't blink. "Everyone involved is over twenty-one. If they hit it off and decide to get naked, that's not my concern."

"It was a concern of Micah Goldman's, and he ended up dead."

Rebecca was lingering at the bar, and out of the corner of my eye I had seen her down two drinks in quick succession. Now she came over and slid into the narrow space between the chair and the table, with inches to spare. Her cheeks verged on sunken, and her arms were too thin for muscle tone.

"I think I know who killed my brother." She spoke so softly that her words were in danger of being drowned out by the drone of the high-speed blender at the other end of the bar.

"Maybe you should keep your speculations to yourself," Baranski said, visible annoyance now openly competing with a strained smile.

Rebecca reached over and took a sip from his drink. She avoided Yuri's irritated look and spoke to me directly, her voice taking on a defiant tone. "He's a driver for Avenue L. Nikolai something."

"Why would you suspect him?"

"Because I was in the back seat of the limo when Micah confronted Nikolai in the Avenue L parking lot. My brother banged on the hood of the car and called him a pimp and a child molester. I'm twenty-two, for God's sake."

"How did this Nikolai react?" I asked, hoping the flush of anger I felt suffusing my face would go unnoticed. *Not that I recall* is what Nikolai had said when I asked whether he'd known Micah. If he had such a low opinion of my detective skills, then why had he bothered to hire me?

"He locked the doors and waited it out. After a while Micah left in disgust. I tried to apologize for my brother's behavior, but Nikolai said to forget about it, that he'd been called a lot worse in Russia and that I should be happy to have a brother who cared enough about me to go on such a rampage. At the time I thought he was being sweet."

"And now?"

"Looking back it doesn't seem natural, his staying so calm in the face of Micah's accusations. Maybe he was already planning to get even and didn't want to arouse my suspicions."

"Have you talked to the police about this?"

"No, she hasn't," Baranski broke in.

Rebecca shot him a resentful look. "Yuri is concerned that a messy investigation of one of his employees could result in a deluge of bad publicity and taint his precious reputation. He has an upcoming show in Moscow."

Yuri shrugged. "Few of us are without conflict of interest. But I'm not as cold-hearted as she paints me. We'd like your help in getting to the bottom of this, Ms. Epstein. The police here are methodical, but slow."

His remark about conflict of interest hit home. "I'm afraid it would not be ethical for me to accept you as a client. But maybe we can continue to share information." I offered my card to Rebecca, and she took it. "Let's keep in touch."

"She'll consider it," Yuri said. They both rose from the table, as if at some hidden signal.

"You're leaving here with more information than you brought with you," Baranski said, patting me on the shoulder. It wasn't easy, but I managed to repress the hostility his paternal posturing aroused in me as we shook hands and went our separate ways.

YOU RUINED MY SISTER AND NOW YOU WILL SUFFER!

It made sense to me now, but somehow I didn't see Micah Goldman as the author. His style had been direct, confrontational, and he would have sent the original, not a Xerox copy. It was more likely that someone else wanted to make the police believe that Micah had sent the notes, so that Nikolai would become their prime suspect. This someone was also in possession of a murder weapon covered with Nikolai's fingerprints. Which made me wonder why, having the power to send my stepfather away for the rest of his life, the blackmailer was biding his time. Was he planning a more complex extraction of revenge?

There was also a possibility that Nikolai had sent the notes to himself. That he had made up the entire story. But why fabricate evidence that pointed to yourself?

Feydor watched in dismay as the same woman he had seen entering Little Dog's house on the night of the murder left The Mantle, where she no doubt had been talking with Rebecca Goldman. The fact that she had managed to track down the girl shattered his complacency. It wouldn't take an acrobat to take the leap in logic that led to his door.

He had counted on isolating his prey, cutting him off from the herd. Now it looked like he would need to change his tactics. All because of this redhead, who he assumed was Little Dog's daughter. He wondered what she would be like in bed and then took an angry swipe at the intruding thought, as unwelcome as a horsefly biting his ass. He was a married man, proud of the fact that he had never strayed.

If this was Russia, it would be so easy to apply the easy solution, an ambush or a car bomb. But such an act in Manhattan would bring out more law enforcement than Putin used to tame Moscow after he was elected in 2000. Still, the woman was creating underwater rocks he'd have to steer clear of, until he could find a way to neutralize her. She provoked in him a heady mixture of admiration mixed with frustrated rage, disorienting yet energizing. But no one, let alone a meddling woman, was going to prevent him from making Little Dog pay.

Two months ago, he had come across his enemy as unexpectedly as a thunderstorm flares up over Moscow in summer. Nikolai Kharpov, standing at the corner of Avenue M and East 18th, violin in hand, bidding goodnight to his fellow players. The scum was so secure in his new life he barely looked before crossing the street—Mr. Everyman—an ordinary citizen of Brooklyn, striding down the street toward his apartment building as if he were headed for the podium.

They had passed within inches of each other, but Little Dog had been oblivious to the stranger, whose eyes could easily have burned a hole in the back of his skull. The street had been dark and deserted. Feydor struggled to control feelings that had been pent up for decades and were demanding instant action. A rush of adrenalin had threatened to overwhelm the edifice of rationality he had so carefully constructed since arriving in America. He struggled with himself, drawing upon his training to hold himself in check. Only a fool would surrender to impulse and forego any chance of exacting true justice.

And now, finally on the verge of reaping the rewards of his self-control, he had a new complication to deal with.

CHAPTER SIX

Driving north on the West Side Highway, my pleasant thoughts about wiping the smug expression, one pore at a time, off Yuri Baranski's self-satisfied face were rudely interrupted by the first few bars of "This is the End" (The Doors, circa 1968), which were no longer as cute as I thought they'd be when I first downloaded them to my cell.

"The son of a bitch called me." Nikolai's voice was thick with drink. "He said I belong to him now—that my instructions will come in the mail. My life is over. What can I do?" There was a dangerous mixture of fatalism and rage in his voice. All I could do was try to keep him focused on the details.

"Did you recognize his voice?"

"I would have told you if I had."

Yeah, like you told me about your confrontation with Micah Goldman. "So how did his voice sound? Was it clear or hoarse?"

"Muffled, like under a blanket."

"By any chance did you see his number on your cell phone display?"

"I am not clueless, Jo. I looked for a number but there was nothing. He has his line blocked."

"What time does the mailman come tomorrow?"

"Not 'til three o'clock."

"Call me if you get another package."

The first thing I did when I got home was to move Nikolai's bloody clothes from the top shelf in my closet to a more secure spot behind the refrigerator. I was still not ready to dump them down the garbage chute in the hallway. For one thing, destroying evidence from a crime scene was contraindicated by all my professional training and experience. More to the point, I couldn't take such a drastic step without being sure of my client's innocence. My mother had said she couldn't live without him. From my point of view, even basic coexistence was going to be a challenge.

As was my habit, I worked on my case notes before retiring and was in bed by one. Approaching sleep but still struggling with stray thoughts about Russian prisons, folk art carved with messages, and émigré entrepreneurs, I was jarred back to wakefulness by the two-tone chime of the doorbell. Immediately afterward, there were three deliberate-sounding knocks on the door, as if someone wanted to convince me they were really there.

I slipped out of bed and threw a sweater over my nightgown before entering the living room, where I retrieved the Lady Colt from my purse. Tiptoeing to the door, I looked through the peephole. Something blocked the view, maybe a hand. I stepped back and stood quietly listening in the dark for a full twenty seconds as my eyes adjusted to the gloom. Nothing. Whoever was in the hall had either left or was waiting for me to react. Something rustled as it slipped beneath the door, gliding toward me on the smooth hardwood floor. Instinctively I jumped backward, and it was all I could do not to cry out. I held my breath and heard footsteps receding down the hallway. Looking through the viewer this time, I caught a glimpse of a darkly clothed figure turning the corner leading to the elevator.

I bent down to pick up the envelope, then thought better of it and retrieved a pair of latex gloves from a cabinet in the kitchen. Using a thin steak knife as a letter opener, I gently liberated a photograph. Staring up at me and across the years, Dad's eyes locked with mine. The picture had been taken in Vietnam, a week or two before they shipped him home with a collection of shrapnel permanently embedded in his leg. His hair was cut so short it was hard to make out the red color he had passed on to me, along with the pale complexion and freckles. I flipped the photo and read the message on the back, written in cursive, the blue ink slightly smudged. *This one had courage. Your stepfather is scum.*

I poured myself a shot from the bottle of Jack Daniels I was currently working on and stared at the picture. Dad had posed in front of a field tent, dressed in Army fatigues, a cigarette dangling from his mouth. The look he aimed at the camera conveyed a mixture of defiance and resignation. The same expression I remembered him wearing at the dinner table, in the park, or when kissing me goodnight, during the two years he spent with us after his return.

When I was eleven, Dad disappeared, leaving multiple bottles of painkillers on the nightstand and a shoebox in the closet, stuffed with $2,000 he had won at the track. When she thought I was old enough to handle it, Ruth told me that the police had treated the case as a suicide. "They said if he planned on living, he would have taken the pills with him. But isn't it obvious that if he planned on dying he would have swallowed them all?"

When Dad got his draft notice she had begged him to flee to Canada. She would have followed him anywhere. Instead, he reported for duty. "He had this crazy idea about serving his country, right or wrong. If he had listened to me, our family would still be in one piece, and so would he."

When I asked why she thought Dad had left us, Ruth said, "I'm sure it was because he didn't want to be a burden. He's still out there somewhere, I can feel it." This may have been true, but it didn't prevent her from having my father declared legally dead so she could marry Nikolai. Not that I blamed her.

By that time, Dad had been missing for twenty-two years.

The stolen picture was one of many photos I had stored in a box in my office, waiting to be digitized and burned on a CD for safekeeping. Whoever had slipped it under my door apparently thought that by invading my privacy so blatantly he could scare me off the case. Thinking about this, I felt my fear turn into anger and my anger morph into cold logic. Someone had followed me home from The Mantle, the same someone who had ransacked my office. It was therefore a male who was either a policeman or knew how to impersonate one. Baranski came to mind, but he had asked for my help in finding Micah Goldman's killer, so why try to discourage me? Detective Grimes, although jumpy and secretive, had sought me out when he heard I was looking for him, and Hasim didn't think he was crooked. On the other hand, Veton, the dispatcher at Avenue L, had the right mix of unsavory qualities plus a connection with the victim, Micah Goldman. But as far as I knew, Veton had not shown up at The Mantle last night.

Daylight was outlining the window shade by the time I fell into an uneasy sleep. What seemed like two minutes later, the blast of the clock radio pulled me like an unwilling fish from the ocean of my already forgotten dream.

I'm not much of a cook, but preparing breakfast was a good way to sooth my nerves while I thought things over. The smell of burning bacon jettisoned me back to reality. With my life possibly in danger, I should call the police. But until I knew enough about Nikolai's guilt or innocence, bringing in the law was not an option. I owed my mother that much. I was beginning to feel like a rabbit caught in the crosshairs of a high-powered rifle. Now, if only I could figure out whose finger was on the trigger.

My cure for feeling overwhelmed has always been to roll up my sleeves and get back to work. So I put in a call to Detective

Spinelli at the 70th Precinct. The detective was busy on another line. I left my name and number and finished up some paperwork while waiting for him to call me back. Which he did, a half hour later. His opening salvo was not encouraging.

"Kefauver told me you stopped by. I called the editor of *Best of Brooklyn,* and it seems she's never heard of you."

Busted. It was hard to tell if his voice conveyed annoyance or amusement at my deception, but I knew that if he was working on a Saturday he was hitting the Goldman case hard. "I'm a private investigator. You can call Hasim Saleh at the 42nd in the Bronx. He'll vouch for me. I'm looking into Micah Goldman's death."

"As a matter of fact, Saleh called me yesterday about another matter. Your name wasn't mentioned. Anyway, I'd like to meet with you to clear a few things up." This last sentence was cop code for I want to know how the hell you knew Micah Goldman's name before the press did and if your interest in the case makes us enemies or allies. We agreed to meet at two P.M. at a café near the precinct.

I spent the remainder of the morning on the phone, trying to track down the three Matryoshka doll collectors whose names and numbers Marya had given me. When I was done, I typed up my scribbled notes for future reference.

Summary of Interviews with Matryoshka Doll Collectors

Algernon Lewis, 987 Riverside Drive: From my description on the phone, identified doll as number three in a set of six Judges manufactured in 1908 at a workshop in Sergiev Posad. Very surprised to see dolls like these in the U.S.—thought all of them were in museums in Russia. Seemed convinced

that the dolls were stolen and probably
sold to a collector in the U.S. illegally,
but nonetheless offered to buy the full set
for $2,000 and was very disappointed when I
turned him down.

Ishkhan Lamsa, no address provided and the
phone number I called is unlisted. Left a
message—no reply yet.

Stanley Turino, 717 East 4th: Refused to talk
with me unless I told him where I obtained
the doll. I told him I was working on a
confidential matter and could not reveal the
name of my employer.

You'd think I'd been writing these things for years.

Stopped at a red light on my way to Brooklyn, my stomach
growled at the sight of a certain chili dog stand on the southern
perimeter of Washington Square Park. Maybe there was a reason
my breakfast had gone up in flames. I consulted my watch and
decided there was time to spare for a detour.

Sanyo had moved his operation to a prime location—right
across the street from the light brown, filigreed stonework of the
Judson Memorial Church. I hadn't seen him since I drew on
his extensive knowledge of all things graffiti to help me solve a
case last year. The chemistry between us, which I felt bubbling
to the surface while I parked the car, wasn't something either of
us had been ready to act on, at least not yet.

The Square was my favorite New York park, with its walkways
paved with beehive-shaped tiles and perennially scruffy students
sprawled inside the perimeter of the fountain, scribbling in their
notebooks, backs braced against the low circular wall.

Sanyo was serving his specialty to two well-dressed customers
who probably had made a special trip up from Wall Street to

ingest the spicy sausages topped with delectable caramelized onions. When the coast was clear, I approached, hunger having overcome an unusual attack of shyness.

As soon as he saw me, Sanyo's impressive eyebrows shot up slightly and then settled down above his light brown eyes, lit by the same gentle power that drew me to him the first time we met. During a casual conversation over lunch one day we had discovered that we grew up within three blocks of each other in the Bronx. It was no surprise that we hadn't run into each other in the old days, since the gangs that divvied up our neighborhood fiercely defended their territory, block by block, and children were wise to play close to home.

"What's up, Jo?"

"Uh, not much." It's strange how tongue-tied I felt, minus my usual excuse of pumping him for information.

"What will it be?" He scraped the grill clean in anticipation of my requesting a greasy delicacy. But there was a new feature added to his cart—an ice cream freezer—and instead of ordering a potentially messy chili dog that might embarrass us both, I asked for a Nutty Buddy.

"Good choice." He seemed unusually quiet.

"How's life treating you?" I asked.

"Can't complain—business is good, but not much excitement." He took off the white butcher's apron, which never seemed to have a spot of grease on it, and came out from behind the cart, tucking the tails of a deep maroon shirt into his jeans. "You still gumshoeing?"

"Poetry doesn't pay the bills, so I guess I'm stuck." Something in the way he was looking at me encouraged my next question. "Sanyo—there's nothing going on at Scandal's on Tuesday night, so I'm a free agent. How'd you like to go to the Nuyorican? I'll buy you a beer and we can listen to some kick-ass poetry."

"No," he said. My heart sank until I saw his grin. "Not unless you let me treat you to that ice cream."

We stood there gawking at each other, aware that we'd crossed into unknown territory. I felt the color mounting in my cheeks but luckily my cell phone rang (actually it played *I Shot the Sheriff*, downloaded in the car on my way there).

"I'll see you at nine," Sanyo said and we both got back to work.

CHAPTER SEVEN

Traffic was a bitch, and I was thirty-five minutes late. I still ended up waiting fifteen minutes for Detective Spinelli to saunter into the restaurant, wearing dark brown corduroy slacks, a light green Izod shirt, and a brown sports jacket worn deliberately open to make the small holster at his belt visible. Spinelli's Romanesque nose was no surprise, but his friendly manner was. I gave him a wave, and he came and sat down across from me in the booth, reaching over the table to shake hands.

"The grilled asagio sandwich is very good," he informed me. This was no doughnut-eating cop.

"Lieutenant Saleh said you know how to keep your mouth shut. He also said that sometimes you don't share information when you should, so I'll keep that in mind too. What do you have on the Goldman case?"

"Not much," I said. "His sister Rebecca is supposedly a model, but Micah may have thought otherwise." I gave him the details on Yuri Baranski's finishing school slash escort service. The detective leafed through his pad, looking for an information tidbit to match my own. "Goldman worked at Print Plus. It's a copy shop on Flatbush. He was the manager."

The waitress took my order for a turkey sandwich and Spinelli's for a chocolate milkshake, a specialty of the house. We made short work of the food when it arrived, not bothering with small talk.

"So she was hooking, her brother made trouble, and this Russian mafia pimp did away with him," Spinelli finally said. "Everyone knows they kill at the drop of a hat."

I was irritated by Spinelli's stereotyping but I liked the way he was headed—toward Baranski and away from Nikolai. I may have had my own suspicions about my client, but as long I was accepting Nikolai's money I had to put his interests first. "If Baranski is involved, he's got a lot at stake. He's trying to break into the international fashion scene. I'm sure he's got a slew of competitors who would love to see him excommunicated from the church of fashion."

Spinelli shifted uncomfortably in his seat and it struck me that he might be religious, in which case my choice of metaphor had been unfortunate. He took a last gulp from his milkshake. "I'll look into it," he said. I knew better than to piss him off by asking exactly how he planned to do this.

After splitting the check, we walked out to the street. I thought the detective would say goodbye but he had something else on his mind. "When you came to the precinct yesterday, you asked about Detective Grimes. How did you know he had moved to the 70th?"

"Lieutenant Saleh told me to look up Grimes. He thought Lenny might be a good contact for me on the Goldman case."

"Have you seen him?"

"Not yet." The lie just popped out, more instinctive than well thought out. Trusting my instincts, I went with it. "Maybe you could arrange a meeting?"

"No way," Spinelli snapped, clearly displeased that I'd gone out of bounds.

"I'm trying to cover all the bases, that's all." This was my tactful way of insinuating that I might uncover some information he'd missed. Spinelli knew this, but I was counting on him being too much of a professional to display his resentment.

"Suit yourself," he said.

"Nice meeting you, Detective."

"Likewise. Don't make me regret it." His warning tone was well rehearsed, and although it may have instilled the fear of reprisal in his snitches, it had no such effect on me.

I checked my messages. An urgent one from Nikolai required a call back.

"You've got to stop him, Jo." His voice was shaky and it was after three—no doubt the mailman had brought him another "present."

"I wore gloves this time like you told me."

"I'll be there as soon as I can."

I'm not the domestic type, but even by my low standards, Nikolai had let the kitchen go to hell. Dirty dishes in the sink, and not one but two empty vodka bottles lay on the floor near the recycling bin, drunken soldiers fallen short of their objective.

"Mr. Eeks has sent us another present." It took me a moment, and then I realized that Americans didn't have a monopoly on the term Mr. X. I wondered if Nikolai had deliberately chosen this name to convince me he was ignorant of his tormentor's identity.

Pulling on my rubber gloves, I cleared a space on the table and removed the first doll from the plastic bag in my purse, placing it next to the second one. The new arrival was about a quarter of an inch smaller all around, with the same bullet shape and high gloss. The folds in the smaller judge's robes were painted with considerable detail and his eyes glared sternly at us from beneath the wig. There was, however, what appeared at first glance to be a defect. The right shoulder and part of the chest of the judge had been sanded down, the dull wood exposed beneath. I looked closer and the grinning face of a skeleton jumped out at me, framed by the hood of a dark robe, its fleshless hands gripping an executioner's ax decorated with the ace of spades. It looked like a tattoo, precisely rendered in dark blue ink. Was this one of the designs I had seen at The Mantle last night, on the arms of the model in the photograph? I wasn't sure. I put the doll back on the table.

"Why would a judge have a tattoo?"

Nikolai started to say something, then changed his mind.

"You must know what this design means."

"What do you think it means?" he growled at me. "It's obvious. Someone from my past wants to taunt me, to drive me crazy."

If that was the plan, it appeared to be working. "Do you have any idea who it might be?"

"You wouldn't be here if I did."

"Look, if I'm going to help you'll have to provide a picture of those years in your life. You've got to give me something to go on."

Nikolai pulled apart the first Matryoshka, removed the letter, and inserted the second, smaller doll in its place. "What do you want? A blow-by-blow description of torture, murder, rape, and nauseating smells that haunt me to this day?" The audible pain in his voice signaled he was closer to hysteria than his stoic demeanor indicated.

"You can keep asking me until you're blue in the face, Jo, and it won't do any good. I've never talked about this, even with your mother, and I'm not going to start now."

"You're saying you'd rather keep silent and go to jail for a murder you didn't commit? That's insane."

He rose from the table and left the room. I waited a while, hoping he was taking time out to compose himself for further discussion. After a few minutes I got up and peered through the doorway into the living room. He was sprawled in the La-Z-Boy, tipped all the way back, eyes closed, an oddly carefree smile on his face—a moment's release from the ongoing nightmare.

I made a quick stop in the bathroom, and when I returned to the living room the recliner was empty. Walking to the elevator—both dolls safely stowed in my purse—I was followed by the sound of splintering bottles, probably being thrown into the bin. Maybe he needed to fall apart before he could pull himself together.

There was a missed call on my cell with a 718 area code, indicating it came from Brooklyn or Queens. I pressed Talk, heard two rings, then a female voice said a soft "hello?" It was Rebecca Goldman. "I thought about what you said and I'm still not willing to talk to the police. But if you . . . would it be too much trouble to ask you to come here? I live in Bensonhurst."

"No trouble at all—I'm already in Brooklyn. Give me your address."

The modest, two-story wood-frame house in Bensonhurst where Rebecca Goldman lived had retained an air of dignity after losing most of its outer layers of beige paint. The front lawn was neglected beyond redemption, but the columns that held up the porch looked freshly painted. A late-90's Honda Civic was parked in the driveway.

The Rebecca who came to the door had little in common with the pouting sophisticate I'd seen hanging on Yuri Baranski's arm last night. She wore a plain corduroy jumper and tights that made her look at least five years younger. When she spoke, the impression of softness vanished. "Why didn't you tell me you were working for Nikolai Kharpov?"

No mollifying explanation came quickly to mind, so I stepped back and let Rebecca give vent to her anger.

"I just got off the phone with an NYPD detective who said he was looking for you. He said that since you were working for Nikolai, he thought you might have contacted me to talk about the confrontation between him and my brother. You pretended to care about Micah and me, but you're just milking me for information. You're not welcome in this house."

It had to be Grimes who had called her, since Spinelli had no reason to sabotage me. Lenny was clever, I had to admit, and whatever his agenda, he knew how to clear the field. Rebecca stared at me as I evaluated the situation. Maybe if I showed some confidence in her judgment she'd regain some confidence in mine. "What if you're wrong and Nikolai is innocent? You told me yourself that he didn't get angry when your brother denounced him."

Rebecca shifted uneasily in the doorway. "Maybe he was already planning to get even."

"Look, Rebecca, I'd be the first to admit that it looks bad for Nikolai, but I took this case because he's married to my mother and in spite of his many faults, she wants to keep it that way. So yes, you're right, I'm hoping I can prove his innocence. But not at the expense of the truth. Do you think I'd want my mother to stay married to a murderer? And you—you loved your brother. Don't you owe him a thorough investigation?"

Rebecca's answer was to step back to let me in. "My mom's gone out. If she comes back while you're still here, you can tell her you're a friend from school. Lots of the students are, you know, older." Precisely what age group she lumped me into I didn't dare ask. Maybe the strands of gray weren't as well hidden under my kinky red hair as I'd assumed.

Rebecca led me into a small living room, where a family of four would have trouble watching TV without knocking knees. The walls were paneled in fake pine and the carpet so threadbare in places that the floorboards showed through. Even so, the place had a well-cared-for feel and looked as though it had been recently scrubbed, as did Rebecca's face sans makeup.

"Have a seat," she said, pointing to a modern Danish chair with burnt orange cushions. "I'll bring us some coffee."

She disappeared into the kitchen, leaving me to stare at the only art in the room—a Vermeer print hanging over the couch—the stocky milkmaid lit like a duchess, graceful in her own way but definitely not an aspiring supermodel's ideal.

The coffee Rebecca served came with milk, sugar, and dry biscuits made barely edible by dunking. She sat down opposite me on the royal blue couch with matching puffy cushions.

"Why don't we start with your telling me about your brother," I said. "Wasn't he a bit old to be living at home?"

Her laugh was strained. "Micah was divorced. His wife, Aviva, was a Sabra. She was chronically homesick and when he wouldn't move to Israel she left him and he moved back in with us. Our mother would never let him live alone—he was so helpless when it came to worldly things."

"How did you get along?"

"Okay, until he introduced me to Yuri and I started modeling and going to parties. Micah said he wanted me to be successful but he didn't want me taking risks. I tried to explain to him that it was alright, that the escort service was not a call girl operation. He wouldn't listen and we had a big blowup."

"Did he threaten you?"

"My brother hardly ever lost his temper. That's why I was so upset when he laid into Nikolai. He yelled himself hoarse and then he yanked open the door and ordered me to get out of the limo and go home with him." She squeezed her shoulders together, reliving the scene.

"What did you do?"

"I refused, naturally, and Veton—the dispatcher—he was mad as hell and I heard him tell Micah: 'You've got it all wrong and if I tell Yuri about this it will be the end of *na khalyavu* for both of us.' "

"What's *na khal*—whatever?"

"That's what Russians call free stuff, the gravy train, and that's how I found out that Micah was in some kind of business with them."

"But you continued to see Yuri. How could you be sure he didn't have something to do with Micah's death?"

Rebecca flushed defiantly. "I called you, didn't I?"

"What do you think Micah was up to?"

"Who knows? He used to bring home boxes from the print shop and carry them into his room when he thought no one was looking."

"Have you been in his room since . . . ?"

Rebecca examined a run in her black tights and then stared at her out-of-season, white summer sandals for a few moments while considering what I was asking her to do. Then she rose and motioned for me to follow.

Micah's room was an add-on at the back of the house, the bottom of the letter L. It was in shipshape order, except for the walls, which were randomly covered with photographs, all taken in an arid climate, Israel, I assumed. In one picture, Micah stood with his arm around a slim girl in shorts, her hair wrapped in a red bandana. "That's Aviva," Rebecca said. "They met when he was an exchange student, about five years ago."

Under the neatly made bed I found two boxes—both ripped open and containing plastic bags filled with small cloth labels, all made of silk, all of them blank.

"The police took only one box when they saw they were all the same," explained Rebecca. "I think they're dress labels left over from a run at the print shop. What do you think this means?"

It was bite my tongue or tell her that if she'd applied for a student loan instead of going to work as a model, her brother might still be alive. I did neither.

CHAPTER EIGHT

I had forgotten that Monday was Linda's bookkeeping day. I usually made a point of not interrupting her when she was hunched over the cash register, trying to balance the week's numbers. As I walked by, she grabbed my arm. "I may have overreacted the other night. Having you here has benefited the club. The customers like you even though you're tough on them sometimes. I was upset and I—"

"It's OK, Linda. If I were in your shoes I'd have felt the same way. I didn't mean to cause you any trouble."

"Then you'll stay?"

"Let's see how things work out." I was still peeved with her for letting one incident convince her that squads of police would regularly descend on the club as long as I was in residence. I was also upset at not being able to level with her and share my conviction that the intruder was not a cop.

"By the way," she said. "There's someone waiting in your office. He said he was a client."

It wasn't a client. It was Lieutenant Saleh, seated at my desk, leafing through one of the many files strewn over its surface. The usual suit had been replaced by a fuzzy yellow sweater that made him look more like an anxious academic than a thirty-year veteran of the NYPD. I offered him a cup of coffee, which he refused, confirming my impression that this was no social call. Hasim was more fidgety than I've ever seen him, playing with the pens on my desk and avoiding eye contact.

"You've put me in a difficult position, Jo," he said.

I prepared for the worst, assuming he meant that the police had seen through my subterfuge on the night of Micah's murder.

"Although this time it's not your fault," he added.

We've got an unwritten agreement not to dwell on our past conflicts but references do crop up.

Hasim got up and walked around the desk, sitting down on the front of it, so we were face to face. "I've been racking my brains for a way to get you to drop this case. I know you too well to resort to threats."

"Why not try telling me what's up?"

"After you called me looking for information on the homicide in Brooklyn I finally got a hold of Detective Grimes and he told me that . . ." He let the sentence hang there, like a hang-glider stalled over a cliff, and then blurted out the rest. "He thinks someone from the 70th was involved in the homicide." I knew what it cost him to say these words.

I told Hasim about my own meeting with Grimes. "He acted like he was deep into something, and it's obvious that he's very protective of his territory."

Hasim nodded. "Most of the Russians on the force keep to themselves. Old perceptions die hard, and they're not a popular group. That's probably why Lenny changed his name from Grishkuv to Grimes. When he told me about his suspicions, I tried to convince him to come in and talk things over but he refused, said that if he was right he could handle it himself and that if he was wrong, he didn't want me sharing the fallout. Since then, he hasn't returned my calls. All I know is that he's gone to ground somewhere in Brooklyn."

Hasim slid off the desk and ambled over to the bookshelves I had mounted on the wall last month. Just when I was sure he'd decided to alphabetize my collection of *Forensic Science Monthly*, he came to his decision. "I've got a favor to ask of you, Jo. Lenny's got a wife named Joanne. I'd talk to her myself, but I don't want to raise any red flags. Maybe if a woman were to—"

"Ask if she's seen her husband? I'll get right on it."

He handed me a piece of paper with Joanne Lowry's contact information. "I hope I'm wrong about this. Better a thousand enemies outside the house than one inside."

The Lieutenant's proverbs usually signaled the end of a conversation, so I walked him out.

The Latin word *privatus* means "set apart, belonging to oneself, not open to the public." It was a word that in our post-911 world was rapidly losing its meaning, like *democracy*. Case in point, fifteen minutes after logging on I knew Joan Lowry Grimes's Social Security number, her shopping patterns, and the unpleasant details of her divorce from Lenny in 2006 and subsequent use of a much-touted online dating service. Joan had recently taken a second mortgage on her condo in Brooklyn Heights and was carrying in excess of $25,000 in credit card debt. These two facts were undoubtedly related. A few more minutes and I'd dug up her employment history and ascertained that she was currently an Account Manager at Sielko Advertising. Judging from the state of her finances, she wasn't the talented executive who landed their most lucrative soft drink client.

From a block away, the Seilko Building looked like a stack of suitcases piled up in descending order of size. After scanning the directory in the lobby, I took the elevator to the top floor, where, walking into the reception area, I was temporarily blinded by the intense sunlight streaming from the floor-to-ceiling windows.

"I'm here to see Joan Lowry."

The paper-thin lips of the distracted receptionist curled into a smile as she waved me through.

Halfway down the hallway the lighting dimmed. Joan Lowry's office was several steps up from a cubicle but still miles below an executive suite. She looked up from her computer suspiciously. Her complexion was pale bisque, her auburn hair not as red as my own, pulled back severely from a widow's peak. Oversized glasses overwhelmed a long, oval face.

"I need to talk with you about your ex-husband."

"Who are you?"

"I'm a private investigator." She barely glanced at the license I held out for inspection.

It was hard to decide how much to tell her. Too little, and she'd throw me out. Too much, and she could jump to some painful conclusions. "I'm here because my stepfather has been accused of murder and Detective Grimes may be able to help. I need to find him."

"*Not* being found is Lenny's specialty. Ask his daughter. He was supposed to show up on Sunday for her piano recital."

"When did you see him last?"

"He took Sonia to the movies two weeks ago, dropped her off early, seemed nervous. Something about setting up a surveillance."

"Did he tell you where the stakeout was—maybe give you an address where you could contact him in an emergency?"

The *what kind of fool do you think I am* look she fixed on me had had lots of practice. "I can't give out that kind of information, Ms. Epstein. I'm not supposed to know what I know, and you could have printed that license at Kinko's."

"I admit there's no one at the 70th who will vouch for me, but I think you should know that Lieutenant Saleh from Lenny's old precinct thinks that Lenny might be in over his head."

"I had a feeling he was in trouble. Lenny told me that no one at the 70th was to know his whereabouts and that this guy he replaced undercover—" She stopped short.

"And whose name you can't tell me," I filled in for her.

"That's right. Come to think of it, I shouldn't be talking to you at all, Ms. Epstein."

She rose from her chair and walked me back down the hall toward reception. "Lenny's not a bad person but I got tired of waiting up nights, of living on his lousy pay, never going out to dinner for fear that someone might recognize him. It's like he was trying to prove that a Russian immigrant can make good in the police department. After I landed the job here, I told him, 'I can support us both while you make a change.' He didn't go for that, so I told him it was his job or us. Sonia was growing up, I didn't want her to be wondering from day to day if her dad was alive or dead.

The pain in her face looked both old and new. "It turned out to be an easy choice for him." She didn't have to tell me he made the wrong one.

After pushing the button for the elevator, she said, "I hope I've made it clear that I don't want to be involved. If you contact me again, I'll call Detective Spinelli and make sure you're charged with interfering with an investigation."

"Understood," I said and rode down to the lobby.

If Joan Lowry cared as much for her ex-husband as I thought she did, I figured it might be worth an hour or two of my time to see what she was willing to do about it.

Ten minutes later she drove out of the Seilko Building's underground parking lot. A half hour later she parked her Lexus and walked into 1636 Nostrand Avenue, without a backward glance.

CHAPTER NINE

Urine in the hallway, hoarse whispers under the stairs. From my perch on the fourth-floor landing, I could hear Joan Lowry below, banging away on what sounded like a metal-enforced door. She waited for a minute and, when no one answered, took the stairs back down to the street.

The only metal door on the third floor belonged to 3C. The lock resisted at first, but my recently purchased, new-and-improved toolkit turned out to be a good investment.

Inside, dust-filtered light seeped in beneath closed window shades. The first thing I noticed was a piece of paper on the floor just inside of the door. *Lenny call me,* is all Joan's note said. I put it back on the floor for Grimes to find.

Someday, probably not soon, a rivulet, if not a wave of gentrification would reach this street, and a smart landlord would invest in having the filthy oak floors scraped and polished. Until then, the water stains on the ceiling and the rotten molding around the windows provided the perfect atmosphere for a cop's life in limbo.

The only furniture in the living room was a kitchen chair with brown foam erupting from its padded yellow seat. Sparse was an understatement; the apartment was barely this side of empty. But not uninhabited, as evidenced by the headline— "Hung Jury in Child Abuse Case"—slashed across the front page of a week-old copy of the *Daily News.* Food-caked take-out cartons and a cold cup of Starbucks coffee kept the newspaper company on the kitchen table. Whatever else he was up to, Grimes had time to read. In the bedroom, a straight-back chair was positioned in front of the window. An expensive pair of binoculars sat on the sill, presumably waiting for its owner to come back from a break.

Some detectives prefer conducting their stakeouts from an apartment with a bathroom instead of a pee jar and the possibility of hot food to eating junk in the car, but not me. First of all, I worked alone, which meant that if anything went down I would never make it to my vehicle in time to tail the suspect. Second, if someone spotted me I'd be a static target. Unfortunately, if I was going to pick up where Grimes had left off, I would have to use his technique. I picked up the binoculars and took a seat. Gray pavement jumped across the street, bouncing off my eyes. As I scanned slowly upward, dull red bricks turned to black, minus the glow from the streetlamp. Along the face of the building I searched for life behind backlit Venetian blinds, flowered curtains, a hanging bed sheet, and some unusual pricey-looking wooden shutters. One naked window stood out like an empty eye socket, and I zoomed into a blurry, unidentifiable object against an out-of-focus pastel background. Zooming back a hair, I found Jesus staring back at me, crucified on a light pink wall, below him a blue light shining through a fringed lamp shade on a table next to the bed, brown hair spread on the pillow. Nothing out of the ordinary here.

I zoomed out farther and tilted down, returning to the original focal point. Whatever he was keeping an eye on should be in plain sight. To the right, two rusty iron doors lay flush with the sidewalk. To the left, a battered blue mailbox. I moved back to the cellar doors, going with my instinct that this was the target.

I tuned the clock-radio to 97.9, my favorite Latin Mix channel. The blown-out speakers made the music sound like it was being broadcast from El Salvador instead of Manhattan.

A mid-sized Ryder rental truck pulled up, blocking my view of the cellar door. The driver's door was facing me and when it opened, I got a good look at Veton stepping out and walking around to the back. He unloaded what I assumed was a clothing rack, its contents covered by opaque blue plastic.

The delivery was quick, only ten minutes passed between the van's arrival and Veton padlocking the cellar door and starting up the truck. He probably wouldn't be back tonight, so I decided to take my chances.

Out on Nostrand Avenue, a woman leaned on the hood of my car, shivering in a thin cloth coat—yellow with multitudinous stains—that she wore buttoned up to her chin, collar raised—a spy fallen on hard times.

"Where's Frank?" she asked, twirling a strand of her stringy brown hair around her pinky.

"I seen you go up there, so don't look at me like that," she added in response to my puzzled frown. "Frank Mitchell owes me money," she sniffled, wiping her nose on her sleeve, a sheen of desperation on her upper lip, where a cigarette dangled when she wasn't holding it in shaky hands.

"When did you see him last?"

I removed two twenties from the wallet in my purse. It might as well be me who paid for her next fix, rather than some john.

Her hollow eyes flickered—perhaps indicating a brief battle between her conscience and the twenties. "Coupla' weeks ago. He had a guy with him in the apartment and he wouldn't let me in. He said to come back and he'd take care of me. Liar. When he came out he walked right by as if I didn't exist."

"What about his friend? Do you remember what he looked like?"

"No, but I heard Frank call him Lenny."

Grimes. "Did he come back here later, on his own?"

"How the hell should I know?

When I gave her the money, she looked around to make sure we were alone before stuffing the bills in an inside pocket. "If I see Frank, who should I say came calling?" Her Brooklynesque rendition of a British accent made me smile.

"Tell him to call his wife."

Her laugh needed practice but I was all out of jokes.

Retrieving a flashlight from my car, I crossed the street and surveyed the cellar door that Veton had locked up tight. I thought about using the tire iron in my trunk, but even if I succeeded in busting the padlock on the cellar door, I'd awaken enough neighbors to guarantee at least one call to 911. I had to find another way.

It turned out to be as simple as entering the building and pushing "B" on the elevator panel, which lacked a security key for keeping nosy intruders out of the cellar.

The flashlight wasn't much help in the pitch blackness, so I followed the smell of bleach to the laundry room, which was on the street side of the building, opposite a flight of metal stairs leading up to the padlocked cellar door. No other rooms back there, so I backtracked past the elevator. One door, unlocked, led to a storeroom filled with floor lamps and dilapidated baby carriages. The deadbolt on the other door took almost fifteen minutes to yield. Without the new tools it would have been a lot longer.

Using the flashlight, I checked out the room—no windows—before turning on the overheads, fluorescent and bright enough to sew by if you were a seamstress working at one of the five machines on the long wooden table. What looked to be hundreds of dresses were hanging from racks along the wall. And stitched onto the inner back neckline of each dress were labels—replicas of the blank ones I'd seen in the box in Micah Goldman's room—except now proudly exhibiting the Mantle insignia. Guaranteed to open the wallets of the fashion-conscious eager to buy tightly fitting clothes on a tight budget.

Under the workbench I found more boxes of labels, identical to the ones Rebecca showed me under Micah's bed.

If I had it right, Veton and, until recently, Micah Goldman, were running a sweet operation behind Baranski's back. This was not the time or place for deep thinking, but there were implications here about Micah's death that needed consideration.

I helped myself to a dress on the way out, a dark green number with black velvet trim, and stashed it in my car. Not to enhance my wardrobe, although that might be a worthy cause, but on the chance that it might come in handy as evidence or as leverage of some kind in the investigation.

Halfway to Dimitri's Palace, I called Hasim and told him what I'd found. I asked if he could run down some information on Frank Mitchell. I didn't say so, but I was thinking that Grimes had deliberately pointed Hasim in the wrong direction by telling him that someone from the 70th was involved in Micah's murder. It was much more likely that Grimes and Mitchell, who wanted to retire rich, were partners. Two underpaid undercover cops who couldn't pass up the opportunity to skim some cream from a high-fashion knock-off operation. And Micah had probably gotten in the way.

Add to this the fact that Lenny Grimes, aka Leonid Grishkuv, was a Russian native, and I had myself a likely candidate for the title of Mr. Eeks. Maybe he and Nikolai had known each other in Russia, and Grimes didn't want any reminders of his past walking around Brooklyn. Although his wife didn't paint him as a rogue cop, he wouldn't be the first to be sent to live on the dark side and decide to take up permanent residence. It looked to me like Lenny's shady business dealings could have provided motivation for killing Micah—who was in a position to expose him. But as any scientist knows, covering the distance between speculation and proof can be as challenging as teaching evolution in the state of Mississippi, and just as dangerous.

CHAPTER TEN

The owners of Dimitri's had painted the exterior a cheerfully bright yellow. Unfortunately, this only underlined the absurdity of the architecture—yellow submarine meets mid-twentieth century mausoleum. Tonight, half the restaurant had been commandeered as a concert hall. Empty chairs were lined up in front of the plywood stage, ready to be occupied, and there, sitting by herself at the end of the back row, was Mom.

"What are *you* doing here?" she asked, always a pro at turning the tables. I sat down next to her.

I'm here because your husband is up to his neck in illegal activities and may or may not have been framed for murder. "I was invited," I said. "Why isn't Uncle Jake with you?"

"He's sick, remember? I've never seen such a persistent case of the flu. Even so, he insisted on calling the taxi and getting out of bed to walk me downstairs. I told him I've never missed one of Nikolai's concerts and I'm not going to start now."

A soft orange key light illuminated the area of the stage where Ludmilla, her back forming a perfect ninety-degree angle with the bench in front of the Steinway, was stretching her thin fingers and chatting with a tall, broad man whose chest was barely contained by a navy blue blazer. I assumed this was the baritone who Sasha had raved about.

Ludmilla played the blunt chords that began the Polonaise-Fantasie, quickly followed by an ethereal passage that ascended to the highest register of the piano. The magnetic pull of her dramatic flourishes gathered stray audience members from around the restaurant, some of them still wiping their mouths with napkins. I'm no big fan of Chopin, but I hung in there and gradually Ludmilla's soft touch and minimalist style drew me in as well. It was only when the applause erupted at the end of the piece that I noticed that Sasha had taken the seat on the other side of me. He handed me a glossy program.

"So glad you and your mother could come. You're in for a treat."

The Polonaise ended and right on cue a husky man with pink cheeks and a thick five-o'clock shadow stepped with unexpected grace into the curve of the piano. Ludmilla introduced him as Pavel Lebedev. She played a short introduction and then Lebedev's booming voice spilled out into the room, like coffee laced with cognac, invigorating yet seductively smooth.

The program notes were a big help. Otherwise how would I have known that Black Crow was a folk song from Southern Russia that told the story of a soldier who, as he lay dying on a battlefield, asked the black bird to fly to his mother and girlfriend to say goodbye.

The big surprise was a jazz ballad, "My Foolish Heart." I hadn't known Ludmilla liked that kind of music and her solo knocked me out. I complimented her during the intermission. "It's nothing original," she demurred. "I learned it note for note from the record."

"The point is, you made it your own," I insisted. She was trying hard not to show how pleased she was.

At ten-thirty Ludmilla stepped off the stage, heading toward the seat that Sasha had saved for her. Then Nikolai made his dramatic entrance, holding his violin in front of him like a baby for us to admire. An expectant hush fell over the room. I hadn't realized what a local celebrity he was in Brighton Beach. I'd heard him play only once before—at his own wedding to my mother—but I'd been too drunk to pay attention.

Softly, almost imperceptibly, he coaxed the opening notes from his instrument. It was a piece that seemed vaguely familiar. "One of his originals," Sasha whispered to me.

I closed my eyes—a habit I have when I'm listening closely—and was surprised by the intensity of feeling conveyed by Nikolai's playing. It was as if the man had stepped aside for the music, allowing all the pain and joy of the world to be pulled by an unseen hand from the strings of his violin.

I opened my eyes as thunderous applause greeted Nikolai's closing notes. He bowed deeply and then looked over at me, a perplexed expression on his face. "Where's Ruth?" he mimed.

I turned my head, expecting to see Mom sitting beside me. The seat was vacant. I scanned the faces in the audience and hers was not among them. She must have made a beeline for the bathroom as soon as the music ended. Old age isn't for sissies. I got up and went to check the ladies' room. No luck.

Nikolai joined me. "She gets confused." His words evoked a picture of Mom's bewildered face that hung in the air in front of me.

Ludmilla appeared at my elbow. "Have you seen Ruth?" I asked.

"Wasn't she sitting next to you?"

A swarm of people rushed over to congratulate Ludmilla and Nikolai on the concert. I told Sasha that Mom seemed to have wandered off. "Maybe she's gone to the kitchen to ask for a glass of water," he said. "I'll take a look."

Sasha came back shaking his head. And that's when the fear jolted through my chest like the first tremor of an earthquake.

"If she's outside we need to find her fast," Nikolai said. "Why did you not keep an eye on her?" He shot this recrimination over his shoulder while pushing his way through the crowd toward the exit. He was right. If Mom had wandered out in front of a car or fallen down some basement stairs in the dark, it was my fault. A wave of guilt and anxiety came over me as, gulping for air, I followed him. What was I going to say? That the beauty of his music had distracted me so much that I failed to notice my mother leave her seat?

By the time we exited the restaurant, I had forced my emotions to the background and was able to focus on the task at hand. At Nikolai's suggestion, I took one side of the street and he the other. We combed the avenues and alleys of Sheepshead Bay, peering into every doorway, investigating every shadow. If a cat jumped off a stoop or a piece of paper swept by on the wind, I stopped in my tracks, senses fully alert. Nikolai would do the same, each of us watching the other for a sign of hope.

We were slow and thorough, and by the time we reached the waterfront park, it seemed like hours had passed. Walking the dimly lit pathways, I called her name, unable to push away mental pictures of her lying face down in the ocean or crippled in a ditch somewhere.

I had been phoning the apartment every few minutes in case Mom had found her way home, and finally, while Nikolai combed through the brush at the far end of the park, I called Hasim. His sleepy "hello" was barely audible on my cell phone. I told him my mother had disappeared during a concert and that she might have been abducted. I had no evidence to support this theory, but it seemed to me that if Nikolai's nemesis had committed murder and blackmail, he was not going to draw the line at kidnapping.

There was a long pause before Hasim spoke. "Didn't you tell me that she's not, how shall I say it, always there? What makes you so sure someone took her? Isn't it likely she wandered off on her own?"

"My stepfather has enemies." Taken out of context, the words sounded implausible, even to me.

"Can you be more specific?"

"I'm sorry, Hasim. I shouldn't have bothered you."

"You can file a missing persons report, but I'm afraid that unless you can give me something tangible to go on—"

"That's not going to happen."

"Honesty is the first chapter of the book of wisdom. When you're ready to tell me your secrets, feel free to call." Hasim and his damn proverbs. The trouble was, I knew just what he meant.

When we were both exhausted, Nikolai flagged down a cab. Seated next to me, his posture rigid as a soldier's and his violin cradled in his lap, he told me he'd decided to turn himself in. "If I give that bastard what he wants, then he'll stop hurting the people I . . . the ones who I. . . ." He took a deep gulp of air but finishing that sentence was simply too much for him. I pictured him getting liquored up to propose to my mother. Did he actually say the terrible "L" word then? When this was all over I would have to ask her.

"We don't know *what* he wants," I said. "Not yet."

The driver ran the red light at Avenue P and brought the car to a tire-squealing stop in front of the building. Nikolai paid, and we went inside. We were both too tired to face climbing the stairs, so we rode up in the ill-fated elevator.

A package lay on the welcome mat in front of 5J. Nikolai picked it up gingerly, as if it might explode. He unlocked the door, and I took the box from him, carrying it into the kitchen, where I placed it on the table. Pulling on my latex gloves, I removed the brown wrapping paper as delicately as I could, in spite of my conviction that there were no fingerprints to smudge. Doll number three was a likeness of the "judge" character and just this side of an inch smaller than doll number two. No tattoo this time. Silently, Nikolai handed over the note that came with it, composed with the same cut-out letter technique as the first two.

DO EXACTLY AS I SAY, OR YOUR WIFES DEAD.

There was no apostrophe used in *wife's*—which could mean the note was pasted together by a non-native English speaker. Maybe the Russian-born Lenny "Leonid" Grimes. Or perhaps an American in too much of a hurry to bother finding a punctuation mark in the newspaper. Why Mr. Eeks chose not to compose the notes on a word processor was hard to say. Unless he wanted to evoke the past by using the old cut-and-paste technique. Something to think about later.

The phone rang and we both jumped. "I'll use the extension in the bedroom," I said. "When you hear me say 'now' pick up."

Nikolai followed my instructions, and we answered the call simultaneously. There was a brief pause before an unnaturally deep, electronically altered voice came on the line.

"At eight o'clock tomorrow morning, take your precious *skreepka* to the southbound platform of the Avenue M station. I will call with further instructions."

"I don't have a cell phone," said Nikolai.

"No matter—your shadow does. Ms. Epstein—I assume you're listening in—you must give me your number."

I complied, after which Mr. Eeks said, "If you call the police you will never see your mother again."

"Please! Let me talk to Ruth," Nikolai cried as the line went dead.

I sat on their unmade bed, imagining Mom dipping a brush in the water glass on her cluttered worktable, adding a new color to a painting she would then tack up on the wall—there were dozens of them—before stepping back to admire her latest creation. *Please help me do whatever it takes to make sure it isn't her last one,* I asked whoever might be listening. Then I went back to the kitchen.

What's a *skreepka?*" I asked Nikolai.

"A violin."

My exasperation with him must have been written on my face to make him put up his hands the way he did, palms facing outward, his eyes pleading.

"We'll bring her home. He won't hurt her—"

"How the hell do you know that? If you love her then call the police and let the professionals handle this."

"I know how much you care about her, Jo, but you've got to trust me. He will know if we call the police. This is not a risk we can take."

I looked at this unreadable man, who had deceived me at every turn. How could he be so certain that Ruth would survive? Was he fooling himself? Or worse yet, was he hoping these events would relieve him of the burden of caring for my ailing mother?

The trained professional and the daughter fearing for her mother's life were both advocating a call to the police. But for all my doubts, I knew that if Ruth had any chance of survival, I had to follow Nikolai's lead. He was the only connection to Mr. Eeks—and to Mom—that I had. Which was why I promised to meet him at the station at seven-forty-five in the morning, and that I would come alone.

When I was little, Ruth took a week off from her secretarial job at the Art Students League to stay home and nurse me through a bad case of the measles. In between dunkings in cool baths to bring down the fever, she read to me and shared memories from her own childhood, some sweet, some frightening, all of them fascinating to a five-year-old. Bits and pieces of these stories followed me into adulthood, but the one I remembered most clearly involved some boys from her neighborhood. They had made a playhouse out of a big plywood crate, and I could see Ruth in her flimsy summer dress with a big smile on her face, thrilled to be invited inside to play cards.

They must have been sure she'd be an easy mark, and they could bluff her out of her milk money. Instead, she surprised them—her father had taught her how to play poker when she was three—and while she was busy admiring the two shiny nickels she'd won, they had crept outside, closing the makeshift door behind them and taping it shut, sealing her up in the darkness. She had struggled to find a way out, punching at the walls, trying to find the door. When she heard them leave she had cried for what seemed like hours, until her voice grew hoarse and then she lost it entirely. No one came.

Twenty-five years later, when she told me this story, the panic in her voice had been so real that it had cut through my feverish haze and made me cry. I was still that child now, facing the fact that my mother, who had protected and cherished me as best she could, was once again trapped in the dark. There was no way I was going to cool my heels until morning while she was out there with a killer.

CHAPTER ELEVEN

If Grimes had followed me to the concert and kidnapped Ruth, I had a pretty good idea of where he might have taken her.

I parked around the corner from the building on Nostrand Avenue that Grimes had under surveillance and sat in the car for a few moments, considering my next move. If I burst into the basement sewing room, he might do something rash. But if I didn't, he might kill her anyway. Maybe he planned to pin her murder on Nikolai. The thought paralyzed me momentarily and then I pulled myself together and got out of the car.

Since I wanted to get inside unannounced, walking into the building and riding down in the noisy elevator was out of the question. The only other entry point was from the street and blocked by two iron doors, padlocked shut and lying flush with the sidewalk. I'd seen Veton open them, but he had the advantage of using a key. It took some low-volume swearing and some elbow grease, but I jimmied the locks and wrenched the doors up and apart. The flashlight illuminated the old coal chute. Holding my breath, I took a rough-and-tumble ride down to the basement, praying that the racket I'd made had not already announced my arrival.

I was surprised to find the sewing room door had been left open. There was no time to check every nook and cranny in the basement for someone hiding in ambush. I said the hell with it and entered the room. No sign of Grimes or Ruth but on closer inspection it was obvious that someone had been here after I left.

The boxes under the workbench had their lids torn off like someone had rifled their contents in a hurry. There was one box that had survived the rampage and was still sealed shut. Tearing through layers of tape, I pried the lid open and within layers of bubble-wrap, found hundreds of small plastic bottles. *Lipitor, take once daily to control cholesterol.* I got out my camera and took some pictures that might come in handy later.

The counterfeit meds stored in this room were worth a lot more than the dresses. Had Micah known he was party to an abysmally corrupt scheme that could have fatal results for hundreds, if not thousands, of people at risk for heart disease?

I explored every inch of the basement, hoping to find Ruth. It was a maze of hallways and storage bins. Across from the elevator, I found a dismal room where pipes crisscrossed the ceiling, pieces of loose insulation hanging from them like banner advertisements for asbestos disposal. A furnace that looked to be barely of twentieth-century origin occupied the center of the room and in the far corner lay the rotting hulk of a huge decommissioned boiler. The beam of my flashlight picked up something green and shiny on the floor in front of the boiler. It was a man's wristwatch with a wide leather band, the digital display glowing in the dark. I opened the door to the boiler, shining the light as I peered inside, and saw something that sent me crashing back against the wall—the figure of a human being, wrists bound and pressed up against the curved metal shell.

I swallowed my fear but there was nothing I could do about the beating of my heart as I forced myself to crawl into the boiler again for a closer look.

The body wasn't Ruth, thank God. It was Lenny Grimes.

I took the elevator up to the first floor and stepped outside for some fresh air. Leaning against the wall, I willed the shudders that ran though my body to subside. For two seconds I considered calling Spinelli. Bad idea. He'd question me for hours and destroy any chance I had of rescuing my mother.

An anonymous call was the best I could do. They would find the knock-off operation but it would take them a while to connect any dots leading to my client. Meanwhile, Nikolai and I would have enough breathing room to do whatever it took to bring Ruth safely home.

Merging onto the Belt Parkway, I felt my hands start to shake. The Protégé veered to the left and I heard brakes screeching, horns blaring, as I fought for control of the car. I pulled over to the side of the road and turned off the engine. I sat there for a quarter of an hour, helplessly reliving the five seconds during which I had assumed that the dead body in the boiler belonged to my mother.

Back home, I spent the rest of the night in suspended animation, staring at a watercolor my mother had given me for my birthday last year. It was a subway-car scene, several riders seated in a row, one of them knitting, another reading a book, while above them two figures floated at ceiling level, holding on to the straps.

I was dressed and out the door by six-thirty A.M., but that didn't keep me from white-knuckling it all the way to Brooklyn. It was exactly seven thirty-five when I arrived at the Avenue M Station and took the stairs, two at a time, from the stationhouse to the southbound platform. Nikolai was sitting on a bench, looking pointedly at his watch. I got out my cell phone and switched it to speaker mode before handing it to him. Then I surveyed the scene.

The station was above ground, but not by much—surrounded by a dozen or so pre–World War I apartment buildings on both sides. I knew Mr. Eeks could be watching from any one of them. At the other end of the platform, a bunch of students from Edward R. Murrow High School were flirting and cursing, filling the air with pre-school cacophony. They piled on to the Q train when it arrived at seven forty and that's when Nikolai took his violin case by the handle and stood up. We walked to the south end of the station, where the platform ended and the tracks continued on before descending into the ground.

At eight A.M. my cell phone played the first two notes of "I Shot the Sheriff," and Nikolai flipped it open. A northbound train rumbled into the other side of the station, and I had to lean in close to hear, even though the speaker was set on high. It was the same low-pitched, synthetic voice.

"Go to the Rockaway Boulevard station and I'll contact you. You have one hour." The caller ID was blocked, no surprise there.

I ran downstairs, got a map from the station booth agent, and returned to Nikolai. "Is it possible? Can we get there in time?" he asked.

I waited until I'd pulled him on board the southbound Q train before explaining that we had to change for the S train at Prospect Park, get off at Franklin Avenue, and then catch the A train all the way to Rockaway. It was going to be close, but the only alternative was driving through gridlock rush-hour traffic, a guaranteed disaster.

"He's probably going to move us around until he's sure we didn't bring in the police."

"You didn't, did you?" Nikolai demanded.

"I gave you my word and I kept it."

We made the trip with five minutes to spare and were standing on the northbound platform of the Rockaway Boulevard station at eight fifty-five when the call came. I took it this time, as Nikolai listened in.

"Listen carefully, Little Dog. I will say this only once. Take your *skreepka* out of the case. Go down the service stairway and look for the red ball. When you find it, put the violin on the tracks—in the middle, not to the side. After that you will have very little time to retrieve the ball—it has a message inside. Your choice will be simple—your violin or your wife."

Without a word, Nikolai opened the case and gently removed the violin, holding it by the neck. As we walked along the platform toward the north end of the station, I saw him stroking the front of the instrument—the part musicians call the belly.

I scanned the tracks and located a gleam of red peeking out from under the insulated covering of the third rail. Nikolai saw the ball too, because he stopped for a moment. When we reached the end of the platform, I followed him down the narrow service stairway and on to the tracks. On the street-side of the station, the sun bounced off a sign advertising a dry cleaning store.

"Wait here!" Nikolai hissed, and I watched his round shoulders, stooped and weary, as he made his way through the black watery grime between the rails, the violin at his side. He had walked what looked like thirty feet, when two headlights became visible, moving around a curve in the distance—maybe a half mile away. I knew he'd spotted them, because he picked up the pace—stumbling awkwardly over the rail ties until he reached the place where the ball was wedged under the third rail.

I ran up the stairs and down the platform to a spot overlooking where he was. I saw him kneel and, with great reverence, place the violin behind him on the tracks. The sacrifice was in place. If I had any doubts about Nikolai's capacity for placing my mother's welfare ahead of his own, they were put to rest then.

He bent down, braced for the jolt of 600 volts that could kill him and then, when it didn't, pulled the ball free. He held it up in triumph and in that instant the rumbling of the oncoming train shook the entire station and him along with it, causing him to drop the ball. It bounced weakly, up and away from him. He staggered forward, leaning down and stretching out his right arm, palm extended upward, swatting clumsily at the red orb, miraculously making contact so that it came flying over the platform's edge, high enough to give me a few seconds to get under it and pluck it from the air. I heard the scream of air brakes and swiveled around to look for Nikolai. The A train thundered into the station. I fell to my knees, disbelief and deadly certainty competing for my consciousness. I shouldn't have let him go—he'd be alive if I hadn't let him boss me around—why hadn't I told Hasim the truth and let him handle this? It was one thing for a violin to be pulverized . . . I squeezed the red ball until my hand ached. Perhaps whatever was inside would tell me my mother's whereabouts, but it would not bring her husband back to life.

The doors to the train opened and an announcement blared from the speakers, telling the passengers to get off. I stood and found myself looking into the anxious brown eyes of a young transit cop, his shaved head gleaming like an eggplant under the fluorescent lights.

"You with that guy?"

"Yes."

"What an idiot. The engineer didn't even see him until he was halfway into the station. I was in the back car. He radioed me. I thought we had another jumper."

"Where is he?"

"There's a catwalk—it's hard to see from here. I sent for an ambulance, just in case. As soon as the passengers are out, we'll open the doors on the other side and have a look."

The platform was filling with passengers, some disgruntled,

others excited and curious about what had happened. I followed the cop three cars down and then into the train. The door on the street side opened and the cop leaned out. "You okay, buddy?"

"You took your time. Help me up—I've got a cramp in my leg."

Nikolai was dirty, disheveled, and disgusted, but unhurt. He also had his story ready. "I'm sorry for all the trouble, officer. I dropped my wallet on the tracks and thought I had plenty of time to retrieve it. There were some really important papers inside and—"

"If you're sure you're alright, I'll cancel the ambulance." I could see how relieved the cop was that no one was dead. He let us go with a warning—"You look like you've had enough of a scare that you'll never do this again"—and we hurried over to the southbound platform before he could change his mind.

Once on board the southbound train, Nikolai used the pen knife on his keychain to slice the red ball into two hollow halves. The note inside—composed with the usual patchwork of pasted newsprint—read: CALL THIS NUMBER AND RING TWICE. I'LL KEEP MY WORD. YOU DIDN'T.

I punched in the number on my cell, clicked Send and then clicked Quit after two rings. "Now he knows we've obeyed his fucked-up commands. I'm really sorry about your violin."

Nikolai nodded. "Ruth had better be home when we get there."

"So tell me," I asked. "Why does he call you Little Dog?"

"Not now," he said, and I let it go, the adrenalin in my system having worn off, replaced by a bone-tiredness that thrust me into sleep for most of the ride back to Kings Highway.

The redhead had no idea how lucky she'd been. If she had chosen to come to the apartment, instead of the basement across the street, he would have shot her without a second thought. When she emerged from the building, he couldn't tell from her body language whether or not she had found the body, but if she was any good at what she did, she had.

Killing a fellow officer was something he had never anticipated, and the guilt would always be there. There had simply been no other way to deal with Grimes's clumsy interference.

To give himself credit, he had done his best not to frighten the old lady. She was sweet, and it made his blood boil to think of her being tricked into marrying a beast like Little Dog. He was sorry he had drugged her, but it was the only way he could be sure she wouldn't escape while he was gone.

And then, at the station, it had looked like all his prospects for obtaining meaningful revenge would be obliterated by the A train. What relief had flooded him, stronger than the overflowing Volga in spring, when he realized that Little Dog had survived to die another day, on the day he chose and not one moment sooner or later than ordained.

CHAPTER TWELVE

"If she's not home by nightfall, I'm going to call the police. They have resources and we have lots of leads we can give them. We owe it to Ruth to do everything we can. You must know this."

"We will wait," is all he would say.

"I don't need your permission, goddamn it. She's my mother."

"If you call the police you won't have a mother."

We kept arguing back and forth until the sound of a key unlocking the front door brought us both up short.

She stood in the foyer, looking from him to me and back again. Nikolai swept her up in his arms and burst into tears.

"What's the matter?" Her voice was muffled in his chest.

"We were worried about you," I said. "Are you okay?"

"Why shouldn't I be?"

Nikolai looked over her shoulder at me and we exchanged puzzled glances. I was about to question her further when he released her and pulled a wad of crumpled bills from his pocket. "Jo will go for take-out," he said, thrusting the money at me and motioning toward the door.

"I can't go. I need to be sure she's alright," I said.

"Leave us be. This is not the time for questions."

"Get some potato salad too," said Mom. "I'm starved."

As soon as I got back, we dug into the pastrami sandwiches,

mayonnaise-rich potato salad, and cream sodas I'd bought at Edelman's Deli—comfort food times two. It took a while to get the whole story out of Ruth, but what it boiled down to was that when she came out of the ladies' room at Dimitri's, a "nice man" had approached her and said that Nikolai didn't want her to tire herself out and had asked him to take her home right after the performance.

"Where did he take you?"

"I'm not sure. We rode around in his police car for quite a while."

"See, I told you. No police," Nikolai said.

"Was it a blue and white?" I asked Ruth.

"No. But it had a big yellow light under the dashboard—the kind they put on top of the car when they're chasing someone. I know these cars—the plainclothesmen use them—I've seen them at Duane Reade keeping an eye on the girls." Like a flashlight with unreliable batteries, Mom's acuity seemed to flicker on and off at random.

Nikolai squirmed in his chair, probably wondering how much Ruth knew about his part-time job driving for Avenue L. Ostensibly unaware of the bombshells she was dropping all around her, my mother continued. "He took me to a place where he said I would be safe, told me to drink a chocolate soda and lie down and get some rest. When I woke up there was sunlight shining on my face from the window and I heard church bells. It was ten o'clock and he wasn't there and I was scared, being there by myself, but then he came back with some sandwiches and I ate everything, even the cookies. After that he said to wash my face and that if I wanted to see my husband I should go for a walk with him and not ask any questions. When we got to the library he told me to go in and stay there until eleven and that after that I could go home. He said that's what you wanted, that you were very busy, and if you knew I was there you wouldn't worry about me. Oh, I almost forgot. He gave me something to give to you."

She stood up and retrieved a crumpled blue Post-It note from the pocket of her skirt, handing it to Nikolai. "After I clear the table, let's have some coffee in the living room."

Nikolai's face hardened as he read the note. He tucked it into his shirt pocket.

"What does it say?" I inquired. As usual, he was forcing me to ask for information that should have been forthcoming.

"Later," he said, carrying the coffee tray into the living room and helping Ruth get settled in the recliner, tenderly tucking a blanket around her. It hit me then how unstable and helpless she truly was. The slightly confused but predominantly lucid Ruth I was accustomed to had been replaced by this woman who depended on Nikolai for everything, from grocery shopping to finding the senior bus pass that was never in the drawer where she insisted she kept it.

I could see now that I'd chosen her good days for my visits. Dementia was notoriously fickle in its timing and I had been unwilling or unable to recognize the signs of her decline. And of course, she'd always been good at hiding unpleasantness.

By the time Mom went to bed, my anger at Nikolai had reached its peak. He must have sensed this, because he pulled out the blue Post-It and handed it over.

Four words: *Kak pozhivaet tvoya sestra.*

"What does this mean?"

"Happy Birthday."

"I don't believe you," I said, making a show of copying the words on the pad I kept in my purse before returning the note to him.

"It doesn't matter," he said.

"Hear this, Nikolai. If you won't be straight with me I can't do this anymore."

He put his hands up in mock surrender. "You win Jo—as of tomorrow my life will be an open book."

"Why not now?"

"Please, Jo. I need to collect some of her things and to explain to your mother why she must go and stay with her brother. Tomorrow you can take her back to Queens. Can you be here at noon?"

It crossed my mind that Nikolai might be trying to con me, but it was hard to imagine him fleeing the scene, given his willingness to sacrifice his precious violin and knowing as he did how much Ruth needed him. "Alright," I said. "She can stay the night. But if you come up with some excuse not to tell me what this is all about I'll turn you in to the cops myself."

His loud phony laughter summoned Ruth back into the room to ask what was so funny. "It's a secret," he said, playfully punching my shoulder, making it hard to resist the impulse to knock his block off.

"I'm so glad you two are getting along. Maybe a little trouble is what this family needed to bring us together."

An endearing quality, my mother's total lack of irony.

CHAPTER THIRTEEN

A line of people snaked along East 3rd Street, all of them waiting to get into the Nuyorican. The rain had failed to dampen their spirits, and the street buzzed with talk among groups sharing umbrellas. Sanyo waved to me—he was holding a place up front, which meant he'd been there for a while. Tiny droplets of water glistened in his thick ebony eyebrows.

It was hot inside the club, patrons packed to the ceiling. Trying to squeeze through the crowd, we got stuck between two retro-hipster guys in black turtlenecks and gold medallions and a short chubby teenager with maroon lipstick glistening like candy on her burnt chocolate face. Everyone seemed immensely casual, careful not to show how thrilled they were to be making the scene at New York's premiere poetry venue. No disloyalty meant to Scandal's, but compared to the Nuyorican, our slam was strictly minor league.

We grabbed the last two seats available at the bar, and I took off my jacket. With a maximum occupancy of 150 maximum and at least 400 people crammed into the club, no wonder the place was a steam bath.

"I like your outfit, don't think I've ever seen that color." He was referring to my silk chartreuse blouse, a present from my mother.

"It's ugly, isn't it?"

"Not with you in it," he said without embarrassment, slipping his arm around my waist and giving me a slight tug toward him. I resisted the urge to snuggle against his chest and concentrated instead on keeping my balance on the bar stool. It's not that I wanted to play it cool with Sanyo—I'd waited a long time for this night—but this new dance between us made me nervous, and I didn't want to fall flat on my face.

"How've you been?" he asked.

"Broke the stress meter."

"Maybe we can do something about that." The words were sincere and not an unwelcome presumption.

Taylor Q was the featured poet, introduced to thunderous applause that amounted to more than hand-clapping—it was a gift of energy from an audience that expected to be knocked on its collective ass. Taylor's ceaseless flow of images began even before he reached the microphone. His words rode on the circular breath of a saxophone player, crackled like castanets, forming rapid-fire phrases that told of monks in Vietnam who chose to soak themselves in gasoline rather than sanction war, that described the heat from their flaming bodies and how it had failed to thaw the millions of souls frozen in front of their TV dinners thousands of miles away.

Sanyo hadn't moved a muscle since the performance began. Either he was as spellbound as I was, or he was rigid with disbelief. When the applause and whoops and hollers died down, he turned to me and said in a quiet voice that I had to lean in to hear, "I never knew you could stop hearing the actual words and still get the meaning."

In the dim light it was hard to tell if the moisture on his face was sweat from the overheated room or honest-to-god tears. Then he leaned over and whispered in my ear, "This guy's gonna be fighting the ladies off with a stick." Fortunately, the slam master chose this moment to leap on stage, and I was able to hide my embarrassment at being caught laughing and crying at the same time.

The emcee provided the fastest rundown of slam rules I'd ever heard. "Six poets, five judges, scores from one to ten, drop the highest and the lowest numbers, eliminate two poets, and see who moves on to the next round."

First came the ritual of the "sacrificial" poet warming up the room. He provided three minutes of doggerel about all the ways we can derange our senses (a tribute to Rimbaud that he may not have been aware of), giving the judges a chance to calibrate their scoring techniques. Then the competition began in earnest. The first two poets pulled off bombastically lackluster performances (an accomplishment in itself), but things picked up when a petite Asian girl delivered, "This Thai Won't Die." The judges gave her insultingly low numbers—a two, a five, and three sevens—and in turn the audience berated the judges with boos and hisses. Some of the rudest sounds were coming from the man sitting next to me. Sanyo had thrown himself totally into the slam.

The fourth poet, a pale beanpole in his twenties whose tight-fitting t-shirt revealed his navel with every breath, floored us with a series of haikus on the physics of sound and light, pithy odes to the invisible worlds beyond our senses. He garnered a perfect score of thirty. The fifth and sixth poets bombed out, enabling the Thai girl to survive her low scores and move on. Sanyo was ecstatic and gave me a lingering kiss, which caused me to completely space out the second round.

I figured we'd be there to the bitter end, but Sanyo surprised me by asking if we could skip the upcoming head-to-head round between his two favorites.

"They're both so good," he said, "I don't want to see either one lose."

I felt the same way and told him so.

Across the street at a neighborhood bar we picked a quiet table and, over a bottle of decent cabernet, agreed that since

Sanyo lived nearby, it would be easier for me to go to his place than vice versa.

Five blocks and one more bottle of wine later, we sat naked, cross-legged, facing each other with knees touching on the Navajo rug in front of the gas fireplace. Since Nikolai called four days ago, I'd been going nonstop. It was good to feel the warmth from the fire working on the tense muscles in my back and I stretched my arms above my head.

"Hard week, huh?" said Sanyo, his eyes trained on my belly button in a way that made my nipples harden. "We'll have to eat breakfast out. I don't have guests here that often. Actually, never," he murmured as he opened my legs and gently pulled them over his own. I held on to his shoulders and arched my back as he slid in, driving slow and easy, the way I knew he would.

After time resumed, we slowly returned to earth, inhaling our musky aroma, sweaty bellies shaking with laughter. The relief of having what you didn't know you'd needed so badly. Or something like that.

I wanted to ask him why he'd been living like a hermit, but it was late and we were sleepy and maybe I wasn't so eager to fill in the gaps between our respective childhoods in the Bronx and our first encounter five years ago. It was like sleeping with a stranger and at the same time enjoying the comfort level of being with someone who might remember what you looked like when you were ten.

I woke up in Sanyo's bed, to the strains of Salsa leaking in from the apartment next door. He gave no signs of stirring while I dressed, so I took the opportunity to explore his apartment. I assumed he wouldn't mind, given that he'd dubbed me *"avorosa,"* last night, which is Fijian slang for busy body.

The most interesting thing in Sanyo's living room was an

urban totem pole, which managed to dominate the room in spite of being relegated to a corner. The brown face, a shade or two darker than Sanyo's own, was intricately carved, but in such close harmony with the grain of the wood that it suggested genetic engineering rather than sculpture. It took a moment to register that the pupils of the eyes were plastic caps from dish-washing bottles and that the iridescent irises were circles cut out of DVD disks.

"I stopped making those after my wife threw out all my junk," Sanyo said, standing in the bedroom doorway, a towel around his waist. "That didn't stop her from taking most of my pieces as part of the divorce settlement."

"Oh. For a second there I thought you were married." My relief must have been in plain sight, prompting Sanyo to grab me and plant a big wet one. "You've been nosing around my house," he chided. "You're my little *avorosa.*"

I was half out the door before he said, "I'll call you."

I mostly wanted him to, except for the woman in me who, after two failed marriages, was oh so gun-shy. Actually, given my profession, this phrase was misleading. "Arrow-shy" seemed more apt when it came to me and Cupid.

Outside, the wind had picked up, but it was still unseason-ably warm for October. I headed down 6th Street to East River Park, the perfect place for a post-coital walk and reflection. The river was choppy, my mood serene. It was a pity I didn't have a gaggle of girlfriends à la *Sex and the City* to tease me when they found out I'd been getting some. Since moving back to New York from Los Angeles five years ago, I hadn't had much time for socializing—unless you count hanging out with my competi-tors at the slam, and even then I had to keep an eye out for the disorderly ones I might have to evict later in the evening.

CHAPTER FOURTEEN

My feelings were mixed when I got home, the glow of having connected so sweetly with Sanyo more than partially eclipsed by my discouragement at having squat to show for a week's work on a case involving an irascible stepfather who worked with me one minute and choked me off the next. Add the unassailable fact that I had neglected to keep watch over my mom, and the result was a splitting headache.

I used an online Russian-English dictionary to translate the words from the blue Post-It: As I had suspected, *Kak pozhivaet tvoya sestra* did not mean *happy birthday.* It meant *How is your sister?* It made no sense to me, but I was determined that by the end of the day it would.

On the way to Brooklyn, I thought about what I would do if Nikolai broke his promise to "tell all." Something had to give—either my patience or his stubbornness. I had to get him to face the fact that the police were poised to pull him in and that Mr. Eeks would give them everything they needed to put him in prison for whatever years beyond his sixty-three were left. After what had happened to Ruth, maybe I'd be able to convince him that we should go to the authorities with the blackmail materials, that we had at least one ally in the NYPD—Lieutenant Hasim Saleh—who was willing to help us. But convincing Nikolai to come out into the open would be harder than coaxing a cat into a dog pound.

I let myself in, and there was Ruth, standing in the middle of the living room as if seeing her surroundings for the first time. I gave her a few moments to recover. Her memory lapses were getting more frequent but she always seemed to recover right when I thought she'd spun off into space. A minute went by before she sat down on the couch and motioned for me to join her.

"He's gone, Jo." It was clear she didn't mean gone as in gone out to buy groceries.

"His suitcase is missing and so is his passport." She closed her eyes.

You won't find him inside your head, I thought.

"He left me a letter. It's right there, on the counter near the sink. I've read it a million times and I still don't understand it."

My dearest Ruth,

When I came to this country I thought I had escaped what I can only call the fate of being Russian, of belonging to a people who for centuries knew no personal freedoms and have been conditioned to expect none. Once again, I am manipulated by forces beyond my control, trapped with no way out but exile. First east to west, now west to east.

You have been my refuge, both from the past and from the dark side of myself. That I could put a luminous smile on your face seemed to make up for my many shortcomings. That I now will cause you pain is the most unbearable burden.

You accepted me without knowing certain details about my past that might have caused you to reconsider, but I am not sorry that I lied. If I had told you everything, then our time together would not have been so carefree, your paintings so bright and hopeful. Your capacity for empathy—one of your greatest virtues—would also have been the downfall of our marriage. No man wants pity from the woman he loves.

Please forgive me and know that if it is humanly possible for

*me to return and for us to go on as before, you will see me
again.*

All my love,
Nik

It was so quiet I could hear the clock ticking in the kitchen.

"You never liked him much, did you?"

If she was blaming me for my stepfather's flight, she might
have a point. In spite of my suspicions that he might leave the
country, I had done nothing to change Nikolai's course.

"You're thinking of when your dad left, aren't you?"

I had misjudged her. Mom did not have a recriminating bone
in her body. I sat down at the table. "Well there is a parallel."

In the days after my father dropped out of sight, my mother
and I stopped talking, at least about anything of consequence. I
was a morose preteen, neither of us was good at chitchat, and to
talk about the whys and wheres of his departure was simply too
painful. Over the years we'd remained friendly but the reserve
had stuck. And now here we were, forced to face the departure
of another man—she more vulnerable and less capable of
recovery than before; me reluctant to open channels clogged
with a mass of unexpressed feelings.

"Mom, is it okay if I look through Nikolai's things?"

She nodded assent, already lost in her loss. There would be
time to comfort her later.

Their bedroom, which served double-duty as Ruth's painting
studio, was in its customary state of chaos, clothes strewn on
the bedposts, canvases stacked to the ceiling on Ruth's
worktable. The top drawer of Nikolai's pine dresser was open,
playing host to a catch-all of old key chains, empty checkbook
covers, half a book of stamps, ancient phone bills, insurance
papers and other outdated and useless documents. The surface
of a small desk next to the bureau was entirely occupied by a
huge computer monitor that looked like it dated back to the

days before Google tamed the Internet. I pressed the blue button on the tower lying on its side beneath the desk, and the machine booted up. Windows XP—no password, thank goodness; I'm no hacker. The first place I looked was the history menu in his browser—the last two sites visited were Expedia and Hotels Online. On the Favorites menu, I found *Build Your Own Trip—JFK to SVO,* and followed that link to a list of several flights with that day's departure date and Moscow (SVO) as the destination. I opened Outlook Express and found a confirmation e-mail for Aeroflot 316, probably already in the air. I memorized the flight number and deleted the message, making sure to empty the trash folder after doing so. It appeared that Nikolai was rapidly burning his bridges, including the one that led to me.

Back in the kitchen, Ruth was rummaging through the white metal cabinet where she kept dry goods. "I was sure there was a can of tuna fish left," she said. "If he comes home for dinner, what will I do?"

"Mom, I need you to think. Is there a friend or relative who Nikolai calls in Russia, someone he stays in touch with? Maybe a sister?"

"Yes, there is a sister. Her name is Olga, and she has a different last name than his—Sadekov. He doesn't like to talk about her. Something bad happened between them."

How is your sister? It all fell into place.

"Do you have Olga's address?"

I followed her into the bedroom, and after prolonged rummaging through the drawer in her nightstand, she came up with an envelope. "It's a birthday card she sent him. He refused to open it, so I kept it. Sometimes people change their minds."

The return address was written in Russian. I took the card out before folding the envelope and putting it in my pocket.

"How about you make us some tea?" I asked, and waited

until Ruth had left the room before continuing my search.

In the middle desk drawer I found the smallest Matryoshka yet, number four. It was not a diminutive judge, as I would have expected, but a prisoner, complete with striped uniform and multiple tattoos. One word, in Russian, was burnt into its heavily varnished chest, the Cyrillic letters like wounds made with a hot knife.

There was also an envelope with my name written on it in Nikolai's flowing cursive hand.

I placed the doll on top of the desk and was opening the envelope when I heard a series of dull repetitive thuds that could only mean that someone was pounding on the front door. It had to be the police, and I was in no mood to be detained and questioned. I crammed the envelope into my jacket pocket and used up a few precious seconds clearing the history and favorites cache on Nikolai's computer before turning it off. I then retrieved the key from the ledge above the window frame, opened the metal gate and pulled up the window as far as it would open. In the distance the lights of the Verrazano Bridge twinkled.

I crept out onto the fire escape and was carefully closing the window behind me when I remembered the doll.

"When did your husband leave?" It was Spinelli's voice, coming from the kitchen.

"I told you, I'm not his keeper." Good old Ruth.

Despite the moment's dread seizing upon me, I removed my shoes and climbed back into the bedroom. I grabbed the doll off the desk and tiptoed toward the open window. Halfway there I slipped in my threadbare socks and grabbed the bedpost for balance. The doll slipped from my hand and clattered across the wooden floor.

I slid under the bed and waited, grateful that the bedspread had such a long skirt and that the mattress coil poking through near my head was blunted at the edge.

Spinelli's suspicion-filled voice was accompanied by his footsteps entering the room. "Is someone else here?"

"It gets windy in here when the window is open," Ruth said. Feet moved across the room. The window closed, and the draft receded. "I'd better put this somewhere safe." Ruth's slipper-clad toes came close to my head, and I heard her opening and closing the nightstand drawer.

"Please don't touch anything else, Mrs. Kharpov. When the technicians get here we'll be giving this room a thorough search."

"I love my husband, Mr. Kharpov, but Ruth Epstein is how I sign my paintings, and that's who I am."

Uncomfortable as my situation was, I couldn't help but smile. This was Ruth's standard line, what she said to everyone who made the same mistake.

As soon as they vacated the room, I retrieved the doll from the nightstand and headed for the window. As I climbed out, I heard Spinelli tell Ruth, "When your daughter returns for her shoes on the fire escape, tell her she has twenty-four hours to report to the 70th precinct for questioning, voluntarily, or we will bring her in for impeding an investigation."

I shut the window and flew down the fire escape stairs to the platform one story below. It took some persistent tapping, but finally the curtain was pulled aside, and Sasha's ruddy face peered out at me. In a moment he had the window gate open and I was inside the Volodya apartment.

"Ludmilla's sleeping," he said, the polite host, not one word about my unusual entrance. "But I'm sure she won't mind waking up to see you."

Before he could leave the room, I grabbed his arm.

"Sasha, this is not a social call, and I don't have time for explanations. There are some people upstairs I don't want to talk to. I need to borrow your biggest, bulkiest coat, and a hat to go with it. Then I need you to ride down in the elevator with me and walk me outside."

Like I knew he would, Sasha rose to the occasion. From the hall closet, he brought out a coat for me to wear that a whole family could have lived in and crammed an equally massive fur hat on my head. But for the shoes, a battered pair of Reeboks, no one would recognize me.

As soon as we reached the lobby, via the stairs, he began firing Russian phrases at me and kept this up until we'd walked past the uniforms and out into the street. It seemed that when it came to avoiding the authorities, there was no better company to be in than a Russian's.

We fast-walked it to my car, parked on Avenue P, and I gave Sasha back the coat and hat. I also showed him the latest Matryoshka. "Can you tell me what this word means?"

He examined the letters burnt into the doll's chest and frowned. "*Fraier*. In Russia it's what they used to call a newcomer to prison. In the old days."

I then gave Sasha the envelope with Olga Sadekov's return address. "Can you translate this?" He pulled a bank deposit slip out of his wallet and wrote Olga's address on the back, in phonetic English.

"I've got one more favor to ask, Sasha."

"You want me to get Ruth and bring her here so you can take her back to her brother's house. No problem." All it took was a nod, and he was walking back, strolling as casually as if he were on his way to pick up some tea cakes at the bakery.

I called Uncle Jake and told him he'd be having some unexpected visitors. Then I opened the letter from Nikolai. Ten one-hundred-dollar bills were stuffed inside, along with a note that read: *Jo, I know you tried but enough is enough. Take care of your mother and pray for me. I'll be where I cannot be found. N.*

The wait seemed interminable, but only ten minutes went by before Ruth was sitting beside me in the Protégé, giving me an argument.

"I want to stay in the apartment. What if Nik comes and I'm not here?"

"Mom, I don't think it's a good idea for you to stay there by yourself."

"What are you talking about?"

"He's left the country and I don't think he plans to return anytime soon."

"You blow everything out of proportion, Jo. He's always staying out late playing music, giving lessons."

I'd seen Mom demonstrate her ability to disconnect in times of crisis before. One of my earliest memories was of my father passing out in the hallway of our Bronx apartment building, where we'd taken refuge from the poisonous fumes released after he cut the freezer coil in our ancient ammonia-cooled refrigerator. Ruth had calmly stood over his unconscious body, chatting with Mrs. Gonzalez—who had put a mustard plaster on my father's chest with no visible results—about a recent burglary on the third floor and wasn't it a shame. She fell apart as soon as dad was loaded safely into the ambulance.

Most people don't know that the largest Chinatown in New York City is actually in Flushing, Queens. On Main Street, there are usually dozens of spiky durian melons dangling in their plastic mesh bags—stinky to western noses but deliciously aromatic to eastern ones—in front of shop windows that also feature oxtail at four-oh-nine a pound. The movie theaters play melodramas in numerous Asian languages, and the whole conglomeration brings Hong Kong to mind rather than Amsterdam, where the original settlers of this area hailed from.

Uncle Jake's fourth-floor one-bedroom apartment was

sparsely but tastefully furnished with scattered tatami mats, a futon couch and chair (both of which doubled as sleeping accommodations), and a rectangular Chinese lacquer table with cushions for seats. His view overlooked the back of the East Lake restaurant. "Smells like shrimp dumplings, with an undercurrent of Wu Gok," said Mom in a moment of clarity reminiscent of the old days, when she stood strong in her refusal to be typed as a little old lady from Brooklyn.

"Jo! I can't believe you're here!" exclaimed Uncle Jake. His perpetually tanned face lit up with pleasure, not even a trace of resentment that for more than ten years I'd been in touch solely by phone. Not deliberate, but neglect all the same, and of someone who had always been there for me. It was Uncle Jake's exploits in Air Force intelligence, related to me in great detail during his unannounced but eagerly awaited visits to our dead-end neighborhood in the Bronx, that resulted in my eventual decision to go to criminology school. After I got my license, almost twenty years ago, I had consulted him often, and he always went out of his way to help me to obtain hard-to-get information. Tonight, I was asking for much more.

"You've brought my sister back to brighten up this dreary place. Excellent!" he beamed at both of us. With typical generosity he had relieved me of the burden of telling falsehoods in front of Ruth. Jake was the consummate quick study. And so was Ruth, when she'd shoved aside the signs of intermittent memory loss.

"It's obvious you brought me here because you think I'm incapacitated and can't manage on my own," she said, pinning me with a fierce stare reminiscent of childhood battles. "Since when are you my survival instructor? I seem to remember your giving away your best bottle caps to some hoodlums on the roof who you wanted to like you."

"I was nine years old, Mom. I'm hoping you'll see I have

your best interests at heart," I said as gently as I could. If she heard even a tinge of frustration in my voice she'd close down tighter than Spandex on thunder thighs. "Nikolai is in a little trouble, and someone wants to send him to jail. I'm going to find the evidence that will clear his name and allow him to come home. But if I'm worried about you, I won't be able to do my job. Your part is to stay here, to stay safe."

"I'll think about it," she said, taking her suitcase into the other room to unpack.

"Give her some time to settle in," advised Uncle Jake, coming out from behind the counter—cluttered with books, newspapers in several languages, and five empty Sake bottles—that separated the tiny, make-do kitchen from the living area. "Remembrances of a great party," he explained unnecessarily. "Sorry you missed it." He was looking more fit than I remembered. At seventy-five, with a full head of dazzling white hair, he had an energy level that put the sedentary computer game generation to shame.

I filled him in as we chewed on some strudel I was sure he had run out to buy after I called.

"If there's one thing I learned working in intelligence it's that you've got to employ your peripheral vision. What about this Spinelli who came to arrest Nikolai?"

"Yeah. Spinelli's a bully but I don't think he's dirty. He's just convinced that Nikolai should be put away for murder."

"Murder!" Ruth's backlit silhouette in the bedroom doorway was ramrod straight. "You said he was in trouble, but you didn't say anything about murder. How could you lie to me that way?"

"I didn't lie, Mom. I told you someone was trying to put Nikolai in jail and when you didn't ask for the specifics . . ."

Her tears could always trounce my excuses. This is exactly what I'd been dreading. "I'm sorry. Sometimes it's hard to know how much to tell you."

Ruth sank down on the futon and grabbed a pillow that she proceeded to beat into shape instead of me. "Don't you see that when you treat me this way you're saying that I'm not a person? Yes, I'm old, and maybe I forget things, but losing your mind doesn't mean losing your feelings. Inside here,"—she pounded her chest so hard I was afraid she'd hurt herself—"inside here, it's still me!"

"I know Mom . . ."

"Do you? Then talk to me, Jo. Tell me what happened at our house that night. I know it must have been in the paper, but Nikolai said I shouldn't read about it, that it would make me too anxious and it really had nothing to do with us. That wasn't the truth, was it?" The realist in my mom had shoved aside its fuzzy competition. For the first time in months she gazed steadily at me from behind eyes that had traded soft Lapis Lazuli for laser-like china blue.

"Yes, Mom. He lied. But you have to realize the man was in shock. He had been forced to fire a gun, to kill someone in cold blood."

"Who did this to Nikolai? Is it someone we know?"

"I don't think so, Mom. It's someone who holds a grudge against him from way back. Nikolai hired me to find this man—we call him Mr. Eeks—but we ran out of time. Now Mr. Eeks has given the police enough manufactured evidence to send Nikolai to jail for the rest of his life. Nikolai had to leave the country before they could arrest him. I also know he was worried about his sister, and that's why he chose to go to Moscow."

Ruth's shoulders sagged but her eyes stayed dry. She took my chin in her hand. "Thank you for trying to help."

Jake served us some homemade California rolls—"leftovers, nothing fancy"—and after a while Ruth said, "I've decided to stay here, if Jake will have me, for as long as it takes for you to bring Nikolai home. All I ask is that you tell me where he is, as soon as you find him."

"You have no idea where he might have gone?"

She gave me that look again.

"Okay, Mom. I promise."

She was looking exhausted, and she wasn't the only one.

"Thanks, Uncle Jake. I'll be in touch."

"Sure thing, Jo. And if you need some help . . ."

"You're at the top of my list."

"Good night, Jo."

"Sure you don't want to stay over?" Ruth asked. "Last week there was a carjacking . . ."

"Mom!"

Terminal Three was packed with Saudis in traditional Thobes and Koreans in shiny suits. I didn't know why I'd come—Nikolai's flight had been scheduled to depart three hours ago and it was long gone.

I dropped in at the Aeroflot office on the mezzanine and asked the agent, a pert, ageless Italian who looked like she might have graduated from stewardess school in the '50s, how quickly I could get a Russian visa. "A two-day turnaround is the quickest service we offer but you'll have to either Fed-Ex or hand-deliver your passport to the consulate in Manhattan. They're very strict about that." I filled out the forms and took down the address of the consulate.

In the lounge a handful of afternoon drinkers, mostly businessmen, were bending their elbows at the bar. "Missed your flight?" inquired the bartender, an indication that I looked as forlorn as I felt. The single malt went down smooth, but failed to take the bitterness with it.

Last year he had taken his wife Karen to Russia for the first time. There were certain arrangements that had to be made while he was there, but she adored museums and was happy to have him drop her off for a day at the Tretyakov Gallery or the Armory Museum in the Kremlin while he went about his business. His side trips took him only a few hours from Moscow by car, so he was able to get back in time to take Karen to a few of the many new restaurants that had opened since his move to the U.S.

He also took her to the Moscow Circus and was amazed at how the acrobatic extravaganzas catapulted her back to her childhood, so much more innocent and impressionable than his own. Her rapt face had fascinated him more than any of the predictable spectacles in the ring.

As was often the case, what he thought would be his most difficult task had turned out to be the easiest. An elderly friend of his uncle had kept in touch with the son of one of Ishkhan's "associates." The *vor*, who went by the nickname Squint, had at first been reluctant but finally agreed to meet him in front of the telegraph office on Tverskaya. Squint was astounded to learn what was wanted, then amused, and finally intrigued. "If what you say is true, and your father was treated unfairly, then I don't want your money," he said. "Maybe later, a favor. We'll see."

Feydor hid his distaste at the idea of a trade. Yes, he needed this man's cooperation. But what was owed to Ishkhan was not to be trivialized.

CHAPTER FIFTEEN

The November sun was out, a prime opportunity to walk rather than ride across Central Park. At the Russian consulate on East 91st, I delivered a stack of original documents to the stiffly polite official. She now had enough information about my life to grant me asylum, much less a visa.

On the way back across the park, I stopped at a sidewalk stand for a hot pretzel and soda, wondering if there'd be similar treats for sale on the streets of Moscow. Passing the East Meadow, I saw some hardy souls picnicking on a grassy hill and was considering joining them when my cell chimed. I fished the gadget out of my purse in time to hear Hasim's voice. "Did you hear about Grimes?"

"Yes. I'm sorry about your friend, Hasim." I was also sorry that I couldn't tell him it was me who had found his colleague's body. Why drag him deeper into conflict of interest than he already was?

"Spinelli thinks Nikolai Kharpov is good for Lenny's murder. He also claims to have an airtight case against Kharpov for the Goldman killing and told me that you helped your stepfather flee the country. You're at the top of his most-wanted list, Jo."

"I didn't help Nikolai run, but I can see how it might look that way." I told Hasim how I had tampered with the computer.

"Brilliant, Jo. You've given them everything but the handcuffs. But be that as it may," continued Hasim in the archaic manner he used when dealing with the unreasonable, "I thought you'd like to know that Spinelli followed up on a tip and found a gun in a dumpster near Kharpov's house that matches the slug taken out of Micah Goldman. Forensics lifted a clear set of prints from the stock, identified as belonging to Kharpov."

Mr. Eek's timing was a little off here. "Don't you think it's odd that the gun was still in the dumpster, when the murder took place more than a week ago? I know trash collection in New York isn't what it used to be, but that's stretching it a bit. The gun is an obvious plant."

"The fingerprints are real enough," Hasim countered.

"Anything on Frank Mitchell yet?" I asked, ready to change the subject and aware that this might be our last chance to talk before I became a pariah.

"I called personnel and they told me that Mitchell's been on leave in the Bahamas. He's due to retire and is using up his vacation time. Your addict must have had her days mixed up when she said she saw him with Grimes. No surprise there. Looks like you've hit another dead end."

"You've got to admit that someone's done a bang-up job framing Nikolai," I said. "I can't say I blame him for running."

"A wise man doesn't stand in a place of danger trusting in miracles." Another pithy signoff from Hasim, and in this case applicable to both Nikolai and myself. It was a sure bet that Spinelli would raid my apartment. If I hustled, maybe I'd make it home in time to pack my gear and incinerate Nikolai's bloody clothes before the police came knocking.

Whatever misgivings Sanyo may have had at the sight of my overstuffed suitcase, he did a good job of hiding them. He'd been sweet on the phone, but I could only imagine how it had felt to be asked for shelter by a woman he'd known intimately for exactly twenty-four hours.

"I cleared out some space in my junk room." He didn't need

to tell me how much of a sacrifice this had been.

"Where did you move your art supplies?"

"Have a look," he said, leading me into the small bedroom, where the collection of scrap metal he used in his sculptures was now neatly stacked on floor-to-ceiling shelves.

"Thanks, Sanyo." I slid the suitcase into an out-of-the-way corner. "I'll be here for two days, three at the most. There are some people who would be very angry if they knew I was leaving the country."

"You're off to Moscow, no date of return. I'm heartbroken." In spite of the joking tone, he looked like he meant it, which brightened my day.

"Sanyo, when this is over maybe we could go away for the weekend. I know a great place in the—"

"Jo, I know you mean well, but you don't owe me a thing. Let's see what happens." He planted a key in my hand and a kiss on my chapped lips. "I've got a meeting at a gallery that won't keep, but I'll be back in a couple of hours. Catch you later."

It was warm in the apartment, and I opened the suitcase to look for a short-sleeved shirt. On top of the hastily packed clothes, I had thrown the latest Matryoshka doll sent to taunt Nikolai—the one I had stolen right out from under Spinelli's nose and would be taking with me to Russia.

Following a hunch, I used Sanyo's iMac to Google *Russian prison tattoos*. It took a while, but I found what I was looking for. The "grin tattoo" on the doll represented the Angel of Hell on Earth, and the skeleton with the ax was the executioner of those who were condemned by the thieves' court. I picked up the doll and ran my fingers over the grisly picture. Nikolai, you're in deep shit.

I didn't realize how exhausted I was until I sat down on the couch. The next thing I knew Sanyo was guiding me into the bedroom, and we were making love. I woke in the middle of the night, completely disoriented and wondering where I was. I felt my way through the darkness to the kitchen, trying not to knock over any sculptures on the way, and poured myself a glass of water.

Despite Sanyo's warm hospitality, it felt like the door to my life had been slammed shut, and there was no friendly neighbor with a spare key who could let me back in.

In two hours I'd be on my way to the airport with a Russian visa in my passport and an international cell phone in my purse. After making arrangements for the Protégé to be parked indefinitely at a garage on Avenue B, I noticed that Sanyo was keeping his distance. Said he hated goodbyes, to which I said ditto.

He was finishing a new piece, and I watched him use a blow torch to melt a beer bottle, carefully pouring the amber-colored liquid into tiny molds laid out on his work table. After the glass cooled, he glued the luminescent brown eyes onto the flat wooden face. The eyebrows he shaped with shoelaces; the nose he cut from an aluminum can.

"What's his name?"

"I don't usually name them." He squinted at his creation, rubbing teak oil on some invisible spot he had missed. "I think I'll call him The Emigré."

"Nikolai would hate that."

"So why are you doing all this for a man you can't stand?"

"It's my mother I'm thinking of."

He placed the giant face on the windowsill to dry, where it watched us impassively. "I understand that, but why can't your uncle go instead. Isn't *he* the world traveler?"

"Jake is retired. Besides, he knows I like to finish what I start."

"Russia's a dangerous place. You could get finished yourself."

"It's not the mob-infested jungle it was a few years ago, although I've heard that civil liberties have been traded in for security. Sound familiar?"

Sanyo sat down next to me on the couch, which was covered with bright Mexican blankets and sagged in the middle. "You don't speak the language, and knowing you, you'll be going places where most Americans never go. I want you to promise not to take any unnecessary risks."

"How much worse than New York could it be?"

"She's hopeless," he said, addressing The Émigré.

"I have flashbacks in my bathtub and you talk to sculptures. I wonder what other eccentricities we have in common."

"Mmm, let me see." He pulled me close and pretended to pull something out of my ear. "What's this? Very odd." It was a bright blue plastic Easter egg. He pulled it open. "Curiouser and curiouser."

Hollow dolls and now a hollow egg with something inside it. But it wasn't a cryptic clue, or a threat—it was a silver chain, and dangling from it was a miniature of one of Sanyo's sculptures. He got up and walked around to the back of the couch, reaching over to fasten the clasp, then kissing the back of my neck. He didn't have to tell me what it was. I knew a good luck charm when I saw one.

★ ★ ★ ★ ★

PART TWO:
MOSCOW

★ ★ ★ ★ ★

CHAPTER SIXTEEN

We took off forty-five minutes behind schedule, with me scrunched between a priest (at least that's what I thought he was, given the ankle-length dress and enormous cross) and a young man whose cracked leather jacket could have benefited from a dose of the oil slathered on his hair.

Right out of JFK the plane took a steep curve and I traded anxious glances with a woman across the aisle. Only her frightened eyes were visible beneath the enveloping head scarf. To distract myself, I wrenched a copy of *Aeroflot Magazine* free from the pouch in front of me. It was packed with reassuring phrases like "Up in the sky, hope returns," and "Sometimes the most important decisions in one's life are taken during a flight." My important decision was to take two Xanax and try to sleep.

At midnight New York time (eleven A.M. in Moscow) I woke up groggy and dry-mouthed. Walking forward to the galley in the front of the plane to ask for a glass of water, I drew a look from the flight attendant in first class that was more amused than disapproving. On either side of the extra-wide aisle "busynessmen" feasted on fruit and cheese and sipped orange juice that I suspected was spiked with champagne. There were a few "busynesswomen" too, although as far as I knew this term was absent from the Russian magazines on board, at least the ones that were translated into English.

As I passed the last row in the forward section, on my way back to the cheap seats, my eyes were drawn to a silhouetted face, framed in the window against a background of pink-tinged clouds announcing the dawn. It took a few seconds for me to recognize him. Yuri Baranski. His ears were covered by silver headphones, and he didn't look up.

Along with the passengers from Flight 114, I trudged through the dimly lit corridors of Sheremetyevo Airport, clean, functional, and dismal as an unrestored, black and white movie. With no taped lines on the floor or roped-off areas to guide us, we flowed into the Passport Control room and merged with an unruly, amoeba-like mob that grew from all sides in no discernable pattern. Two women cut in front of me, experienced travelers, equipped with fans to keep them cool as they carved a swath through the crowd. Stifling the urge to scream obscenities, I focused on keeping Yuri Baranski in sight. He was well ahead of me in the jagged line approaching the control booth. Was it just chance, us being on the same plane? If he spotted me, he'd be asking himself the same question.

My obvious distress at being trapped in the crowd and about to lose Baranski was picked up by a well-dressed man in the "line" next to mine. He tapped me on the shoulder and said, "You should try the Diplomatic booth. I think they don't mind people passing through when it's not being used by officials." His voice was British, smooth, cultured. "Why don't you try it yourself?" I asked.

He seemed to find this question amusing. Evidently I was meant to be the guinea pig. Well, why not? In a moment I was at the Diplomatic window with my passport and immigration card at the ready. The officer laughed and said something in Russian to her companion behind the glass, but she stamped my passport and let me through. Looking back, I saw the Englishman still patiently awaiting his turn, unwilling to take the same chance. I winked at him before stepping into the baggage claim area. My first hour on Russian soil, and I'd already broken the rules. I felt like a native already.

Since my only luggage was a carry-all, I walked past the carousels and took the quick route, following the green line all the way out to the street. The air tasted of metallic smog and something else I couldn't identify—was it cabbage?

I had just taken my place at the end of the *Taksi* line when Baranski emerged from the automatic doors and hailed a circling BMW limo. I threw my bag and myself into the back seat of the nearest Volga—provoking some indignant shouts in Russian that I was glad I didn't understand—and tried out my first Russian words, straight from the dictionary in the back of my phrase book. *"Slehdahvaht toh mashina."* Follow that car.

With no visible sign of surprise, the driver stomped on the accelerator and followed the BMW out of the airport and on to Leningradskoe Highway. I calculated that since I had 10,000 rubles in my money belt (roughly 400 bucks) and a few thousand more in my shoe, I was well prepared to pay the ten rubles per kilometer fare, even if we drove all the way to Chechnya.

Maybe it was the grime on the cab window, but the outskirts of Moscow seemed to project the persona of a crumbled empire, tired of keeping up appearances, with only the occasional Georgian mansion or gilded church dome breaking the monotony of socialist cement. Then, as we crossed the river and drove down Tverskaya Ulitsa into the city center, the wide sidewalks began to fill with people. Even at a distance I could see that many in the crowd out-dressed the most elegant Fifth Avenue shopper. As if on cue, the haze lifted, and I found myself in a sunlit, prosperous European-style city, bustling with energy.

Our creep slowed down to a crawl, and although the streets were so wide they made the Avenue of the Americas look like a hiking trail, I felt we were in danger of being spotted by the occupants of the BMW.

"*Ahdeen mashina zah,*" one car between, I said to the driver, sounding each word out painstakingly from the phonetic dictionary in the back of my phrasebook.

"*Da,*" he replied without taking his eyes off the road, and then, "*Moskvich,*" referring to the ancient vehicle that now served as a one-car cover between us and the limo.

"*Spahseebah,* thank you," I said, feeling inordinately satisfied at this small success in communication.

"No problem," he replied in quite passable English. "We just now crossed Sadovaya—the Outer Ring road. This man you follow, he is your husband?"

"No. Watch out. They're turning."

If my map was right, the BMW had turned onto Tverskoy Bulvar, which is part of the Boulevard Ring and one of four Ring Roads that fan out in concentric circles from the Kremlin. A strip of park ran down the middle, with elegant mansions on both sides, remnants of the nineteenth century that lent an air of stateliness, punctuated by imposing statues of Russian cultural heroes who I wished I had time to visit.

Baranski's destination was a pale pink, baroque-style hotel. From our spot behind a pickup truck bristling with gardening tools, I saw the doorman greet Yuri like an old friend. What I didn't see, until it was too late, was the man who jerked open the back door of the taxi and stuck a gun in my face.

"Give him your money. Is best," said the cab driver without turning around, as if he were telling me to tip the porter. But it wasn't my money this guy had come for. It was me.

"Out!" he ordered, nodding his head toward the hotel. I was quick to comply, and once he saw that I offered no resistance, he shoved the gun beneath his long leather coat and pulled out his wallet. "I pay. You go hotel. I bring luggage."

Service like this you don't get every day.

"You're late for brunch. I hope the coffee's not cold." Yuri's third-floor suite had all the amenities you'd expect at a ritzy New York hotel, except that the antiques were for real. He was lounging on a couch upholstered in red satin, a good match for his bloodshot eyes. I helped myself from the silver urn on the coffee table and stood by the window, keeping an eye out for more surprises.

"You didn't need to strong-arm me. Why not a polite invitation?"

Baranski unbuttoned the collar of his starched lavender shirt and loosened his tie. "Grisha meant no harm, Ms. Epstein, but in New York you invaded my life and tried to convince my mistress that I killed her brother. I cannot let you cause that kind of trouble in Moscow." The menace in his tone was like a big cat's snarl.

"Have a biscotti," he offered, downgrading to a purr.

There was a knock at the door and a woman I recognized as one of the models from the party at The Mantle entered the room, a few high-heeled steps behind her fragrance. Her olive complexion was a perfect compliment to the tangerine mini-dress and dark green bolero jacket.

"Jo Epstein—this is Mimi Romanovna, my assistant." She nodded vaguely, but she was checking me out.

"Mimi, I need you to pick up my voice messages. My day-timer is on the desk in the den."

Mimi walked by me and into the adjoining room, her expression disdainfully neutral, as if prepared for a camera to capture her arrogance at any moment.

Baranski poured a coffee refill into a delicate glass cup etched with flowers that looked like it was made for a Czarina. "You were right about one thing. I do have an interest in the case you're working on. I want to find out who killed Micah Goldman. My reasons are different than your own, but why not work together? I have resources I can put at your disposal."

"I don't need your help."

"That's where you are wrong. Mimi can be your driver—you will be hopelessly lost or worse if you wander around Moscow by yourself. And then there's your appearance. If you do not fit in you will learn nothing.

"We're throwing a party tonight—it's Fashion Week and all my biggest customers will be there. Rebecca will be modeling and you can talk to her if you wish. But first we must do something about your clothes. You look like—how can I say it—a bumpkin. Mimi will take you to pick out something appropriate. It's on the house. It will be what you call in America a makeover."

His impudence was astounding, but I stifled my anger. If he wanted to keep tabs on me, let him. I'd learn more about him than he would about me.

"Where are you staying?" he asked.

"The Sovietskaya." This lie elicited derisive laughter all-round.

"How chic," Mimi said, following me out the door.

Riding down in the elevator she set me straight. "The Sovietskaya is in St. Petersburg. You lie not so well."

As our shopping expedition progressed, Mimi thawed out. She was an expert at selecting clothes that flattered what was, at least in comparison to hers, a voluptuous figure. An hour or so later I walked out of The Plashch, which meant mantle in Russian and was a near-duplicate of Yuri's boutique in Manhattan. I was wearing dark red leather sandals with two-inch heels (the highest Mimi could talk me into—thank God it wasn't snowing), a short skirt in black denim interwoven with gray angora and fake rabbit skin, and a tailored silk shirt, black with malachite buttons. The bulge created by my money belt somewhat spoiled the sleek look, but for both ethical and practical reasons, I had drawn the line at buying a matching rabbit skin purse (nothing fake about it). Still, no problem blending into the well-dressed crowd strolling down the Arbat. By the time I'd had my hair cut and layered as finely as a Persian cat's fur, even Ruth would have had trouble recognizing me.

That evening, as we entered the cavernous showroom, Mimi explained that Fashion Week in Moscow was the biggest event of its kind in Eastern Europe, and that this year, for the first time, Visa Corporation was a co-sponsor. The folding chairs on either side of the runway were almost completely filled, or I should say half filled, by the chic rear ends of fashion devotees from around the world. Pointing out an empty seat in the back row, Mimi abandoned me for more exalted company.

Shortly thereafter, Rebecca Goldman strode down the runway, elegant and cool, as if she hadn't a care in the world except looking fabulous.

"Welcome. Tonight you will experience something very special that all of you have been waiting for. Yuri Baranski's designs combine elegant hand-tailoring with the exaggeration of sharp lines and military-style detailing. His new collection adds a dark twist that is both modern and retro. Yuri is a master at blending warm fabrics such as velvet with the rich textures of suede appliqué. The embroidery has a geometric feel often found in Slavonic work."

The music came up, techno-beat mixed with what could have been balalaika samples, and a parade of fashion followed, six or seven models who took turns jaunting down the runway, their toothpick legs apparently stronger than they appeared, exuding the air of extroverted nonchalance that was essential to acceptance, let alone success, in the fashion world. They wore exotic pieces, ranging from a sexy business suit with a low bust-line that could get the wearer jumped in the boardroom to a full-length silken evening gown splashed with fur and spangles. The exotically cut sports clothes would have fallen apart at the mere sight of a muddy playing field. It was all sublimely ridiculous and made me keenly aware of how pedestrian my own tastes were.

I was so absorbed in the show that I almost failed to notice that Rebecca was signaling me from across the runway, pointing toward a door that I assumed led backstage. I stood up and edged my way through the row of sleek fashion aficionados, catching glares from those who had to pull back their million-dollar legs.

In the dressing room, temporarily empty of models, Rebecca handed me a plastic grocery bag. "I was restringing Micah's guitar to give it to one of his friends. It didn't sound right, so I looked inside and there they were."

The bag was packed with the same silk labels she had shown me in Micah's room at home, except that each label now featured a large letter 'M,' for Mantle, printed in a flowing blue script.

"You brought these to Moscow?"

"They are perfect imitations," Rebecca said. "Micah must have printed them at work for someone who was knocking off Yuri's designs. I was going to show them to Yuri, but he's totally involved in a deal he's trying to close with Target. Then I heard that you were here."

"Why would they store the labels separately?"

"It's a common practice. They manufacture the knockoffs overseas, usually at the same factory as the fashion house. At night and on the weekends the *fabreechnee* produces overruns of handbags, dresses, watches, whatever's selling."

"Where does Yuri do his manufacturing?"

"In Ivanovo—very convenient—only a few hours from Moscow."

"If someone were using this factory to produce knockoffs, how would they get the dresses out of the country?"

Rebecca answered without hesitation. "They ship the clothes without labels so they can pass through customs without too many questions. The labels are sewn on in New York, before they deliver the knockoffs to one of the outlets on Canal Street. Little risk, big profit."

For Micah, big risk, but in the end, no profit.

I was on the verge of telling her about the basement sewing room on Nostrand Avenue, when we were interrupted by a trio of models rushing in to change for the next round. Ignoring us, they pasted rhinestones into their belly buttons above hip-hugging wide patent leather belts and took their time refreshing their made-up faces, so caked with gunk that I wondered if their pores might ever see the light of day. After they had swooshed out in a cloud of perfume, I asked Rebecca, "Do you think Yuri found out what Micah was up to?"

"It's possible. He has a terrible temper and that's why—" She tripped out the door ahead of me before I could hear the end of the sentence, using a model's neat footwork to avoid the implications of her words.

Baranski was waiting outside the dressing room when we emerged. He dropped his cultivated manner to hiss at Rebecca. "You were supposed to introduce the evening dresses and the furs. Mimi had to fill in when we couldn't find you. What were you thinking?"

That you may have killed my brother for stealing your designs would be my guess. Rebecca smiled and took his arm. "I'm sorry, darling. The strap on my dress broke and Jo here was kind enough to help me fix it. When does the party start?"

"Right now."

The three of us made an awkwardly moving triangle as we strolled outside. Judging from the amount of noise coming from within the tents, the post-show parties were going strong. In contrast to the miles of white canvas in the parking lot, Baranski's tent was buttercup yellow. It was full of self-important guests, and as the evening progressed, I wondered if the number of dresses purchased was as big as the number of drinks consumed. Somehow I doubted it.

We got back from the party at two A.M. Mimi showed me to a plush room in Baranski's suite, where I pulled on the silk thermals that I had wisely packed and mulled over why Detective Grimes, to the best of my knowledge, did not tell Spinelli about the knock-off operation on Nostrand Avenue. What if Grimes had been working for Baranski and was paid to kill Micah and blackmail Nikolai? If that were true, it made sense that Baranski would have disposed of Grimes before leaving for Moscow. No loose ends threatening to ruin his meteoric rise in the fashion world. But the pieces didn't quite fit. Why would Baranski go to such elaborate lengths to force Nikolai to return to Moscow?

It was three P.M. the previous day in New York, and I decided to do some time traveling. I punched in a string of numbers on the global cell phone I'd rented for the trip via the Internet and after only three tries, reached Hasim at the 47th Precinct in the Bronx.

"Hiding your stepfather's clothing was an amateur move, Jo. You'll lose your license and will probably go to jail."

"I know."

"Are you also aware that your stepfather has a second murder charge pending? I feel responsible, Jo. I'm the one who told you to look up Lenny Grimes and now he's dead."

The palpable pain in his voice made me wince. "I'm sorry, Hasim. But you can't believe that Nikolai killed him."

Hasim's silence spoke volumes.

"Did the police close down the knock-off operation that Grimes was keeping tabs on?"

"I don't know what you're talking about. What I *do* know is that Spinelli's got an APB out on you and that officially I should be tracing this call. Don't call me again, unless you're ready to come in."

Between Hasim hanging up on me, knowing that I was still persona non grata in New York, and all the theories spinning around in my head, I didn't get much sleep that night. One question hounded me, relentless as a yapping Chihuahua. Hasim had indicated that the police were unaware of the knock-off operation. So, how had Veton managed to relocate his stock of pills and dresses before the cops arrived on the scene? Either he was tipped off by the murderer or by someone inside NYPD. The other possibility was that the Avenue L dispatcher killed Grimes himself, but that didn't wash. Not even a fool would kill someone and then leave the body in close proximity to illegal goods that the police would be delighted to confiscate.

I showered in the morning, choosing my comfortable blue jeans over yesterday's mini-skirt, and shared a continental breakfast with Mimi. She said Baranski had gone out. There was no sign of Rebecca, and given what she'd said last night about Yuri's temper, I hoped she hadn't made the mistake of confronting him.

"Where are we going today?" Mimi asked, when I rolled my carry-all out of the bedroom.

"I need to visit a relative in the suburbs."

"You will stay there? Is that why you bring luggage?"

It's none of your business. "I'm bringing clothes to my aunt."

She thought this over. "Clothes are useful but you must also take flowers and instant coffee."

After purchasing the recommended items at a market around the corner, I told Mimi I had no need for a driver. "I've got a map and plenty of rubles. I'll take the Metro."

"Don't be silly. Yuri will not forgive me if I desert you." As per Baranski's instructions, she was sticking to me like fake lashes on a beauty queen. Yesterday, she had served as a useful connection with Baranski's world—today I had other plans.

I gave Mimi the address, and we settled into the gray leather seats of the silver BMW, which was more of a traveling advertisement for Golden Moscow perfume than a mode of transportation. Mimi wove in and out of traffic like a slalom skier. When we reached the Sparrow Hills neighborhood, she pointed out the spire of Moscow University, one of the "Seven Sisters," she said, built by Stalin after World War II to "glorify socialist architecture." To me it resembled a 1930's American skyscraper with baroque Kremlin overtones.

Mimi double-parked in front of a wide brick archway. "This is it." She insisted on waiting for me. "No matter how long, I have book."

Carrying the plastic bag of goodies and wheeling my carry-all, I walked through the archway in full view of the car and entered the inner courtyard—surprised to see so many trees and a fully equipped playground. From the street one would have no idea there was a park back here where children could play, safe from the traffic zigzagging along Prospect Vernadskogo.

The *babushka* patrolling the lobby glommed on to me immediately, and it took a while to find the right phrases in my little book to convince her that all I wanted to do was leave the building by a different door.

Ducking under a clothesline packed with less than fashionable underwear, I emerged onto a side street that I followed for a few blocks before returning to the main boulevard. By my best guess, I was within a half mile of Olga Sadekov's last known address. I hoped Mimi's book was a page-turner.

He wasn't a religious man, so why did he feel so moved when the first *lukovitsas* appeared on the horizon as he drove toward Moscow? He was glad that the onion domes figured, albeit peripherally, in his plan. They had graced the tops of Russian churches since the sixteenth century, creating an illusion of permanence that he appreciated, even as he embarked on a path he knew led to chaos.

The domes reminded him of his mother Galya, who had considered herself a religious woman in spite of her cohabitation with a thief. Feydor had never heard his mother disparage his father's profession. Quite the opposite. To her, he was a *vor-v-zakonye*—a respected thief-with-a-code-of-honor—with little or nothing in common with the pickpockets, extortionists, and black marketers who populated the band he led and for whom his word was law.

The fact that Ishkhan's cohorts killed him in the end only served to strengthen Galya's conviction that Ishkhan was superior to the criminal world he ruled. But she also knew that her son, who had been forced to witness the brutal killing of his father, would never be crowned a *vor*. Hard as it was to let him go, she was relieved when Feydor moved to Moscow to live with her brother. Unless the *vory* recovered the *Obchak*, Feydor would remain on their hit list. The *vory* code may have prohibited murder, but they had already imposed the death penalty on Ishkhan for stealing their communal fund. There was no reason to suppose they would spare his son.

Although Galya knew that Feydor's experience with the *vory* had filled him with hate for the criminal class, she found it hard to hide her disappointment when he called from Moscow to tell her that he'd been accepted by the Vladimir Special Militia School and would be training as a *militsioner*. She knew how disappointed Ishkhan would have been to see his son become a policeman.

During the year following his father's death, Feydor slept in the kitchen of the communal apartment in Moscow where his uncle Mikhail reluctantly permitted him to stay. The other tenants took pity on him and gave him odd jobs in return for food rations. He was so homesick that he often thought about running back to his mother in Tula, in spite of her warning that the *Obchak* was still missing and the *vor* were looking for him.

That first year at Lyceum #17, his fellow students learned, after one or two challenges, that Feydor was not your typical peasant transplanted from the country. He could write master equations, memorize chemical formulas, or use his fists as required. They continued to taunt him, although at a safe distance, until he was finally relegated to the status of barely tolerated outsider. By his second year he no longer fantasized about joining the KBG and sending the lot of them to the gulag.

Feydor was twelve when Uncle Misha died from a bout of pneumonia, contracted during an unusually harsh winter when their building ran out of coal. Galya sent her son money. She didn't say where she'd gotten it, but he knew that Ishkhan had managed to leave her with some means, in spite of this being in violation of the *vory* code. He used the rubles she sent—along with some others he had earned running errands for the elderly woman downstairs—to convince the other tenants that the most "humane" thing to do was to bury Mikhail in secret and let his nephew move into the vacated room.

At fifteen, after completing his basic education, Feydor wanted to continue his academic education. His school advisor disapproved. "Go to a *Technikum* and train as a machinist. You'll be better off becoming a good proletarian worker and staying out of trouble. One day you'll thank me." Feydor ignored this advice and went on to complete Senior Secondary School.

At eighteen, he joined Komsomol, the youth wing of the Communist Party, hoping his membership would provide opportunities for advancement. He soon discovered that, although the Moscow intelligentsia had been cowed into pretending they had no class prejudices, all this meant was that they were better at hiding their elitism. How he longed to tell them that he was the son of a powerful *vor!* He could have told them stories that sent them crying to their mothers. Instead, he kept his distance and learned to rely on himself alone.

With his School Leaving Certificate, he found it remarkably easy to enroll for training as a policeman at the Vladimir Special School. In the '70s, they had already begun to ask fewer questions, as long as you had the right documents, which could always be gotten for a price. Since he bore his mother's surname of Marov there was no way for them to trace his *vory* "pedigree."

At the Militia school, for the first time he felt accepted on his merits, and this encouraged him to work hard. He graduated with honors and threw himself into police work with the same zeal his father had applied to his position as a thief-in-law, but with far different motives. His superiors were impressed with Marov's relentless energy and had no idea that he was driven not by professionalism but by hatred. If his commander noticed that *militsioner* Feydor Marov killed more than his share of those "resisting arrest," he probably put it down to the fact that Marov had an uncanny knack for unearthing scum and had detained more criminals during his six years in the *militsiya* than most policemen did during the course of their entire careers. From Feydor's point of view, every thief he sent to jail or to the grave was another limb hacked off the collective body of the *vory*.

During his years in America, he had come to accept that he was powerless to punish the *vory* for their merciless execution of his father. What he *could* do was to use the same code that had condemned Ishkhan to destroy the one person most responsible for his death.

CHAPTER SEVENTEEN

There was no doubt that Olga looked like Nikolai. It was as if his rough-hewn features had been scaled down to fit the delicate oval of her face, and then framed with soft white curls.

"I look for your brother," I said in elemental Russian, "my mother—his wife," holding on to the edge of the heavy door, my fingers in danger of being smashed to a pulp if she slammed it in my face. She stared at this stranger who had appeared on her doorstep, claiming to be a relative. A few beats later, she made up her mind.

"This is not the place he is, but now you are here . . . come inside."

Relieved to hear that she spoke English, I followed her into the apartment. The red flowers on Olga's housedress matched the artificial roses that brightened the foyer; her feet were bare. I took off my shoes and followed her down a long hallway, the scratched parquet floor partially covered by a tattered rug, the only furniture a mahogany table covered with photos and knick-knacks. One wall was almost entirely taken up by an oil painting of a windswept scene, a peasant woman—potatoes gathered in her apron—running though the *taiga*, her baby on her back, both pairs of blue eyes focused on the storm clouds of World War II closing in on them.

"It's beautiful," I said.

"It was painted by my father," she replied.

We passed several closed doors and I wondered if this had

been a communal apartment, with each bedroom housing an entire family. "I rent now to students, one only per room." Olga had immediately picked up on my appreciative curiosity, and this gave me hope that we would be able to communicate.

The kitchen was an ode to petroleum products, with two chairs covered in vinyl, a yellow Formica table, and plastic lace curtains providing a filigreed view of the courtyard. Olga located a vase for the flowers and placed the chocolates I'd brought on the windowsill. She motioned for me to join her at the table, where she served the instant coffee I had brought with me. Freeze-dried Nescafé has never been my favorite, but it seemed to perk up Olga. "You live in Brighton Beach?"

"Not too far from there. Your English is good."

"I worked hard for improving it when I had job at Intourist. Now I am, how you call it?"

"Retired?"

She poured herself a refill. My own cup was still half full.

"Yes. I stay home now where I am safe. Today all the young ones are joined with criminal gangs and the girls who come to Moscow from the countryside have only one choice, is prostitution. So much for their new Russia."

I wondered if she missed communism, but I wasn't here to talk politics.

"Why are you looking for Nikolai?" she asked.

I explained my relationship with Nikolai as best I could, how he had fled the country, and the necessity of finding him and bringing him home to my mother.

"This boy who was killed, he was Jewish?" Olga asked, showing no signs of shock that her brother was a fugitive from American justice. Maybe she knew already.

"Yes, he was."

"Maybe it was a skinhead that did this."

This was a logical supposition, given the hate crimes that had bloodied the streets of Moscow in the '90s and continued to sporadically target minorities and foreigners. "It was an undercover detective who killed Micah—I still don't know why. What your brother needs to know is that if he comes home he will be able to prove his innocence."

To encourage Olga to talk about Nikolai, I shared my frustration—easily called up—with his pathological secrecy and general rudeness.

"He never was likeable, even when a boy," she responded, and for a moment I could see the two of them knocking heads over the ownership of a Soviet teddy bear stuffed with sawdust.

"You're older than him?"

"By three years. Nikolai and I, we had privileges as children, not like most others in those days. Even in wartime, we lived well, because our father was high in the Party. Nikolai had the best music teachers to cultivate his talent on the violin. A bright future they planned for him."

"Brighter than yours?"

Olga's smile was rueful. "You are asking was I jealous. Yes, of course. But there would have been no problem if he showed the respect owed to the eldest. I looked after him; it was me who gave him food from my mouth when he was sick. But Nikolai was arrogant and self-centered and treated me like a servant. He took pleasure in causing me to hate him, in the way that some children do. Maybe he thought my hatred extended also to our parents and this made it easy for him to blame me for what happened."

Olga gave me a questioning look. Did I really want to hear all that gloomy family history?

"You were saying?," I said, afraid she would decide to stop.

She drained her glass and continued with her story. "Following the war, Nikolai was accepted at the Music Conservatory. He was only fourteen and our parents threw a party for him at our dacha outside of St. Petersburg—it was called Leningrad in those days. After dinner Nikolai went for a walk. When he returned, our parents were gone, arrested by the KGB. We never saw them again."

She looked me in the eye when she said this, to make sure I understood what she meant. "They would have taken me too, but the officer in charge recognized me. His daughter Zoya and I were schoolmates. He told me to hide in the attic and he would make sure they did not find me."

"Why were your parents arrested?"

Olga shrugged. "There is no logical way to explain these things. In Stalin's Russia, people were more likely to ask why you were *not* arrested. Nikolai assumed I was interrogated and had informed on our parents in return for my freedom. There was no way for me to tell him otherwise. By that time he was living in the Home for the Children of Enemies of the State."

"And you?"

"I stayed hidden at the dacha for as long as the food lasted. After that, I went to stay with Zoya's family."

"You took refuge with the man who arrested your parents?"

"I know how this looked, especially to Nikolai. A few weeks later, Zoya's father himself was arrested but by that time the damage to my relationship with my brother was permanent. I lived with Zoya and her mother until I graduated from the university."

Olga rose from the table and busied herself, surreptitiously wiping her eyes as she poked around the refrigerator to locate some kielbasa and cheese. She sliced the sausage on the cutting board with deliberate strokes, as if calming herself with the familiar task

"When did you last see Nikolai?"

Olga brought the edibles to the table and waited for me to take a few bites and nod my thank you before she answered. "I dropped off food at the Home but they refused to let me inside. I did not see Nikolai again for thirty years. Well, not exactly. I recognized him on television. By then he was a famous orchestra conductor, on a world tour with the Kirov Ballet. He was calling himself Kharpov, no longer Sadekov."

"Sadekov is your family name?"

"Yes. I never married. But Nikolai did, and when I read in Pravda that his wife committed suicide, I thought about contacting him, but it was too late—my brother and I were dead to each other. So you can imagine my surprise when he came to see me. He said he was going to defect to America. He seemed greatly changed and hinted at things in the past that he had cause to let go. And then he said, 'I forgive you, Olga.' This impudence was even more than I expected from my brother.

"He sent me his address in Ohio and I wrote to him once a year. When he moved to New York he sent me a card. After that, nothing. I thought I did not care, but now, there is no denying I would like to see him before I die."

"So you're telling me you haven't seen him lately?"

The question, along with the implication that she might be lying, hung between us like a blast of car exhaust, neither of us daring to inhale.

"Have I not been helpful, telling you all our family secrets?" She started to clear the coffee cups from the table, a signal that she wanted me to leave.

"I understand your loyalty, Olga. But I have reason to believe that Nikolai has returned to Russia and that he thinks you might be in danger."

"I take care of myself very well, thank you."

"At least tell me the name of the prison where Nikolai was held."

"Vladimir Central," she said softly.

She wiped down the table with a sponge, forcing me to move

my elbow. "I think the time is now for you to leave. I am sorry."

In the front hallway, I put my shoes back on and fussed with the laces, hoping she'd change her mind.

"You need not to worry about me," she finally said. "My brother has not been here himself but he has provided someone to protect me—a man who stops by the apartment every so often.

"I'm glad to hear it," I said.

As she closed the door behind me the conflicted feelings that my visit had stirred up followed me out into the hall and down the stairs. In spite of all that had happened, Olga obviously still cared for Nikolai and had suffered from losing his love and respect. He must still care for her, I thought. Why else would he have bothered to arrange for her protection?

Using its spire as a landmark, I walked toward Moscow University. Mimi would be angry when I failed to return to the car. Or maybe she would dismiss me as yet another spoiled, irresponsible American.

At the Internet café on the MSU campus, surrounded by the buzz of multilingual conversations, I logged on and printed a train schedule and metro map. I then proceeded over to the mall adjoining the *Universitet* metro to collect some badly needed rubles from the *bankomat*. Next door, at the ticket desk, I bought a *billeyt* for less than four dollars and wheeled my carry-all onto a steep metal waterfall of an escalator, packed with commuters riding deep into the ground. On the platform, waiting for the train, I admired the brown marble walls, eerily lit by art deco lamps. A far cry from the fluorescent funkiness of New York's MTA.

All signs were in Cyrillic, but with the help of the table in my phrasebook, I was able to transpose the mysterious letters on the map into the Latin alphabet and reconstruct the names of the stations. After that, it was easy to catch the Red Line going north. I got off at metro Komsomolskaya, the stop closest to the Yaroslavsky Railway station, where the guidebook said the suburban *elektrichka* left for Sergiev Posad every hour.

"May I see your documents?" The request came from a no-nonsense member of the militia. I pulled out my passport and immigration card.

"You are not registered. This is serious," he said, his face deadpan. No room for argument.

"How much?" I asked.

"One thousand."

Rubles. He made no pretense of filling out paperwork. Why bother when everybody knew he would keep the money for himself? "Make sure you register as soon as possible," he warned me as I handed over the rubles. "Two infractions and you are to be arrested."

Under the arched entranceway to the Trinity Monastery of St. Sergei, a half dozen tourists stood in rapt attention, listening to the faultless English of their guide, whose navy skirt and white blouse fit the setting perfectly. With muted enthusiasm she related the story of two brothers who ventured into the wild forest in the fourteenth century, and how the one named Sergei stayed on to found the hermitage in 1345. I followed them into the Cathedral of the Trinity, where we joined a long line of the faithful inching toward the crypt containing the remains of St. Sergei. The vaulted ceiling seemed to swell with song, the aching harmonies of pilgrims, many of whom, the interpreter informed us, were sick and in search of a miraculous cure. Their faith was timeless, a devotion that had withstood centuries of foreign invasions and sieges and had miraculously survived Stalin's zeal for the destruction of the Russian Orthodox church.

Afterward, I waited outside the monastery walls, built in the mid-sixteenth century, while the guide loaded her charges on the waiting bus. Her practiced smile was complemented by a rigid, almost military, bearing and short dark hair, cropped close for easy management.

"Excuse me," I said. "Would you be available to translate for me at the toy factory?"

"When?"

"Right now. I know it's past five o'clock and they may be closing, but it's very important that I go today. I can pay extra."

Her appraising look made me wish that I was still wearing my Fashion Week outfit, instead of the blue jeans and a fleece sweatshirt I had worn to my meeting with Olga. "It is no problem," she said. "I will telephone them to make our arrangements."

Her name was Larissa and she seemed nice enough. Within ten minutes, we were driving through the narrow back streets of Sergiev Posad in her immaculate but well-used green Passat, my carry-all stowed in the trunk.

Our destination turned out to be a low-slung, rambling wooden structure, more like a horse stable than a factory. A blonde, sixtyish woman in a bright blue smock waited for us out front. Larissa introduced her as Elena Malinov, the factory director. Maybe she had met all her quotas during the Soviet era, and they had kept her on after the transition to exploit her expertise. Larissa translated as Elena asked if I wanted a full tour. From the looks of things the factory could use the income.

Our first stop was the lathe operator's workshop, where wood shavings covered every inch of the floor, not a safety goggle in sight. A craftsman in tight-fitting blue overalls refused to break his concentration and acknowledge the visitors, choosing instead to dazzle us with his speed and accuracy. Starting with a hunk of rough wood, it took him less than five seconds to turn out a smooth, hollow doll about three inches tall. He barely paused to add the new doll to the collection on the bench beside him before beginning a new one. "Leonid has worked here for thirty years," Elena said. "The last of his breed."

In the adjoining workshop, three women artists, faces intent, hands steady, painted intricate fairytale designs with the tiniest of brushes.

Elena led us into the factory store, well stocked with a collection of traditional and modern dolls for sale. I showed her a photo of one of the *Matreshki* that had been sent to Nikolai. The one I had chosen was minus the markings made by Mr. Eeks. "Was this one made here?" I asked. "It would have been long before your time."

"To be sure." Elena hacked out a laugh indicative of many years of breathing the same heady mixture of shellac fumes and wood particles that enveloped us now. "If this is the doll I think it is, the original was manufactured right here sometime in the 1920s," she said. This confirmed what Marya from Russian Treasures had told me.

Larissa's eyes asked me *what are you up to,* as she continued to translate Elena's words. "A few years ago, a customer brought in a set of six dolls for restoration. I remember them well. They were formed in the shape of bullets, very unusual. Business was slow at the time and he paid generously." How horrified Elena would have been to hear that several members of this valuable set had been defiled with prison tattoos.

"May I ask who ordered the restoration?"

"Perhaps you can find something you would like to buy." The proposed trade seemed reasonable. I picked out an elaborately painted set of *Matryoshki,* each doll decorated with a copy of a famous painting at the Tretyakov Gallery in Moscow. The price was 6,000 rubles, about $200—well above market value, which meant that the director could take her bite without damaging the apple. "The name on the receipt is Ishkhan Lamsa," Elena said, without consulting either ledger or computer. Apparently she had an exceptional memory. "Mr. Lamsa paid us five hundred dollars for the restoration. He is a well-known collector." She was right about that. Lamsa's name had been on the list of collectors that Marya had provided. My coincidence meter jumped into the red.

I thanked Elena and was about to leave with my package tucked under my arm, when she said, "You're not the first person to ask about that set of dolls. There was a gentleman here yesterday."

"Was he in his sixties, with a crooked nose?"

Elena snorted. "Yes, but half the men in Russia have broken noses from fighting when they are drunk."

She couldn't resist pulling my chain.

"And his age?"

"You have that right," Elena admitted.

Nikolai.

"If you share what this is all about, maybe I can be of assistance," Larissa said, possibly in response to my brooding silence as she pulled out of the driveway of the *Matryoshka* factory. Beneath her schoolmarm manners, I sensed a lively, active mind.

How do you explain to a total stranger how a bunch of disconnected pieces of evidence, most of them obtained in another country, refuse to fit together and may not even be part of the same puzzle? Sitting in her Passat in front of the train station, I did the best I could.

Larissa had the rare ability to actively listen, so that as I spoke I felt she was seeing pictures rather than hearing words. When I got to the part about the tattoo of a skeleton holding an ax, she stopped me. "That means a revenge killing."

She had confirmed my recent research on the Web, but I

asked her anyway. "How do you know this?"

Larissa phrased her answer carefully. "Everyone in Russia has at least one ancestor or family member who has been in prison. These tattoos have become part of our folklore."

By the time I finished bringing my guide up to speed, they were announcing the train to Moscow. "How long a drive is it, from here to Vladimir?"

"Two, maybe three hours," she said. "If your stepfather was a prisoner in Vladimir Central, they will have records. We can also request information about this man called Ishkhan Lamsa who had the dolls restored. They may have served time together."

My story seemed to have left her totally undaunted. In comparison to the conspiracies, corruption scandals, and hardships that are part of everyday life in Russia, she may have seen Nikolai's troubles as trivial. She also seemed to take it for granted that I needed her services. "We will need to drive sixty-five kilometers to Pereslavl-Zalesskiy and then another one hundred forty to Vladimir. We can spend the night at the Vladimir Hotel and visit the archives and the prison in the morning."

"Don't you have other work you need to attend to?"

"I am freelance. Most of us, we work by the day."

She agreed to a daily rate of $150 and I told her how much I appreciated her help.

According to the guidebook, Vladimir is a small city, located in the "golden ring" of towns northeast of Moscow. It has a population of 300,000, and that evening it seemed all of them were outside, strolling through the streets, eating in restaurants, or drinking in beer garden tents that looked hastily assembled and were probably stored away each winter. The buildings along the main streets were smaller and less imposing than those in Moscow. As a result the people seemed taller, more full of life.

Larissa and I checked into two rooms at the Vladimir Hotel. Exhausted and jet-lagged, I fell asleep to the pulsing of bass and drums drifting up from downstairs—a high-energy mixture of folk music and disco that filled my dreams with visions of dancing bears.

At eight A.M. sharp Larissa met me in the lobby, and we went to breakfast, which was served in the same banquet hall that had hosted last night's party and included an unidentifiable but delicious meat roll in addition to the ubiquitous instant coffee.

"Americans never visit Vladimir Central Prison," she told me, "but many Japanese make the journey in honor of their relatives buried in the cemetery next door. There is even a monument."

After breakfast, we drove through town, and she pointed out a few glass factories and ironworks left over from Vladimir's industrial past, as well as the famous Assumption Cathedral.

The Vladimir Regional Archive was housed in a box-like, three-story building on Baturina ulitsa, one of a cluster of buildings patterned after the Georgian style so popular in prerevolutionary Russia. A large photo of Putin—still undeniably the most powerful man in Russia—was mounted next to President Medvedev's, in the same spot on the wall behind the reception area most likely used by their predecessors to assert their authority over this starkly functional room. All around us, shelves overflowed with musty ledgers. Ominous-looking file cabinets were stacked precariously from floor to ceiling.

Larissa explained to the clerk, a woman whose parchment skin matched her surroundings perfectly, that we needed to see the records of two prisoners, Nikolai Kharpov and Ishkhan Lamsa. The government worker looked us over doubtfully, mumbling something in Russian before disappearing into another room. She came back ten minutes later carrying some files that she slapped on the desk in front of us. The phone rang. The clerk stayed on the line, listening attentively, then dropped the old-fashioned receiver into its cradle like a hot pirogue and addressed Larissa in a no-nonsense tone of voice.

"What is it?" I asked.

Larissa didn't bother to conceal her annoyance. "She says she is sorry but today they will be closing early."

A bald-faced lie. I knew that the workday started and ended late in Russia. It was eleven A.M., and many employees were still arriving, clutching their briefcases as they climbed the stairs to their offices.

"I want to speak to your supervisor," I said. Larissa translated my words, and then, to my surprise, she accompanied the now-hostile clerk to the back office. That left me with just enough time to peer inside the file folders and slip two brown envelopes that looked like they contained photographs into the kangaroo pocket of my sweatshirt.

When Larissa came back she was shaking her head, and I gave her my best resigned smile. "Let's go. Maybe we'll have better luck at the prison."

I barely breathed as we walked back to the car, expecting at any moment to be stopped and searched. Inside the Passat, I was so happy I almost hugged my guide—then decided she'd be better off not knowing what I'd done. When we were out on the road, I waited for the first sharp turn and, while making a show of holding on to the strap for balance, leaned toward the passenger door and slipped the two envelopes under the seat.

The guard at the gate to Vladimir Central Prison scowled when he saw us approaching and immediately picked up the phone. I was sure we were going to get the runaround, but we were soon admitted, first to a room where our passports were collected, and then through three security gates, each of which clanged somewhat ominously behind us.

A guard led us up a narrow staircase to the second floor of a nondescript building overlooking the prison yard. A young, thin woman in a beige business suit was waiting by the door of the museum. "This is Alexandra," Larissa said. "She will guide us through the museum."

Alexandra began our education by explaining that the ancient-looking skeleton keys she used to open the museum doors were the same as those that the guards used to lock up the prison cells. "The design has never been improved upon," she said.

It's amazing how more than two centuries of suffering can be condensed into a few exhibits behind glass. Alexandra told us that in Czarist times prisoners were branded on the forehead and cheeks with a hot iron. Other instruments of torture on display included a twenty-kilo wooden block that was hung around a prisoner's neck and spiked dog collars that made it impossible for the wearer to lie down.

"After the Second World War, all of the clothes from the concentration camps were passed on to the gulag, and it became customary to dress the most dangerous prisoners in striped robes." By dangerous she meant political. "Today," she continued, "they are all dressed the same."

According to Alexandra, the first political prisoners to be incarcerated in Vladimir were participants in the Polish rebellions of the eighteenth century. The prison went on to become "home" to Bolsheviks arrested on Bloody Sunday in 1905; Soviet dissident writers like Solzhenitsyn; and many Russian Orthodox priests incarcerated by Stalin. I was amazed to hear that Stalin's own son, whose prison name was Vasily Pavlovich Vasilyev, had done time here, along with his cousins, who knew too much and were identified in prison by number only. The exhibit included a photo of the American U-2 pilot Francis Gary Powers, who was imprisoned in Vladimir Central for two years until he was traded for a Russian spy in 1962.

"The more famous prisoners had many privileges," Alexandra said. "They did no work, were given writing materials, and were allowed to walk in the yard twice daily. Stalin's son even had a wooden floor in his cell to keep out the damp. And of course there were the kingpins, the *vor-v-zakonye*, who had the high-caloric food shipped in."

"How did they pay for it?"

"With their *Obchak*. It was a communal fund to which they all contributed, so that those who went to jail would be well taken care of."

After touring both rooms of the museum, I thought we were done, but Alexandra steered us into a room on the other side of the hallway. Here pastels ruled, light greens and blues soothing the eye, soft couches inviting relaxation. "This is where they have, how do you call it, therapy with art. They work with both the prisoners and the correction officers."

The far wall was graced with a softly psychedelic mandala in shades of rose and gold.

"All of our prisoners paint, but we only show the best," boasted an intelligent-looking middle-aged man who put on his tortoise-shell glasses when we came in. *We've come a long way* was the subtext.

Roll call was being taken in the yard, and Larissa told me we would have to wait upstairs until they were done. I watched from a window, as each prisoner stepped forward when his name was called and then walked back to the main building or to work in the bakery directly below us. Afterward, Larissa and I said goodbye to Alexandra and hurried through the empty yard, followed by a guard who carefully closed each security gate behind us.

At the window where we had relinquished our passports, the guard handed Larissa her dark maroon booklet. Then he gingerly picked up my passport, as if examining it for explosives, and removed the immigration card. I was mentally counting out the rubles I would be asked to pay for my infraction of the rules, real or imaginary, when he said, "I'm afraid you must stay with us until this is cleared up."

I wasn't sure I had heard him properly until I saw the color drain from Larissa's face.

"Please, call the U.S. consulate," I said to her.

She gave me a look I found impossible to interpret, dropping her own passport into her purse and snapping the clasp with a firm click, before answering. "Don't worry. I'm sure they have a good reason for detaining you." I stood there, dumbfounded, as she walked away without a backward glance.

Little Dog's shadow, as he had begun to call her, was locked up as tightly as President Yeltsin's liquor cabinet should have been. (Only in Russia could a drunk have given away the entirety of his country's resources to mafia thugs and still remained in power for ten years.) Ms. Epstein's misadventure had been easy to arrange, thanks to Feydor's cordial relations with the Moscow Criminal Police and their colleagues in Vladimir. If his father had known that one day his son would maintain police credentials in two countries, he'd have drowned him in the Don River. He could only hope that Ishkhan would somehow know what an important role these credentials had played in helping his son to avenge his death.

When Galya fell ill, Feydor had moved her to Moscow so he could take care of her. She refused to go to the hospital, so he found her an apartment in an eight-story building—where in the spring the mountain ash in the courtyard were covered by clusters of small white flowers that reminded her of home—and hired a nurse to look after her. The expense gobbled up his entire salary, but what else did he have to spend it on? He joined her for dinner at least a couple of nights a week and on Sundays, but whenever he asked her questions about the old days she refused to answer. Amnesia was a common folk remedy in Russia.

One cool spring evening, he dropped in on her unexpectedly to tell her he had received word of his first promotion. They shared a toast and then sat in silence, watching a performance of Giselle by the Kirov Ballet televised on Moscow Programme. The camera panned across the rapt audience at the Mariinsky Theatre and then paused for a close-up of the conductor, his face the picture of ecstatic communion with the swelling music. "It's him," she whispered. Then louder, "It's him!"

"Who?"

"It's Little Dog—the boy your father called 'my protégé.' He should have called him 'my murderer.' " She pointed at the conductor's plump face. "He's grown famous and fat as a puffin on your father's blood."

"Are you sure?"

"Positive. His is a face I would never forget. Even in those days he held himself to be better than others. It's why he got into so much trouble. Ishkhan chose to protect him, out of the goodness of his heart, and what was his reward?"

She stopped there, unwilling to talk further about the events that had caused his father's death and the destruction of whatever happiness she might have expected from life. But during the days that followed she allowed Feydor to extract the story from her, piece by painful piece. The more he learned, the more he brooded over the injustice of it all. How could someone like Little Dog be allowed to enjoy fame and fortune while Ishkhan rotted in his grave? Feydor's belief in the rule of law— never strong to begin with—faded away, and he lost all interest in chasing criminals. Even murderers had the excuse of being overwhelmed by passion—but what excuse did Little Dog have? Ishkhan had arranged for his escape from prison and would have rewarded him generously for his loyalty. In return, Little Dog had filched the *Obchak*—the insurance fund that each v*or* contributed to in anticipation of their own inevitable arrest and incarceration. By stealing the symbol of Ishkhan's authority, *Obchak,* Little Dog had caused his benefactor to lose not only his life but the respect of his men and the right to have his memory revered by his fellow *vory.*

And there was his mother to think of—she deserved to die in peace and although she had not asked directly, he knew he was obligated to set things right.

The conductor's name was Nikolai Kharpov. Searching the KGB archives, Feydor found such a person registered as living in Moscow in the 1950s—a cellist with the symphony orchestra—but he had died in 1954. In 1957, a new file had been created for a student with the same name, who supposedly came from Minsk and was attending the music conservatory. No one had bothered to make the connection that now set Feydor's brain on fire.

He took two days' leave and drove to St. Petersburg, where he waited in the cold outside the Mariinsky Theatre, prepared to deliver the gunshot that would sacrifice his career, perhaps his life. But he waited in vain. Little Dog never came out the stage door. Perhaps the same luck that had led him to Ishkhan and the fortune in the *Obchak* prompted Kharpov to meet some friends in the lobby and exit from the other side of the theater. It was a colossal disappointment, but strengthened Feydor's resolve to pull the conductor down from his podium and bury him in the dirt where he belonged, no matter how long it took.

A week later, while on tour with the orchestra in France, the man he still thought of as Little Dog defected to the United

States, leaving Feydor to attend his mother's funeral and say goodbye to her in the bitter knowledge that her last wish had remained unfulfilled.

When he left for the U.S. after being recruited by the NYPD during the Brighton Beach "crime wave," he felt his career in Russia had been a failure. Looking back, however, it was clear that one valuable thing he'd learned from his police work in Moscow was how to mount a closely timed operation. The present one would be no exception.

CHAPTER EIGHTEEN

The five-by-ten-foot cell was no museum exhibit. All too real were the paper-thin mattress between my spine and the hard bunk, the cold concrete floor, the humiliating bucket in the corner. The walls had been whitewashed, but some graffiti was faintly visible underneath the thin mixture of lime and water. One drawing, located directly opposite the bunk, had remained untouched—maybe preserved by some perversely appreciative trustee. The silhouette of a woman's face was outlined in barbed wire, drawn using God only knows what for ink. Below the face was a graphically rendered phallus, pierced by a dagger. The erect penis was "standing" on chicken feet and, one of its testacies had sprouted a feather. There were words scrawled underneath, and I had no desire to know what they meant. I just knew that if I had not dropped out of the creative writing program at City College to go to criminology school, I would be looking at this "art" displayed on the wall of some avante garde museum, instead of sharing a cell with it.

A pile of used wooden matches had been left on the floor next to the bunk, presumably by someone lucky enough to have had some smokes. The burnt ends provided just enough soot for me to scratch out a haiku, my contribution to the wall:

> tiny hairline crack
> now a wide and deep ravine
> with no way across

After the confrontation at reception, they had confiscated my purse and cell phone and taken me upstairs, strong-arming me through a maze of hallways that led to what I was sure was a deserted wing of the prison. Since hearing the door slam behind me, I had not heard a voice or a single sound indicating that the place was inhabited by fellow humans. Eventually, a guard opened the door to deliver my food tray—brown bread, meat-loaf, and some suspicious-looking caramel-colored pudding. I peppered him with questions, first in English and then in primitive Russian, but to no avail.

Alexandra had explained that all the cells were located in the upper stories of buildings that were connected by covered bridges, so that, as she put it, "a prisoner's feet never touch the ground." Except, I assumed, when they went to work in the bakery or were allowed to exercise in the yard.

I envisaged what it would be like to remain incarcerated here—possibly forever and at least for the time it took for Mr. Eeks to wreak his vengeance on Nikolai. This brought on a panic attack, and the only way I could calm my overheated brain was to use it to apply some logic to the situation.

First of all, it was obvious that the same Ishkhan Lamsa who ordered the restoration of the *Matreshka* doll at the toy factory was responsible for my being here in this cell. It was simply too much of a coincidence that I was arrested on the same day that I inquired about Lamsa at the Regional Archive. Second, Lamsa must either be with the Federal Security Service or the *Militsiya* to be able to pull the kinds of strings he was using to entangle me. This conclusion raised, rather than lowered, my blood pressure. I decided I'd better start thinking about how to get out of here. It was an all-male prison—maybe I could talk them into letting me take a walk in the yard, and a tourist would see me from the same window where I had observed the roll call and realize that something was amiss. I imagined my predicament being reported in a blog on the Internet and leading to my eventual release.

The lights in my cell flickered before being extinguished, along with my far-fetched fantasy and any comfort it may have brought. I stared into the darkness, fear clutching my belly. I remembered one night, a lifetime ago in Brooklyn, asking Ludmilla if she and Sasha had ever considered going home after the fall of communism. She had scoffed at the idea, saying, "Freedom is my new friend, and I won't give her up." I said I'd heard that things had changed in Russia and that's when she told me not to be naive, that the concept of civil liberties did not yet exist in Russia. "People may be free to buy designer clothes and sell goods imported from China," she said, "but look at our leaders—all graduates of the KGB." And now I was getting a taste of what she meant firsthand.

I conjured up Larissa's frightened face closing in on itself when she saw me being detained. A strong, intelligent woman completely intimidated by the first flexing of authoritarian muscle. I didn't blame her—for all I knew she had relatives who were murdered for daring to speak up in the old days.

Sweat ran down the back of my neck, evaporating on my lower back and sending chills up my spine. I clutched the good luck charm that Sanyo had given me, unfastening the chain from around my neck so I could hold the medallion in my palm. As I traced the face embossed on the metal with my finger, I saw Sanyo's face, concerned for my safety, amused at my foolhardiness, lustful for my return. There were so many things I wanted to say to him, but right now all I could think of was *get me out of here.*

At three A.M. I awoke from a restless half-sleep. Two guards stood in the doorway, their faces barely visible in the dim light of the hallway, bulging holsters at their sides.

"You must come," one of them said. There could be no good reason for moving someone in the middle of the night—unless you wanted them to disappear. I refused, raising my voice to let them know I would not go quietly. This place might be horrible, but at least Larissa knew I was here. I kept shouting, until they retreated and closed the door. Probably going for reinforcements.

I did my best to control the wild speculations offered up by my imagination as I waited for the guards to return, which they did, this time bringing with them some carefully memorized words. "Office of the Administrator. No harm to you. Mistake to be fixed."

There's an international language made up of signs of embarrassment, and the well-fed face of the official behind the imposing desk, most likely the Russian equivalent of a warden, exhibited all of them: blushing complexion, darting eyes, apologetic smile.

"This incident was most unfortunate," he said in heavily accented English, handing me my passport and immigration card. "I regret we frightened you by waking you so early, but if you leave now, it will be . . . better for all of us."

"Who do you mean when you say 'all'? The people who told you to keep me here?"

He looked at me directly for the first time. "It was a case of overzealous enforcement, that is all," he said, confident that if he stuck to the official line this would all go away. "We have a taxi waiting to take you back to your hotel."

A captured animal never hesitates when the cage door opens, and neither did I. Two guards led me through a labyrinth of hallways convoluted enough to give me cause to doubt our destination. Maybe the warden had lied so that I would allow myself to be taken without protest to a more secure location, a quiet wing where they could do whatever they liked. Larissa was the only person who knew I was here, and she had thrown me to the wolves without hesitation.

I was prepared for the worst, which doubled the amazement and relief I felt when the reception area appeared just ahead, unattended at this late hour. And then we were outside, a white Volvo waiting with the passenger door open, as if it were the most natural thing in the world to be picking up a woman at Vladimir Central prison in the middle of the night.

"You Americans, you think you're exempt from all the rules." His English was almost unaccented. I peered into the car to see who was speaking and was met with the flash of a badge. "Feydor Marov, detective with the Moscow Criminal Police."

The roof light revealed thick, salt and pepper hair receding at the hairline, strong features in a pale face that looked like it had seen too many winters, dark gray eyes that looked like they had seen too much.

"Are you arresting me?"

"On the contrary, I arranged for your release and am here to see that you arrive at your hotel safely."

"How did you know I was here?"

"This is the thanks I get, to be questioned like a suspect? Believe it or not, when the American Consulate asks for a favor we Russians do our best to respond. Please, get in."

The interior of the Volvo smelled like leather and aftershave, no trace of chemical air freshener or lingering cigarette smoke. "Where are you staying?" he asked.

"The Vladimir Hotel."

He put the car in gear and waved to the night-duty guard as we drove through the gate. "Your tour guide called Moscow and my supervisor called me. I was on assignment here, in Vladimir. He asked me to handle this matter."

"Thank you for getting me out."

"You are welcome."

The main street was deserted, except for a well-dressed couple walking unsteadily along the sidewalk.

"Why didn't you register your immigration card?"

"I've been busy."

He laughed, swerving the car slightly and then correcting our course. "Give it to me. I'll have it registered and bring it back to you in the morning."

I handed over the card as we pulled up in front of the hotel.

"Is it customary to throw someone into a prison cell for failing to comply with a bureaucratic rule?" I asked as I got out of the car.

"Dos vi danya," he said, and drove off.

After wedging the back of a chair against the door, I brewed a cup of tea and tried to forget every assumption I'd made about this case so far. It was time for another look at Yuri Baranski. He had lots of influence in Moscow and possibly beyond. Was it possible that I had failed to lose Mimi before going to Olga's apartment in Sparrow Hills? That she was more competent than I gave her credit for? Did Baranski have the clout to deny me entry to the archives and then have me thrown in jail? What might I find if I went to the factory in Ivanovo where he manufactured his clothes?

I ordered some whiskey and ice from room service and drank myself to sleep, questions floating around in my head like drifting logs entering the sea from all directions.

A knock at the door, six A.M. glowing on the bedside clock.

Hung over and sleep deprived as I was, my bleary eyes did not deceive me. Larissa stood there, ramrod straight in a soft yellow dress, sheepish smile contradicted by sparkling eyes. "I am so glad to see you are okay."

I invited her in and we sat facing each other at the table by the window. In the distance, onion domes glittered faintly in weak sunlight. "I'm sure you think I abandoned you," she said, correctly taking my silence for disapproval. "Truthfully I was very upset about what happened. This is not the communist Russia, no matter what is being said elsewhere."

"I heard you called Moscow on my behalf. Thank you."

She flushed with embarrassment. "I made some calls, but I am not, as you say in America, connected."

Connected enough to get the job done, I thought. She was probably reluctant to take credit because she was afraid of reprisals. Vladimir was a relatively small town, the kind of place where everybody knows everyone's business. I decided not to discomfit her with more questions.

Larissa removed a steno pad from her voluminous canvas bag and read aloud: "Nikolai Kharpov convicted of train robbery in January 1956 and sentenced to three years—escaped on December 1957."

"Are you sure?"

"Yes, I know it's strange. The official line is that only two prisoners have ever escaped from Vladimir. They climbed over the wall into the nunnery next door and were both caught and returned to their cells the same day.

"I also obtained information about Ishkhan Lamsa, who was convicted of currency speculation the same year that Kharpov started his sentence. Lamsa contracted tuberculosis and was released for humanitarian reasons. Last known address, ulitsa Atamanskaya 13, Tula."

"Where is Tula?"

"A few hours east of here," she said, putting one hand on my arm while using the other to dig around in her purse.

"There's more?" I asked in amazement.

She pulled out the two brown envelopes I'd stolen from the Regional Archives and spilled their contents onto the table. "Did you think I don't know what goes on in my own car?"

"I'm sorry. I wasn't sure I could trust you."

"In Russia we know that sometimes the only way to obtain the truth is to steal it."

"Is that why you've done all this for me?"

She fiddled with the laces of her Adidas before replying. "There are many reasons, Jo. First, I admire that you would come such a long way and brave so many dangers for the sake of a relative. In Russia family is the most important thing. Second, I do not want you should think so badly of Russian people that we would not help in your search. For many years we were taught to look the other way when trouble came. I do not want to be the person who does that."

It seemed I had completely misjudged this woman. Larissa had single-handedly restored my belief in Russian hospitality.

I picked up one of the photos she had placed on the table. If I had not known it was Nikolai, I wouldn't have recognized the handsome young man in the Cossack shirt with the straight nose and expression that dared you to find any fear behind his defiance. The other picture showed a short and barrel-chested log of a man, possibly in his thirties, with a dark moustache hiding his upper lip. I tried to imagine what Ishkhan would look like today, fifty years later—probably not relevant, given his bout with tuberculosis and the fifty-seven-year life expectancy of hard-drinking Russian men.

It doesn't add up. Lamsa must be dead by now. He could not possibly have ordered the restoration of the Matryoshka doll at the factory in Sergiev Posad.

Larissa told me that she was scheduled to lead a tour to Suzdal that morning.

"That reminds me. What about your fee?"

"For yesterday you owe me one hundred fifty dollars. As for today, nothing. I wanted to help."

She gave me her cell number, making me promise to call if I needed anything. I thanked her and said in Russian—self-conscious about my pronunciation but determined to try—"You have shown me great kindness."

"*Pazhaaloosta,*" she said, which is the Russian word for *please.* I wondered what she wanted. And then I remembered. *Pazhaaloosta* also means "please don't mention it." She was gone before I could embarrass her further.

"Mind if I join you?"

It was Detective Marov. He sat down opposite me at the table where I was waiting for my breakfast to be served and slid my newly registered immigration card across the table. "Keep this with your passport. You'll need it to get out of the country."

"The enduring Russian paper mill," I commented.

The detective bristled. "Do you think it's easy for Russians who travel to *your* country? They make us fill out our lives in triplicate."

"So you've been to America. I can hear it in your English."

"We exchanged personnel with the police department in Indiana. I was there for a year."

The waiter came over, and Marov ordered something in Russian before asking, "Where are you headed today?"

"I'm looking for my stepfather. He was in Sergiev Posad a day or two ago."

"Maybe I can help. If he's an American, we do try to keep track of them."

"Don't I know it!"

"Do you have any idea where he went?"

I could lie to this man—who invited suspicion in spite of, or perhaps because of, the way he had sprung me from prison—

but I might not obtain the information I needed. If I trusted him, he might have a hidden agenda and lead me astray. Either way I was taking a risk. I mentally crossed my fingers and opted for cooperation. "Nikolai may be traveling east, to Tula, but I'm not sure."

"Why would he go there?"

"It's the hometown of someone he knew, a very long time ago. They were in prison together." I took the picture of the tattooed *Matryoshka* "judge" out of my purse and placed it on the table between us.

"All I know is that my stepfather knew someone named Ishkhan Lamsa when he was in prison and that something happened between them. The repercussions of this event, whatever it was, followed him all the way to America and are threatening to ruin what's left of his life. Not to mention my mother's."

Detective Marov picked up the photo and examined it. "The tattoo on the judge's shoulder is meant to tell your stepfather that he's a target of the blues."

"He's got good reason to be depressed," I said.

The detective laughed dryly. "The blues are what they call the *vory*—after the color of their tattoos. A *vor* is what in America you call a crime boss. Only here they think of themselves as keepers of the thieves law. Very quaint."

"In Nikolai's case, very deadly."

Marov sipped his coffee. "There are many unpleasant things a woman traveling alone might experience. Why don't you let me drive you?"

I chose to ignore the chauvinism and asked the obvious question. "What would your supervisor say?"

"I'm semi-retired. They use me only on a case-by-case basis."

"So you're a freelancer."

"Not exactly, but no one minds what I do on my own time."

"I'll be fine taking the train, Detective.

"Please, call me Feydor."

"Alright, Feydor. I appreciate your offer, but I'm perfectly capable of taking care of myself."

He looked crestfallen, so much so that, as payback for his part in my rescue, I decided to give him something to do.

"I have one side trip I need to make before I take the train to Tula. If you want to help, maybe you can get hold of the address of Yuri Baranski's clothing factory in Ivanovo."

He looked at me oddly for a moment. "Why so interested in fashion?"

"Oh—just something I need to do for a friend." What I didn't tell him was that I wanted a firsthand view of the factory where someone, possibly Micah's murderer—was knocking off Baranski's designs.

"Alright, leave it to me," he said, and I sensed the detective was eager to join in the chase. Either that or the retiree was zeroing in on a cure for his boredom. In any case, he promised to call me as soon as he got the information, and I went upstairs to pack.

Noon and no word from Marov. I waited as long as I could and then checked out. I had plenty of time to walk to the station and catch the one-fourteen for Ivanovo. There wasn't much street traffic, so it was easy to spot the car that was tailing me. I pulled out my camera, turned around, and walked back. I wanted the driver to know that any harassment would be recorded. It was the Volvo, with detective Marov at the wheel.

"Why were you following me?"

"Following? I was trying to catch up with you to give you the address you asked for, the one in Ivanovo. Let's go."

"Putin was right, you know, when he told your president that we don't want the kind of freedom you people are handing out in Iraq."

We'd been on the road for an hour, and Marov hadn't shut up yet. Which was okay by me. I was learning a lot: how Americans are seen as misinformed cretins gulping down press releases fed to the media by the military industrial complex; how the world has forgotten Russia since they lost their place in the contest for world dominator (or dominatrix as I corrected him); how it's not the Russian people but the greedy oligarchs who are being divested of TV stations and deprived of their civil liberties. It was a lopsided rant, but nonetheless a real education.

"For a policeman, you have some radical opinions."

"Hah! You should hear what my counterparts in the States have to say."

"The ones in Indiana?"

"We Russians travel a lot more than Americans think."

A light dusting of snow covered the tall birch trees on both sides of Route A113 as we drove into Ivanovo and down Shuja Street, where jalopies from the last century competed with the peeling paint on the storefronts for the title of supreme dismalness. This was a bleak factory town straight out of the Soviet past, with no signs of the urban renewal or upscale gentrification that had transformed Moscow.

Marov pulled into a gray industrial complex. "Baranski Textiles," he said, translating the sign over the factory entrance. The only bright spot in this sea of cement was a small but graceful chapel, its red-stained log walls topped by a silver onion dome.

The front office was empty, so we rang the bell on the desk and waited. Almost immediately, a small woman appeared, her hair raised in a bun and the silk suit she wore, along with the pearls encircling her neck, speaking of little or no time spent on the factory floor. To my relief, Marov, who was acting as my translator, refrained from showing her his badge.

"Tell her I'm a big fan of Yuri Branski's haute couture," I said, and he spoke with her at some length in Russian before she replied.

"Her name is Natalia and she is the manager. The director is out sick and yes, they produce all of Mr. Baranski's clothes."

"Does she know if anyone uses the factory when it's officially closed?"

Marov looked at me like I was crazy. "That's not a question she will answer. Let me try another approach."

The two of them continued to chatter away in Russian. Their facial expressions provided no clues to what was being said, but the rubles I saw him slip into her hand did.

Natalia motioned for us to sit in the vinyl chairs near the desk and then disappeared.

"She's bringing us something," is all Marov would say.

She soon returned and, with a tight smile, handed me a rectangular cardboard box. Marov expressed our thanks, and I carried the box, which was very light, to the car. What I found inside was a dress—an exact twin of the green one I'd taken from the basement sewing room in Brooklyn. The only difference was that it lacked a label. And that it might be the evidence I needed to establish Yuri Baranski's motive for killing Micah Goldman.

"Thank you, Detective Marov. You've gone to a lot of trouble to help a stranger."

"You're most welcome. And please, call me Feydor."

"Won't Natalia get in trouble for giving this to us?"

"I doubt if it will be missed. There's a lot more going on in that factory than illicit dressmaking. Russian industry has become, how shall I put it, extremely versatile. I have it on good authority that this coming Tuesday, Umarov's thugs will be picking up a load of Uzis and plastic explosives."

If he was trying to impress me, he was succeeding. "Who is Umarov?"

"Dokka Umarov is a Chechen rebel leader who has chosen to stay and fight for independence rather than live in exile in Turkey."

"I thought the Chechen rebellion was completely crushed."

"That's the official line, but Umarov has visions of a Caucasian Emirate—an Islamic state for all the people living in the North Caucasus. He buys munitions where he can find them, in this case from the *vor* known as Squint."

The underground connections in this country made fiber optic cables look like walkie-talkies.

On the way back to Vladimir from Ivanovo, we passed through the medieval town of Suzdal, where the road was lined with old-fashioned wood framed houses painted in red and green and decorated with intricately carved shutters and latticework. Golden cupolas pierced the sky, symbols of the newly released religious fervor of Russia. In front of the Monastery of St. Euthymius, tourist buses clogged the road like giant white corpuscles. Marov slowed down and found a parking space to squeeze into. "You cannot pass through Suzdal without hearing the bells," he said.

We entered the grounds and walked down the brick pathways, past the whitewashed buildings with tiny windows designed long ago to discourage the nuns from gazing out at the world. In the monastery gardens a symphony of resonant chimes greeted us, the bell ringers performing their magic in the tower high above.

"You timed this perfectly."

Marov nodded stiffly, the intensity to his aura at odds with the peaceful ambience of the monastery. "There's something here you need to see," he said. "There are cells at the other end of the monastery, where many religious and political dissidents were incarcerated during the nineteenth century."

I looked around at the well-kept flower beds and serene faces. "No more prison tours for me, thanks."

"Yes. I understand. But I promise, it will be worth your while."

Something in his tone had changed. I stopped on the path and turned to face him. "Can you be more specific?"

"You will see soon enough." It was obvious he was irritated with me for being so reluctant after he had gone to so much trouble to help me.

"If this place makes you uncomfortable, we can leave." He stood there, waiting patiently for me to make up my mind.

I felt like a fool. Evidently my recent incarceration had made me paranoid. "No problem," I said and we continued walking. There was a museum behind the north wall. It was much smaller than the one at Vladimir Central and the place was deserted, not a big tourist attraction. Photos, ancient handcuffs, and the usual paraphernalia were on display, as they were at Vladimir, but the prisoners here had been priests and nuns, deemed heretical for criticizing church dignitaries or for "spontaneous expressions of atheism." Had the church, by creating this bleak monastery jail during Czarist times, unwittingly set the stage for their own persecution by the Bolsheviks? Was this a precursor to the gulag?

Marov looked around to make sure we were alone, then tugged at a thick metal ring mounted in the floor. Accompanied by his grunt of effort, the trapdoor yielded, releasing a ladder that unfolded downward, into the darkness. "Not many people know about this chamber. It was used for solitary confinement." He gestured. "Ladies first."

"Not me," I said instinctively.

I felt the cold nose of a gun jammed into the small of my back and the chilling truth coursed through my body, bringing back every qualm I had foolishly suppressed after meeting this man. What an idiot I'd been. Stop it! I told myself. You can beat up on yourself later—if you survive.

"Go ahead and call for help," he said. "But it will be your word against mine and people respect badges, even in the new Russia. Better to come quietly."

With every muscle pulling in the opposite direction, I forced myself to descend into the cavernous room, Marov close behind. Would this be my last experience of Russia? The musty smell of an earthen floor, and something else, rose to meet me. Above us, the trapdoor shut with a resounding thud.

"Give me your cell phone," Marov demanded, and I handed it over, watching him bury my best hope of rescue deep in his jacket pocket.

In the dimness I made out a huddled figure.

Nikolai! He stirred, then sat up, rubbing his eyes and squinting against the new light. If he was surprised to see me, the scraggly beard on his face did a good job of hiding it. He greedily devoured the sandwich that Marov had brought.

"Are you alright?" I asked.

"I've been better," he said, "but once your head is cut off, there's no use worrying about your hair."

Now I understood why, even in Brooklyn, Nikolai had kept his wits sharp and exercised his gift for sarcasm frequently. When all else failed, it gave him something to fall back on.

I turned to Marov. "Who is Ishkhan Lamsa?"

Nikolai answered for him. "Ishkhan was Feydor's father. We knew each other in prison. He was a *vor.*"

Something didn't compute. I asked Marov, "How could you become a policeman if your father was a gangster?"

He covered the distance between us and with one angry motion slapped me across the face, hard. "My father had more integrity in his little toe than the entire Russian criminal justice system. And if you understood anything about our culture, you'd know that the *vory* were not allowed to marry. It's my mother's name that I carry." Feydor's face contorted with rage. His veneer of civility had cracked, and the werewolf beneath came to light. All that was missing was the foam at his mouth.

Feydor wasn't the only one who could turn primeval. Spitting out the blood from my bitten tongue, I braced for attack, ready to scratch out his eyes before he could shoot me.

Nikolai struggled to his feet. "You've got *me*, Detective Mitchell, and that should be enough. Leave my stepdaughter alone."

I don't know what shocked me more—Nikolai finally granting me family status or his revelation of Marov's true identity. They both watched me closely as I put it together. *Frank Mitchell, the Brooklyn detective who worked undercover with Lenny Grimes. Frank Mitchell aka Feydor Marov, aka Mr. Eeks.*

"You're right, Little Dog," Marov said. "I need her alive so she can witness your trial."

"And after that?" I asked.

He didn't answer, so I assumed he planned to dispose of me when I was no longer useful. I wiped the blood off my lips with the sleeve of my sweatshirt, tamping down my rage in favor of a clear head.

"They will be here tonight," said Marov, as he climbed the ladder. "Nikolai can tell you all about it."

We could hear him banging around in the exhibit room above us. "He's putting a block of wood through the iron ring in the trapdoor," Nikolai explained. "Primitive but effective."

"His trademark."

Nikolai forced a smile. "Just like his father."

Outside, in spite of the chilly weather signaling the approach of winter, his forehead burned hot and feverish. He was dizzy, but not from a feeling of power or the anticipated pleasure of being swept into the vortex of long-delayed revenge. It was as if the malevolent maelstrom he had worked so hard to create had turned into a debilitating force that sapped the strength of his will. The fierce energy that he had relied on for so long to compel him toward his goal was failing him—like a neap tide falling short of the shore—just as he was about to reach his objective. Everything was working smoothly, according to plan. Why this sudden sickness of spirit?

As he collected the wide-hipped amber bottles from the trunk of the car, he found a name for what he was experiencing. Grief. Insistent and intense, it was a burning sensation in his chest that a weaker man might have mistaken for a heart attack. And in a way it was. Having carried the burden of his unexpressed anguish for so long, his body had chosen this inconvenient moment to rebel. What he most wanted was to merge the sound of his own sobs with those of the bells echoing off the walls until they were both spent. Instead, he forced himself to recall every painful detail of Ishkhan's disfigured face, twisted with pain as they forcibly tattooed a picture on his ass that was so disgusting his son didn't know what it signified until he was much older. He forced himself to hear every scream he had been compelled to listen to, every torment he had been forced to see his father endure.

In a few moments, he had himself under control. Once again, as he had in New York, he could rely on his anger to provide the strength he needed to fulfill his purpose. He would go through with the trial for the sake of his father's memory, and in the process he would try to salvage his own self-esteem. If there was irony in having the distant associates of Ishkhan's executioners pass judgment on the man who had betrayed him, so be it. As long as the *vory* adhered to the code, a verdict of guilty was inevitable.

It was time to get the job done.

CHAPTER NINETEEN

The first one climbed down the ladder at eleven, and by midnight there were three. No introductions were made, but as the trial progressed, I learned the nickname of each judge: Buzz, the twitchy young buck in the stereotypical track suit; Squint, the arms dealer Marov had told me about, who wore a three-piece brown suit and appeared to having nothing wrong with his eyesight; and Priest, a round-faced burgher with a giant silver cross around his neck, by virtue of his age the leader of the group.

In the weak light of a kerosene lamp, they sat cross-legged on the damp earth, sipping the cognac that Marov had so thoughtfully provided. It was Priest who first deigned to notice me. "Who is this woman?"

"Daughter of the accused," answered Marov.

Neither Nikolai nor I bothered to correct him. Our gazes met, and I decided that if we somehow got out of this alive, I would take my stepfather to Scandal's and get him good and drunk.

Marov began the proceedings by saying, "I, Feydor Marov, son of Ishkhan Lamsa, am here to present my case against Nikolai Kharpov."

He spoke in Russian, and Buzz translated, delivering the English words in a dull, formal manner, in contrast to Marov's impassioned voice tone, which grew in intensity as the story progressed.

"My father Ishkhan was a powerful *vor*—proud to be known as the keeper of the thieves law. In 1957 he was arrested for money laundering and sent to Vladimir Central Prison. It was the first time in my short life that my father had left us for any significant period of time, and before he left, he told me not to worry, that he would lack for nothing and even bring me presents when he returned. His confidence was entirely due to the *Obchak*, the fund to which all *vory* were compelled to contribute and that was drawn upon whenever one of them went to prison. My father told me that the *Obchak* was especially important during the war, when the number of *vory* in prison exceeded the number of those living outside.

"When Ishkhan had been away for almost a year, I remember walking home from school and seeing two men in the distance approaching our house. My first thought was *what if I'm wrong and the tall one in the dark blue overcoat and black boots is not my father after all?* As he came closer, he saw me and called my name. I ran toward him and he opened his great coat, enveloping me like a hungry bear. 'There you are,' is all he said but I could feel his joy as he held me. Then he turned me around to face his companion and said, 'This is my good friend Little Dog, you must treat him as a member of the family.' "

As he spoke, Marov moved closer to Nikolai, hissing his words so that the spray of his spittle came close to dousing my stepfather's face. "I remember examining you closely to see why you would be called such a funny name as 'Little Dog.' But I dared not ask Ishkhan since he showed you such respect."

Feydor turned his eyes upward, as if gazing directly into the past through the low ceiling of the underground cell. "Our house was small but well kept, painted dark green on the outside, with bright red shutters and a thatched roof. Ishkhan knew that my mother was not expecting him, which was why he hesitated before entering. I heard him saying to Little Dog, 'I hope she doesn't shoot me. Galya hates surprises.'

"My mother had her back to us and was stirring something on the stove. Ishkhan grabbed her around the waist. Anxiously, I watched for signs of her displeasure, but of course she was overjoyed. She got out a bottle of brandy she had saved and we celebrated my father's return. She even let me take a sip from the bottle."

Marov redirected his burning stare toward Nikolai. "All during dinner Ishkhan sang the praises of Little Dog. He said his escape from Vladimir Prison would not have been possible without you and that he was eternally in your debt."

From that point on in the narrative, whenever Marov said "you," the *vory* judges turned their heads in unison to stare at Nikolai. Feydor had succeeded in firmly establishing Little Dog's identity in their collective consciousness.

"After dinner my father banished me to the loft to finish my homework and sent you outside so that he could be alone with my mother. Through the floorboards I could hear them both laughing. It was good to see her so happy, after all the nights I had listened in the darkness as she cried herself to sleep.

"When Ishkhan had been home for two days, he told us that Little Dog would be leaving in the morning. 'He will fetch the *Obchak* and bring it here, so that I can keep an eye on it while I choose my successor. This is the only way to avoid bloodshed—too many people want what only one can have.' I remember his words well, because after speaking them he had a coughing fit that shook his body so hard that his teeth rattled. The next day, Ishkhan took you aside for a long talk and then you left, never to return."

Feydor addressed the judges directly. "As you know, the *Obchak* contains much more than money," he said. "It is the life's blood of a centuries-old way of life. My father would sooner have cut off his own arm than steal what had been entrusted to him. His mistake was to expect Little Dog to feel the same way."

Marov turned to Nikolai. "Because of *your* crime, they tattooed repulsive, obscene images on my father, covering the prison tattoos he had proudly worn since the age of fifteen. Because of *your* betrayal, they sodomized him in front of my mother and then shot him in the head. Because of *your* cowardice, my father was buried without the honor and respect he deserved. You spit on his soul."

Nikolai bowed his head. I had no way of knowing what he was thinking, but I was sure that if he said one word Marov would have been on him like a tiger.

Feydor resumed his narrative in a voice now on the verge of breaking. "My father suffered unspeakable pain and humiliation, but he never revealed your name to his torturers. You used the *Obchak* to become rich and successful, a great Russian artiste. You are lower than a parasite. Even a parasite permits its host to live."

Buzz stopped his translation as Marov struggled to control his feelings. When Feydor next spoke, his eyes, which moments before had been ablaze with hate, were void of expression.

"Nikolai Kharpov deserves the same punishment he caused to fall on my father's head. You must convict him and order his execution."

It was Priest who spoke for the group. "We must hear from the accused."

Nikolai stood up slowly, the tension in his jaw the only outward sign of stress. "As far as I know, the *Obchak* is still hidden in the place where Ishkhan buried it," he said.

For a moment the only sound in the cavern was the sputter of burning oil. Then Squint queried Marov, "Did Kharpov tell you this?"

"Of course I told him," said Nikolai. "He believes only what

Ishkhan wanted him to believe. A story designed to protect a little boy."

"My father spoke the truth, always!"

"He was a father who was dying from tuberculosis and wanted to provide for his son," Nikolai said. "Inheritance has always been anathema to the *vory* and it is the main reason that, at least in those days, they were forbidden to marry. A thief-in-law's status must be earned, never inherited. It was for your sake, Feydor, that Ishkhan broke the code."

Marov grabbed Nikolai by the shoulders, shaking him in a fruitless attempt to exorcize the painful words just spoken.

"Let him go," Priest said. "We are the ones who will judge— not you. If you interfere again, the trial will be declared invalid."

Marov grudgingly released his hold and stepped back. Nikolai picked up his story, which to my ears at least, seemed to carry the weight of truth. "When Ishkhan sent for me from his bed in the prison infirmary and said he had arranged for us to escape from that hell hole, I was overjoyed. He laid out the escape route as casually as if it were an itinerary for a Black Sea vacation. 'There is a monastery next door to the prison,' he told me. 'Once we are over the wall, they will provide us with clothes and a car. I am very weak and need you to accompany me to Tula.'

"Ishkhan told me his plan. He would pretend that the *Obchak* had been stolen and to tell the members of his collective that he had confided its location to me. He would say that he had trusted me to secure the money and then, when the time came, deliver it to his successor. He would claim that I had betrayed him and then disappeared. Even Galya and his son would not know the truth until later. I owed Ishkhan my life more than once over, so of course I agreed."

His tone softening, Nikolai spoke to Feydor as if the two of them were alone in the room. "Your father knew he would be dishonored and executed, but he did not care. He was dying, he wanted to provide for you, and this was the only way. If I were blamed for stealing the *Obchak*, no suspicion would fall on you or your mother. He said the *vory* would vow to kill me, but since they knew me only as Little Dog, they would never find me.

"It was a good plan. I was to wait for one month and then contact you to make sure that you had found the money and taken it from its hiding place. I followed his instructions, but when I showed up in Tula, your mother recognized me. She said she would kill me if I tried to enter the house and she refused to tell me your whereabouts."

"So you kept the *Obchak* for yourself?" Squint asked.

"No," said Nikolai. "Maybe I would have pinched it if I'd known where it was—I was no angel—but Ishkhan trusted me like a wolf trusts a fox—enough to hunt with but never to share the spoils. All he told me was that he was going to write a note explaining everything to Feydor and leave it in their secret place."

"Liar!" Marov cried. "My father and I had no such hiding place." Again he addressed the judges, trying to quell the desperation that had crept into his voice. "Little Dog stole the money. My father died. What else do you need to know?"

"Have you told them you are a policeman?" I asked. It was a shot in the dark but even before Buzz translated, I could see Priest react. He conferred with Squint—questioning him none too gently—and then stood up, brushing off invisible specks from his dirt-colored suit and downing the last of his cognac. "Am I to understand that we have come here at the request of a *ment*—that you are a foul policeman?"

Marov knew he was in trouble and tried to explain. "I was sent to live with relatives in Moscow. I wanted nothing more to do with the *vory* after what they did to my father. The Militia accepted me when no one else would. They made me feel useful, as if I were helping people."

"How?" asked Priest. "By sending the strong ones to labor camps and the weak to the grave?" He had switched to English, acknowledging my presence for the first time.

"I was not that kind of policeman—in the same way you are not the kind of criminal who kills for the sake of killing."

The three judges walked to the foot of the ladder, preparing to leave. Priest glared scornfully at Marov. "We agreed to come because my brother, rest his soul, knew Ishkhan and believed in his innocence. But you deceived us. Out of respect for him we will let you live. But we cannot continue this sham of a trial."

"If you will not give me justice I will deliver it myself!" Marov pulled out his gun and clicked off the safety. He was going to kill Nikolai and then me, I was sure of it. The *vory* would maintain their neutrality and not interfere. I thought about my Lady Colt sitting uselessly in a drawer at home.

"You never meant a word of it," I told Feydor. "Your talk about justice is as hollow as any *Matryoshka*."

Keeping the gun trained on Nikolai, Marov used his free hand to reach into his shirt pocket and pulled out something that he held out for us to see. It was a tiny judge, the fifth doll. "You betrayed my father and I will throw the last *Matryoshka* on your grave!"

He slammed the doll to the ground and it cracked open. A sliver of white peeked out. Feydor picked up the doll and tugged at it impatiently, releasing a small square of paper. As he examined his find, an incredulous expression came over his face, a child's wonder competing with a man's distrust.

"This can't be true," he murmured.

CHAPTER TWENTY

"This is not my father's handwriting," Marov insisted. "It's a forgery, a transparent attempt to send me wildly chasing a goose." His English was far from perfect and so was his logic. In what looked like a classic case of denial, Marov vehemently maintained that the note had been planted by someone at the *Matryoshka* factory during the restoration process, someone who had been paid off by either me or Nikolai.

"At the time you placed the order in Sergiev Posad, Nikolai and I were busy living our respective lives in blissful innocence of your plans," I reminded him.

"You could have slipped the doll out of my pocket in the car when we were driving to Ivanovo and inserted the note."

"Yes, that's possible, but how would I have resealed it? Oh, I forgot. I always carry a bottle of rubber cement in my purse."

Priest now spoke for the three *vory*, who apparently had changed their minds about abandoning the trial. "You lied to us about being a policeman. If it turns out that you have also falsely accused and persecuted Nikolai Kharpov, you will be held responsible."

Marov started to say something but Priest silenced him with a raised hand. "Does the note say where the *Obchak* is buried?"

"Yes, but—"

"Then there is only one solution. We will keep the accused with us and you will go and investigate his claim. Take the woman with you. She will continue to be your witness. If you do not come back with a full report and bring her with you, we will assume that you have tricked us again and deal with you and any loved ones you have accordingly."

There was no mistaking the fear that swept across Feydor's face. Surely it was not his own safety he cared about, which made me wonder if someone was waiting for him in Moscow or New York. And more to the point, if I would be alive long enough to find out who it was.

Feydor used his cell phone to make some arrangements. As I walked by, Nikolai whispered, "Take care." With far more trepidation than hope, I climbed the ladder and left him to await the results of our journey in the not-so-tender care of the *vory.*

It is impossible to drive around Russia without being stopped intermittently by the Traffic State Police, checking papers, testing the waters for bribes. At each of the two checkpoints we passed through on the way to Tula, I considered asking for help and decided against it. What would I have said? That I was traveling in the company of a police officer with impeccable Russian and American credentials who in reality was a blackmailing murderer? That his *vory* associates were holding my stepfather in a dank underground chamber beneath the Monastery of St. Euthymius and would kill him unless the results of this trip were to their liking? Between my pathetic language skills, Marov's slick cover, and the gun jabbed into my side, my chances of escaping or convincing anyone of anything except my own lunacy were strictly zero.

Marov was weaving in and out of traffic like a commuter terrified of being late for work. "Maybe you should back off on the accelerator," I said. He gave the Volvo more gas and launched into a tirade about how President Bush, now retired safely to his ranch in Texas, had planned the World Trade Center attack.

"It's not crazy, it's consistent with history," he insisted when I told him I strongly disagreed with his theory. "Putin demonized the Chechen rebels in the same way that Bush characterized all of Islam as evil, and that's why, until the world condemned the invasion of Georgia, the two of them were such great pals."

"Just like you and the *vory*," I said.

Instead of taking offense, Marov laughed. "I'm in good company there. Take Stalin. Our most celebrated gangster. He envied the reputation of the *vory* as upstanding criminals so much that he tried to appropriate their traditions and mythology. He thought he could absorb them into his cult of the personality. Never happened."

"I don't know much about Stalin, but I can see a parallel between the *vory*, with their beneficent *Obchak*, and the communists with their guaranteed employment and benefits. They both conned people into believing they'd be taken care of, as long as they were willing to follow their leaders off a cliff. Come to think of it, Hezbollah has an *Obchak* too—and so does the mafia."

Marov twisted around in the passenger seat to face me (now that we were driving in the country and the checkpoints were gone, he had put me behind the wheel). His eyes were lit, not with anger but with interest. A shame that such an intelligent man had such a damaged psyche.

"You're right—there are many who see the *vory* in a romantic light. There will be a rude awakening when they find out their folk heroes have been selling arms to the rebels in Chechnya."

He was referring to the upcoming shipment from the textile factory in Ivanovo. "I thought the *vory* were thieves who did not take sides in politics. So much for their code of honor."

Marov snorted. "When there is money to be made, men forget who they are. And what about your global corporations?

Guilt-free crime machines with faceless stockholders whose main function is to absolve the company of all evil in the name of profit?"

Refusing to take the bait, I drove past an abandoned industrial park and into the town square in Tula, where arching spurts of water from a fountain rained down on prancing horses, their dark energy captured in black stone. Marov explained that it was here that the weapons used by the Red Army to defeat the German invasion had been manufactured. "Since the time of Peter the Great cannons and rifles have been made here. It is a place also famous for their samovars. As they say, 'You don't go to Tula with your own samovar.' " For a moment, his pride in being from this area of Russia had dampened the blaze of hatred that consumed him.

Back on the open highway, the signs were all in Cyrillic, and I had no way of tracking our progress. Marov ignored my questions about where we were headed, but from the angle of the sun I gathered that we were traveling east. We passed through a dense, built-up area filled with factories and what I took to be chemical plants, smokestacks puffing overtime to put God knows what into the air. I breathed easier when the landscape changed to open fields dotted with farmhouses set well back from the road, the only jarring note a new housing development that looked depressingly Californian.

A few miles later the road curved and ran along a river, the water a placid mirror, the banks covered with dry grass and a few scrubby trees, all dimly lit by the setting sun behind us. I caught a brief glimpse of a falcon overhead, sailing on the up-draft. All very beautiful, but as I gazed out the car window I couldn't shake the image of Nikolai's resigned face when we left him in the underground chamber at the monastery. I wondered where the *vory* had taken him and if I would ever see him again. Because no matter what we found in the forest, Marov would have to be crazy to let me go. Unfortunately, he was as sane as any policeman-turned-murderer-turned-blackmailer could be.

The fields gave way to dense oak forest, the trees whizzing by in black silhouette against the azure sky. We passed a sign that Marov told me marked the turnoff for Tolstoy's house, *Clear Glade,* which was now a museum run by the writer's descendants. Soon after, Marov had me pull over behind a pickup truck on the side of the road.

"I've arranged for some transportation."

He held a brief discussion with a laconic, pasty-faced young man, whose bright yellow shirt did nothing to wake up his sleepy, hooded eyes. Money was exchanged, and Marov took possession of a Russian-made pickup, which came with a cavernous dent in the passenger door, a smashed right headlight, and two mismatched fenders. He handed me the keys, and to my surprise, the truck started up on the first try.

After a mile or so, Marov showed me where to turn off on a narrow dirt track, barely visible from the highway, which seemed to grow skinnier as it wound its way through the low hills. The pickup's shocks had worn out half a century ago, and it vibrated and bounced like a mechanical bull in a Texas bar. Fortunately, the big wheels kept us from stalling in the mud or drowning in the swift-running stream that we crossed before driving into the woods. Another mile or two and the road ended abruptly at a wall of trees.

"This is the spot."

It was obvious he was talking about more than geography. For a moment his guard was down, and from his wistful expression I surmised that we had arrived at a place in his past that, until recently, Marov had been sure he would never see again.

At best, twilight would last for another two hours, and I was not happy about going for a woodland hike in the darkness with a seasoned and unpredictable killer. With every step, our shoes sank into the mixture of red sand and brown soil that formed the forest floor. Some light filtered down through the branches, but if there was a path through the trees it was visible only to my companion. Nonetheless, I tried as best I could to memorize our route. I would have to make my move soon and it wouldn't do me any good unless I could beat him back to the truck.

"You're very quiet," Marov finally said. "What are you afraid of, the ghost of the Rostov Ripper?" When I failed to respond, he told me he was referring to Andrei Chikatilo, whose fame had spread all the way to America after he butchered more than fifty children in a lonely strip of forest. "You don't need to worry about your own safety," Marov sneered. "For one thing, you're not a child. And the Ripper was executed by firing squad in 1994."

"Actually, I was thinking that if the *Obchak* is buried here, we have no shovel or pick-ax to dig it up."

"Not your concern," Marov said, picking up his pace.

An hour later, I was consumed with thirst and the growing conviction that Marov was deliberately getting us lost for some dark purpose of his own. He stopped at last in a small clearing, where a gigantic rock embedded in the ground prevented the encroachment of trees. In front of the boulder, hundreds of smaller rocks had been piled into a circular mound to form a cairn.

Marov began to pick his way through the pile, carefully placing each stone he removed to the side. I sat down on a log a few feet away and watched him work, keeping an eye on the gun in his belt. I was biding my time, willing my reflexes to sharpen. The twenty minutes it took for him to completely uncover the ground beneath the cairn gave me time to consider what Marov's options were for dealing with me. If he failed to find the *Obchak*, Nikolai's guilt would be confirmed in his eyes and he would take revenge by killing both of us. If he found the *Ob-*

chak, he might decide to keep the money and kill the only witness, yours truly. Or, and this was my favorite scenario, he could decide to do the right thing and return the money, and me, to the *vory.* Fat chance.

Marov grunted with effort as he jettisoned the last stone and smoothed the earth away from the edge of a symmetrical hole. A dim ray of sunlight caught the gleam of metal. "What is it?" I asked.

"A German artillery shell. My father used it as a hiding place."

Marov reached down, his arm disappearing into the shell up to his shoulder, then planted his feet on the ground to provide leverage as he heaved upward. He grunted with effort but with no results, then tried again and the object broke free, propelling him backward onto the ground. The cylindrical parcel landed on his chest with a thud. It was tightly wrapped in something shiny that, leaning in for a closer look, I identified as black oil cloth, the kind used to make waterproof jackets.

Marov sat up, reaching into his back pocket for a knife. He gingerly cut the rope that secured the cloth around the *Obchak,* letting the American dollars spill out on the ground. Leave it to the *vory* to know their currency. No worthless rubles for Ishkhan. The $30,000 I watched Feydor count would have been deemed an enormous sum in 1957.

If I was expecting him to dissolve into a gel of self-recrimination upon finding the *Obchak* intact, I was cured of that notion immediately. He rewrapped the money in the oil cloth and returned the artillery shell to its hiding place.

"The *vory* will want to see that before they release Nikolai," I said.

"They will want to keep it for themselves."

"So you're willing to sacrifice my stepfather, even though you know he's innocent, to protect this lump of cash?"

In an instant Marov had his Russian-made Nagant pointing directly at me. If I had only a few seconds of life left, I was damned if I was going to waste them. I made a grab for the gun, wrapping my right hand around the stock before he wrestled it free. He whacked my chin with his elbow before shoving me to the ground with his free arm.

I felt for loose teeth with my tongue before scrambling back to my feet. "If I were you, it would not be *me* I'd feel like killing." I left the meaning hanging there for him to pick up.

"What makes you think I intend to kill either of us?" He was suddenly jumpy, distracted.

"Then why the gun?"

He ignored my question, staring at something over my head and slightly to the left. A sliver of light was reflected in his eyes. A nanosecond later came the crack of a gunshot.

Marov fired the Nagant as he fell, grabbing my ankle and pulling my feet out from under me. I landed hard on my back, stifling a cry of pain that would have given us away.

I waited for sixty long seconds, and when nothing more happened, crawled over to where Marov lay. I touched his arm and got a groan in response. His left shoulder was shattered and he'd already lost enough blood to form a large pool on the ground. I scrambled out of my jean jacket and wrapped the sleeve around his upper arm, pulling it as tightly as I could. It wasn't the best of tourniquets, but it slowed the bleeding down to a drip. There was no way to tell if the wound involved a vital artery. I felt his hand on my knee. "Thank you," he whispered. Even in the dim twilight, I could see his face was the color of dirty chalk. On the ground next to him, I spotted a small piece of paper. It was the note that had fallen out of the last *Matryoshka* when he smashed it. I slipped the crumpled paper into my pocket. His breathing was shallow and ragged. "Please tell my wife I love her. She is my treasure, an innocent in all this."

He seemed near the end, so I gave my promise. I was in the middle of telling him to quit talking and save his strength, when a volley of shots flew over our heads.

The gun Marov dropped when he fell had to be close by, but it was too dark to see, and I was afraid that if I fumbled around I would give away my position. I grabbed a handful of gravel and flung it as far as I could to the left. Gunfire erupted, directed at the source of the sound. I threw more gravel, trying to convince whoever it was that it was me they heard thrashing around. I did this two more times and then crawled in the opposite direction as quietly as I could, stopping every few feet to listen for any telltale sounds. None were provided.

When the last of the light faded, I picked up a rock the size of a baseball. This one had to be thrown far enough to convince my adversary I was gone for good. Standing up, I cranked my arms into the same pitching windup I'd perfected as a kid playing stickball in the streets of the Bronx, and released the rock, my left shoulder burning with the effort. The rock arrived at its destination with a satisfying thud, and the reaction was immediate: a shaft of light pierced the darkness. For a brief moment I caught a glimpse of a yellow shirt, but then, instead of aiming the flashlight in the direction of the rock, he aimed the beam directly at my face.

I turned and ran blindly through the trees. I could hear him crashing behind me through the brush. When the sounds of pursuit stopped, I knew he was reloading. Damn it. If only I had retrieved the Nagant.

The exhausted part of me was sorely tempted to sit down with my back to a tree and surrender to darkness and despair. My enemy was probably a local who knew this terrain and could afford to wait me out. What the hell, another part of me said, if it's as hopeless as all that you might as well die trying.

But in spite of my resolution, I ran out of breath and was

forced to slow my pace to a fast walk. This turned out to be a good thing, because after a few yards my extended arms encountered hard cold stone that would have cracked open my skull if I had run into it head first. I explored the surface of the rock with my fingers and found that it extended above my head, maybe a cliff face. I felt for a foothold. At least an ascent would make less noise than running through dried leaves. Unless, of course, I lost my footing and fell.

Placing my right foot on an outcrop, I leveraged myself up, inching upward, hugging the rock face so tightly I feared my hands would grow numb and I'd lose my grip. I have never been afraid of heights, but I was climbing in almost total darkness and each new foothold was loaded with uncertainty. What if the next time I reached up I couldn't find a handhold? What if I dislodged an unseen boulder? What if the cliff was a hundred feet high and my arms and legs gave way before I could find a ledge to rest on? I tried to turn off my mind, which was rapidly succumbing to a mixture of vertigo and fatigue.

I estimated I had climbed about twenty feet when the fingers of my left hand gripped what felt like a large clump of grass. When my right hand encountered the same texture, I felt such a surge of relief that I almost let go. My feet searched for a foothold, but the rock face had become completely smooth. Praying that the crab grass in Russia was as stubbornly rooted as the variety back home, I grabbed hold of as much of it as I could muster and hoisted myself up and over.

I landed in a layer of prickly needles surrounding the massive trunk of a large tree, my ribs making painful contact with the compact mounds of earth that covered the tree's massive roots. A meadow was softly illuminated by a sliver of moonlight. Grateful to be alive, I was about to say a prayer of thanks to the God I sometimes believe in, when a single gunshot, its sound carried from the distance, broke the stillness. Yellow shirt had found Feydor.

I buried myself as deeply under the leaves and pine needles as I could and fell into the drugged sleep of the overtired, oblivious to stars above and danger below.

Morning revealed that what I had mistaken for a meadow was in fact a small pond surrounded by grassland. If I had rolled in any other direction than the one chosen, I would have been soaked to the skin and a good candidate for pneumonia. As it was, I had a bad case of the shivers, brought on by the hours I'd spent curled up in the cold and damp.

I quenched my raging thirst in the stream that fed the pond and then followed the water downhill, until it diminished to a trickle that flowed under the road. The sun was up, and using the shaded areas by the side of the highway for cover, I forced my aching legs to walk in the direction opposite to where the fading light had been visible the night before.

I found the Volvo still parked in the spot where Marov had exchanged it for the truck. What a stroke of luck that he had made me drive. I dug the keys out of my jacket pocket and had my hand on the gearshift and my foot on the gas before it dawned on me that if I left the *Obchak* behind in the woods, I would also be leaving Nikolai to the merciless justice of the *vory*.

On second thought, there was a fifty-fifty chance that Yellow Shirt was at this moment receiving a reward for delivering the money to whoever had hired him to kill Marov. Even if I could talk myself into going back into the woods, I had no food or water to sustain me for the hours, or days, it might take to locate the spot where the artillery shell had been so cleverly hidden. My best bet was to race back to the monastery as quickly as possible and hope that my wild explanations would affect Nikolai's release. I had to get the hell out of there while I still could. The adrenalin from the night's adventure would carry me only so far.

Москва 195. The road sign was a welcome sight. Add the kilometers from Moscow to Suzdal, and I was looking at a four-hour drive.

CHAPTER TWENTY-ONE

The tourists at the monastery had a bit of a shock when, right in the middle of their guided tour of the museum, the custodian appeared and frantically shooed them aside, using a crowbar to force open a trapdoor in the floor. Russians, however, are experts at minding their own business. They've had plenty of practice.

Aleksey the custodian had agreed to help me when I told him that a friend of mine could be trapped in the chamber below, and the door seemed to have gotten stuck. Instead of asking me what the hell we had been doing down there, he cooperated willingly, and I wondered if he had been bribed to provide assistance and make sure that I didn't call the police. I was sure the chamber would be empty, but I insisted on his opening it because I had this crazy idea that the "judges" might have left a message indicating their whereabouts. No such luck.

I used Aleksey's cell phone to call Larissa, who interrupted my increasingly incoherent narrative to suggest that I save the details until my arrival at her apartment. It was close to one A.M. and the Volvo was sputtering on empty by the time I parked it in front of her building in northeast Moscow. She took one look at my bedraggled state and insisted I take a shower and spend the night. When I thanked her for all she had done, she said, "Walls are useless. Only friends can protect each other." If

Hasim ever ran out of proverbs, he'd find plenty more to his liking in Russia.

On Sunday morning, with my toes poorly protected from the increasingly cold weather by a pair of Larissa's Reeboks, I walked from the Ismailovky Park metro station to the Vernissage Market and made my way through the stands filled with old Soviet posters, military uniforms, coins, cameras, and everything a souvenir hunter on a tight budget could wish for. Larissa had provided instructions on where to go, what to say, and to whom. How she had obtained her information, I was forbidden to ask.

In spite of our preparations, I was sorely lacking in confidence. If the *vory* were involved in arms dealing, what could one life possibly mean to them? What if they had decided to dispose of Nikolai as an inconvenience? Or maybe they'd released him, and he'd gone to ground, in which case he'd be harder to find than the lost tribes of Israel.

The currency exchange was just where Ludmilla had said it would be, in a tall Nuevo Deco building on the far side of the market. I followed the arrows to the waiting room and got in line with a bunch of tourists, easily identified by their backpacks and sandals, along with some locals toting their signature plastic bags. When my turn came, I was admitted to a small windowless room containing two exchange booths. An "observer" kept watch on the patrons while pretending to read a newspaper. There was barely enough room to turn around in, much less attempt a robbery.

I traded 500 American dollars for the equivalent amount in rubles—about 15,000. The exchange took place in silence, and the clerk, a sour-looking woman with a huge mole on her cheek, looked annoyed when I broke protocol and addressed her directly. Reading phrases from a card that Larissa had given me, I told her in Russian that I needed to see Priest about an urgent matter and would she please tell him I was here.

She looked at me blankly, and it struck me that she might think I wanted to see a real priest rather than the elderly *vor.* Gamely, I repeated my careful pronunciation of the phonetic words. This time a connection was made and she nodded at the heavy-set security person, who folded his newspaper and raised himself with difficulty from the chair. He motioned for me to follow him into the lobby, where he unlocked the elevator and rode with me up to the third floor.

Priest met us in the lift, impatiently toying with the silver cross around his neck, looking none too pious. He dismissed the guard and walked me down the hall toward his office. "It is Feydor Marov we are expecting," he said, in hesitant but service-able English.

"Marov is dead, killed by the man you sent."

He kept walking, not a break in his stride. "We sent no one."

"I don't really care. The *Obchak* contains thirty thousand dollars. It is buried in an artillery shell in the forest outside of Tula. If you release Nikolai, I will tell you exactly where. A fair trade."

Priest turned to face me at the door to his office, having changed his mind about inviting me in. "This will not work. You have put the order backward. You must first bring us the money and then your father will be seeing his freedom."

He had the edge, and he knew it. "Since you are returning to Tula, you should visit Yasnaya Polyana. Is very popular with tourists," he remarked. "The grave of Tolstoy is there, and the mansion they have preserved, even the school he built for the peasant children. Too bad you had no chance to see it."

I told him I'd already seen enough. "How do I know you will release Nikolai once you have the *Obchak?*"

"You have my word. We will give you twenty-four hours to bring back what belongs to us. After that . . ." He did not need to spell it out for me. I gave him Larissa's number to call if he wanted to contact me. As far as I knew, my own cell phone was in a dead man's pocket. Priest did not offer to share his number and I knew better than to ask.

Back at Larissa's, I scribbled a note and then went out and gassed up the Volvo. I also bought a new cell phone and stocked up on some supplies for the trip. Driving though downtown Moscow in the direction I hoped led to the highway going east, toward Tula, I recognized some of the buildings—as far as I could tell I was near the Arbat, where Mimi had taken me shopping only a few days ago.

I knew that even if Yellow Shirt had failed to steal the money and the *Obchak* was still sitting inside that artillery shell, my chances of successfully backtracking through the woods to retrieve it were slim to none. Frantically, I ran through a mental checklist of possible ways I could obtain the money without going on this fool's errand. My credit card had a limit of $10,000 and was already maxed out. My mother barely got by on her Social Security and Uncle Jake's gambling habit had gobbled up his savings long ago. Thirty thousand dollars was probably chump change to the *vory,* who were demanding its return as a matter of honor. To me it might as well have been a million.

Traffic was heavy, and I wouldn't have noticed the tail if the driver of the dark green Ford Focus hadn't been so keen. He changed lanes in tandem with me several times, prompting me to keep tabs on him. Then a second Focus, a black one, joined the game by covering the lane to my left.

I swerved to the right and zigzagged through a maze of residential streets, desperately searching for a place to stash the Volvo. A furniture delivery truck was parked in a driveway, and I squeezed in behind. Just as I got out of the car, the green Focus sped by and squealed into a U-turn. I cut through a short alley that came out onto the wide expanse of a tree-lined boulevard. Fast-walking down the sidewalk, I was about to duck into a market for cover when I saw the entrance to a pedestrian underpass and decided that would be a better move.

I ran down the stairs, almost knocking down a slim girl in jeans and high heels who cursed me out in Russian. "*Izvenitzye!* Excuse me!" I called over my shoulder and plunged into the tunnel, slowing my pace to blend in with a crowd milling past artists at their easels and old women selling tiny kittens, kerchiefs, and fresh baked goods. I reached the far end of the passageway, confident that I'd avoided the web. Unfortunately, the spider waited at the top of the stairs, small craters sculpted into his face, an athlete's physique, and the outline of his shoulder holster visible beneath the milky blue of his tracksuit jacket. He grabbed my arm just as the black Focus pulled up alongside.

I was to be kidnapped in broad daylight with no one on the busy street seeming to notice or care. I tried to break free from my captor, hoping to make enough of a scene that someone would remember seeing a hysterical American woman being forced into a car near the Arbat. Right then the driver of the Focus leaned out the window and flipped open his wallet to show me his badge. "*Militsiya,*" he said. "You must come."

Seen from outside, the brown stone facade of 38 Petrovka had little in common with the smooth concrete walls of Manhattan's One Police Plaza, except for a foreboding presence that transcended architectural style. I was escorted through security and into a windowless room where a bored-looking woman wearing rubber gloves took my photograph and fingerprints, providing a wet paper towel afterward to wipe off the ink. My next stop was a large but spartan office on the third floor. Major Desho of the Moscow Criminal Police came out from behind his desk to introduce himself. He stood at about five-ten, a handsome man with a swarthy complexion and trim black mustache that made me wonder to which of Russia's many ethnic groups he belonged. My guess was Assyrian.

Desho's English was as polished as his laced-up black boots, and, unlike some of the New York cops I'd met, he didn't bother to hide the intelligence in his eyes. He offered me a seat before returning to the executive chair behind his desk. "I was still a young trainee when Feydor Marov left for America," he said, "but I knew him well enough to appreciate how hard he worked, how dedicated he was. Which is why I was so upset to hear from the Tula police that his body had been found in the woods." The Major paused to wipe his glasses, and I could see that his grief was genuine.

"And now you turn up in Moscow in his Volvo—it was a rental, so you see . . ." He shrugged his shoulders in emphasis of the inevitability of his conclusions.

I had a flash of what it would be like to permanently occupy a cell in Vladimir Central Prison, endless legal appeals from Silas Harding falling on deaf ears, my own government unwilling to help someone already facing felony charges back home.

"We're conducting some tests, and we will have the results soon. Meanwhile, you can tell me why you came to Russia."

I told him the truth. This was no time to prevaricate. And although my story seemed outlandish, even to me as I told it, Desho gave no sign of disbelief. On the contrary, he nodded in agreement when I mentioned where the *Obchak* was buried. "They found the artillery shell. Interesting hiding place. What is even more unusual is that the Tula police turned over the money to the Moscow Organized Crime Squad." Apparently there were more honest policemen in the new Russia than he had counted on.

The Major's phone rang, and he listened for a while. "The

ballistics tests have ruled out the Nagant we found in the woods as the murder weapon, Ms. Epstein. However, you still need to explain the presence of your fingerprints."

Feydor. Even in death you're the master of the frame. "Just before Marov was shot he threatened me and I tried to take the gun away." The major thought this over for a while.

"Can you give me one reason I should let you go, Ms. Epstein? You spin a good story, but you were driving a car stolen from a murdered man and your fingerprints were found on a weapon that had been recently fired. I'm afraid I have no choice but to detain you."

"What if I had something to give you that would change your mind?"

"I know what you Americans think about the Russian police. That we are all unclean handed. I am not like that, Ms. Epstein. And, whatever else he may have done after he left the Criminal Police, Feydor Marov took no bribes. He was a conscientious policeman who put in a lot of overtime. We did that in those days. Now is a different story—the police are lazy, to them it is only a job. It is the criminals who benefit."

"You don't understand. I need that thirty thousand dollars. If I don't return it, the *vory* will kill my stepfather. What I can offer you in return is a chance to bust a ring of weapons dealers and earn the undying gratitude of the Russian government." This got his attention, and I repeated what Marov had told me about the upcoming transaction between the *vory* and the Chechen rebels, everything except the location and name of the factory.

"For all we know, the armaments have already been delivered," he said.

"I don't think so. According to Marov, it was going to happen on Tuesday—that's tomorrow."

Desho picked up the phone and talked in Russian for a while.

When he finished the call, he said, "You have an arrangement. But you will need to stay here for a while, until we—"

"Not a chance!" I interrupted. "My father's life is at stake. You must take me *and* the money with you to Ivanovo. Afterward, I'll need a special escort back to Moscow so I can meet the six P.M. deadline, and then a ride to wherever it is that they've taken Nikolai."

I was taking a chance by dictating these terms—he could easily choose to throw me in a cell until I coughed up the information he needed—but Tuesday was fast approaching, and I could see he was hooked. After a few more phone consultations, the Major informed me that I would accompany him to Ivanovo. "You're sure of this information?" he asked, as we walked out of the building toward his car. "I've called out a special squad. My boss will not be happy if we have built a house on sand."

"And my stepfather will be dead," I reminded him. The fact that we were equally vulnerable seemed to reassure him, but it didn't do much for me.

As we drove north in Desho's Hyundai, I asked him what he could tell me about Feydor Marov.

"On a personal level, not much. He kept to himself and there were some who said he had a chip on his shoulder." If there was a grand prize for understatement, this one was worthy.

"Professionally speaking, Marov specialized in organized crime, in particular the *vory-v-zakonye*—thieves-in-law. He accused the police of according them too much respect. I recall him saying that one criminal was the same as the next and we should prosecute the *vory* more vigorously. The trouble was, in those days the thieves controlled the entire black market and without them you could not get parts for your car or meat for your table. Every factory had both a legal and illegal shipping department. Just like the plant in Ivanovo we will visit shortly.

But Feydor insisted on following the book. He conducted so many raids that we were all sure he would be blown up before any of his cases came to trial. Luckily for him, he was recruited by your country as part of an exchange program in the 1980s. Leaving Russia may have saved his life. Up until now, that is. He did not stay in contact, but I heard he got married."

Please tell my wife I love her. She is my treasure.

Had Marov thought he could wreak havoc on two continents and simply return to life as usual, Sundays in the park and all that? Or had he known he'd never see her again?

Major Desho parked the Hyundai across the road from the factory. He told me that his team had taken their positions in the field several hours before. "If you move even one foot away from this vehicle during the operation, our deal is canceled. Is that clear?" He waited for me to indicate my compliance, then reached into the glove box and handed me a pair of binoculars. "Watch and enjoy." Walking away, his deliberately casual stride said to anyone watching *this is no big deal for someone as capable as me.*

At nine A.M. a large white truck backed up to the loading dock. The driver remained in the cab for what seemed like an interminable time, in no hurry to pick up the boxes waiting for him on the platform. When he did emerge, it was obvious even from a distance that he had no problem lifting and loading the cargo into the back of his vehicle. To me this indicated that the boxes contained only clothing, as befitted a textile factory. Major Desho must have agreed, because the truck was allowed to depart the complex undisturbed.

Noon came and went, the only entertainment provided by the powerful lenses of the field glasses magnifying the strain taking hold of Desho's face. At two o'clock, a minivan parked across the road, and two policemen came out of hiding to unload boxes of bottled water and a dozen lunch-sized bags that made my stomach growl. Always the gentleman, the Major crossed to the car, gifting me with a soggy but edible bologna and cheese sandwich. I reminded him of the six P.M. deadline Priest had set for returning the *Obchak* and asked if there was any chance of his giving me the money right then. As expected, he strongly rejected this option. "I am nobody's jester," he said.

"It's nobody's *fool,* and I'm not trying to trick you," I said, my point being proved when, at three o'clock, Squint and his cohorts arrived in a cloud of dust kicked up by two Toyota pickups. The six men entered the factory and within minutes came out again and got to work stacking heavy wooden crates on the loading dock that had been under surveillance all day. A half hour later the hissing sounds of air brakes announced the arrival of a semi truck. Through the field glasses I observed three pairs of muscular men turn themselves into human forklifts, pushing the hefty crates up a ramp and into the gaping interior of the big rig.

Desho let them sweat it out for a bit, choosing the perfect moment to project his voice at maximum volume over the loudspeaker. I don't know what he said, but it was menacing enough to trigger a universal flight response almost comic in its intensity. Smugglers scattered in all directions. Not one of the racing cartoon figures was quick enough to escape the police, and to my surprise, not one shot was fired. A picture-perfect police raid.

Within ten minutes all of the smugglers were lying facedown on the ground. The only exception was Squint, who argued furiously with Major Desho, their animated faces filling the field of vision in my binoculars. Whatever Squint had to say must have been convincing, because suddenly the Major threw up his hands in disgust and walked away. Behind him I could see the *vor* yelling at his men, who in one disordered motion rose to their feet and resumed loading the crates on the truck.

In disbelief, I watched as a dozen policemen returned to their cars and drove off. Desho came over and got into the Hyundai. "You were right about one thing. The delivery was scheduled for today. But the purchaser is not Chechen. There is nothing we can do."

"I don't understand. It's illegal to sell contraband. What difference does it make who buys it?"

Desho snorted in disgust, either at my naiveté or the obvious absurdity of the situation. "Yes, if it were allowed, we might recover enough arms and explosives to blow up half of Tbilisi. But we cannot touch these men or confiscate the weapons they will sell to the foreign minister of Abkhazia."

"I don't understand."

"The so-called Republic of Abkhazia is a country that exists only in the eyes of Russia. Abkhazia wants help from Russia to defend itself against Georgia."

"So?"

"You are a typical American, ill-informed about the world. Suppose that California were to secede from your country and declare itself a republic. This is what Georgia did. Then imagine that Los Angeles, like Abkhazia, declared itself independent of California—in our case Georgia—and sought the help of the United States in defending itself. Our politicians do not want the world to know they have been sending Abkhazia weapons to be used against Georgia."

"And this means what?"

"It means that if I interfere with this shipment I will lose much more than my job." He nodded at the truck fully loaded with weapons. "Nothing changes."

"So you are backing out of our deal?"

The Major shook his head indignantly. "We made a bargain. I will drive you back to Moscow myself." A fine offer, but

Priest's deadline was now impossible to meet, and even if I returned the *Obchak* to his captors, Nikolai's life was forfeit. He would die because Marov had given me the wrong information and because, even with the Russian police on my side, I had failed to find a weakness in the *vory* that I could use to my advantage. Or maybe not . . .

"Major Desho, is it true that the *vory* take an oath not to join the army or collaborate with the government in any way?"

"Yes, those of them who still adhere to the code."

"What about Priest?"

Desho smiled. He knew what I was getting at. "You're right. Priest is of the old guard, and Squint has violated a prime directive. The consequences for him could be dire." The Major's quaint expression seemed appropriate for describing criminal rules of conduct that were forged in the late nineteenth century. "Maybe if our young policemen were as dedicated to law and order as the *vory* are to their rules and regulations, our crime rate would not be reaching the sky."

I waited impatiently while Desho put the pressure on Squint. When the policeman returned, he looked pleased with himself. "Squint will help us locate your father in return for my keeping Priest in the dark about his activities on behalf of the Russian government."

I would never understand the intricacies of the *vory* code or the convolutions of Russian politics, but no matter—after wandering around for days, blindfolded and lost in a maze, I had apparently found my way out.

I stepped out of the Major's car, and he handed me the *Obchak*. It was hard to believe that this unpretentious package had caused so much death and destruction. To my relief, the money inside was as well preserved as its ancient oil-cloth wrapper.

"I wish I could accompany you to your journey's end, but it is better I do not."

"Much as I enjoy your company, Major Desho, I imagine your face is too famous among the *vory.*"

He smiled at the compliment. "I am happy to say that one of my men has volunteered. Private Taksa speaks some English, and he knows the area well. He is also a new recruit and won't be 'made' by the *vory.*"

I grinned at the Major. He had finally nailed down an Americanism.

"When you make contact with the *vory,* you will be on your own. There can be no official involvement by Moscow Criminal Police in the payment of a ransom." Desho winked at me and then summoned a fair-haired, blue-eyed youth in plainclothes who shook my hand. Taksa smiled vaguely, but his arrogant slouch made it plain how grateful I should be for the favor of his company.

The Major walked us over to a dark blue Renault. Squint was hunched down in the back seat. He looked dejected, but in the manner of a losing politician rather than a felon, if you didn't count the handcuffs. "He will remain in Taksa's custody until your father is free," the Major explained.

Taksa took the wheel and I got in beside him. I rolled down the window so that Desho could reach in and shake my hand. *"Udachi,"* he said. "Good luck."

As Private Taksa drove past the abandoned houses of the Kostroma region, potent symbols of Russia's decline in population and the dissolution of the old economic system, my belief that I would find Nikolai alive began to waver. We were two hours past the deadline, and it had been four days since I had last seen my stepfather at the Monastery of St. Euthymius. I imagined Ruth's face collapsing as I told her that her husband was dead because I'd failed to get to him in time.

It was early evening, and with its unlit streets pounded by

heavy sheets of gray rain Isupovo had the look of a ghost town. The only visible sign of life was a lone plume of smoke wafting up from the chimney of a log house high up on the hillside.

Squint mumbled something in Russian that prompted Taksa to pull off the road and kill the engine. "Give it to me," he said.

"That's OK. I can deliver it myself," I responded, tightening my hold on the bulky package. Taksa reached over and made a grab for the *Obchak*. I tugged at the door handle—my relief at hearing a sharp click changing to shock when it registered that the sound had actually been made by the safety catch of his gun. The firearm, pointed straight at my heart, seemed to occupy the entire cramped space of the Renault. A sharp mental picture of being shot in the back kept my flight response in check. "Give it to me," Taksa repeated. "Or I will—"

A choking sound replaced whatever words he might have used to threaten me. Squint had thrown his arms over Taksa's head, yanking back hard on the chain connecting the handcuffs to cut off the policeman's air supply. With one hand, Taksa tugged frantically at the metal crushing his larynx. With the other he continued to clutch the gun, his face growing red, struggling for a breath that would never come. The pistol wavered back and forth, Taksa holding on even as the light faded from his eyes. One twitch of his finger would send a bullet slamming into my chest. Seeing his blond head slump forward, I started to grab the gun, then pulled back, afraid that if I touched the weapon it would fire. A second later a deafening explosion shattered the window behind me and my left arm seemed to catch fire. "Shit!" I yelled, as Taksa fell back on the seat, dropping the Nagant on the floor.

I retrieved the gun, shoved the door open and got out of the car. Examining the left sleeve of my denim jacket, I found no blood, but when I touched the area around my bicep the pain shot clear down to my fingertips.

Squint emerged from the back of the Renault. Was his wry smile sinister or bemused? It could go either way.

"Let me see your arm."

These were the first words I had heard him speak in English. I gratefully accepted and stood very still as, in spite of the impediment of the handcuffs, he performed the delicate task of extricating my left arm from the tight-fitting sleeve. While trying to keep my cries to a minimum, I bit my lip, which only made it worse.

The wound turned out to be a deep graze, rapidly swelling but not traumatic—the bullet having saved its most lethal effect for the car window. Squint hunted around in the Renault's glove compartment and found a dull silver flask. "One hundred proof," he warned, giving me a second to grit my teeth before he splashed the wound, and my arm went up in flames. In the States, an unmarked police vehicle might have carried a flask of whiskey, but it would also have been equipped with a first aid kit. Lacking this amenity, we made do.

A movement on the hillside caught my eye. Someone had appeared on the porch of the house, no doubt prompted by the gunshot. Squint followed my gaze. "I'll go," he said.

"Not without me."

He held out his wrists, bloody from the debacle with Taksa. "This is not the time to argue. Will you help me find the key?" Squint had saved my life, there was no denying that. But in the process he had also saved his own—Taksa would not have left a witness. And given what the *vor* had already accomplished while restrained, I had no idea what he might be capable of doing if set free.

"I gave you up to the police. How do I know you won't decide to take revenge?"

He answered without hesitation. "We are the same, you and I. With us, family comes first. Everything you have done has been to help your stepfather, and you are not even related by blood. I respect you for this."

It took me a while to get up the gumption to re-enter the car. As long as Taksa's body was out of sight, so was the reality of his murder, if that's what it had been. There's nothing like going through a dead man's pockets to bring home the reality of his demise. Fortunately, I did not have to do this. The key we needed was hanging from the ignition with the others. I unlocked Squint's handcuffs, and together we dragged the corpse of the greedy policeman out of the car and into the bushes by the side of the road.

The toothless old man who answered the door pointed the Kalashnikov at us more efficiently than might have been expected. *"Gdyeh Nikolai?"* I asked, showing him the *Obchak* but keeping it out of his reach. He pointed at the ceiling.

It was freezing upstairs, in spite of the pot-bellied stove that heated the rooms below. The attic door was unlocked and when we entered Nikolai stood up from the rickety table, where he had been writing by the light of a kerosene lamp. He looked weak and confused, and I wondered when he'd last eaten. Squint helped Nikolai down the stairs, and I followed close behind.

I presented the *Obchak* to the old man, who put it on the table before opening the front door. He stepped back and was motioning for us to pass through when his cell phone played the theme from *Mission Impossible*—another reason that I would always remember Russia as the kingdom of irony.

Whatever was said on the phone caused Toothless to reach for the Kalashnikov. I pulled Taksa's gun from behind my money belt but the old *vor* didn't seem to notice, or if he did, to care. He fired round after round point blank at Squint, who fell out the door and down the front steps, coming to rest at the bottom, his blood seeping into the dirty puddles in the driveway. Being so swift to punish their own, the *vory* would have no reason to spare an equally guilty outsider. I pulled the trigger. The bullet caught Toothless in the shoulder, just as I intended, knocking him across the room like a rag doll as Nikolai pulled me outside and slammed the door.

Running down the steps, Nikolai stumbled and I caught him before he could fall on the ill-fated Squint's lifeless body. Then we were both in the car. I risked a look back at the house as I started the engine. The front door remained shut—it looked like we'd make our getaway. But as I squealed onto the highway, I spotted a black Mercedes in the rearview mirror. It pulled into the driveway behind us and then turned around in pursuit.

CHAPTER TWENTY-TWO

"How could the *vory* have found out so soon that Squint had cooperated with the police?"

"There is no time to be asking questions," Nikolai yelled at me. "Get us to Suzdal. I have an idea."

But getting to Suzdal was not going to be easy. The Mercedes had a lot of weight behind it, and within a mile it had closed to just a car length away. It was almost dark, but in the rearview mirror I made out Priest's face at the wheel, and someone next to him, maybe Buzz. Another few seconds and they made contact, pushing the tail of the Renault from the right side.

I kept my foot off the brake as we spun around and suddenly found myself looking into a stream of oncoming traffic. Jamming the transmission into reverse I backed us off the road just in time. My wounded arm sent up flares of painful protest. The Mercedes had disappeared in the other direction—no doubt Priest was hoping we'd been smashed by the westbound traffic.

If I could get us back on the highway, we had a chance. Not so if the rear tires continued to spin uselessly in the mud. Nikolai got out of the car, and with him pushing—god only knows how in his frail state—I was able to get traction. In a moment he was back in, and we headed east. It took them a while, but the crack of the back windshield shattering into a million pieces signaled that our pursuers had turned around and found us once again.

"Left turn!" shouted Nikolai, and without thinking I obeyed, skidding the car into the other lane and narrowly missing a tanker truck that blared its horn as we bounced over the high shoulder and drove through a wheat field, the plants rustling like a windstorm against the sides of the speeding car.

I risked a look over my shoulder, but the rain obscured everything behind us.

"There are buildings on the other side of the field," said Nikolai, his voice warbling with every bump in the dirt. "It's the Museum of Peasant Life."

He directed me toward a grouping of wooden peasant houses, or *izbas*, located across the road from a convent. The houses, windmills, and churches (their onion domes cleverly painted to disguise the wood as mock silver) were all painstaking replicas of the originals, surrounded by wooden walls, like the Russian villages of old. The place looked deserted.

"The tourists will not be back until morning," Nikolai said as I parked the car and followed him into a barn attached to one of the houses. We climbed into the loft. My upper arm was throbbing at twice the rate of my heart, and I was too exhausted to ask even one of the thousands of questions crowding my mind. As we rested on the straw, the rain pattering on the skylight, what came to mind were the serfs, Jews, Czarists, maybe even Bolsheviks who had at some time been forced to hide out, perhaps in a twelfth-century barn just like this one. I wondered if any of *them* had survived to tell the tale.

It was cold in the loft, but what made me tremble was the thought of my jacket, lying in the middle of a road just feet away from the corpse of the man Major Desho had trusted to protect me. It was small comfort that the contusions on his neck would be linked to the handcuffs used to strangle him, thereby implicating Squint in his death. I knew enough about the eccentric nature of Russian justice to place small confidence in the power of logic to influence it.

"Nikolai, we need to leave the country as soon as possible."

He had so many sarcastic responses to choose from: *Thanks to you, we'll have to hire some smugglers to get us out. But no, that's impossible, since all criminals who come near you drop like flies—Maybe we can get help from the authorities, but no, that won't work either since you're implicated in the death of two of their own.* I was just getting started on my list of self-recriminations when I was interrupted by the feel of something soft being draped over my shoulders. Nikolai had gifted me with his coat.

"I'm Russian—I can deal with the cold," he said. He would never be one for sentimental drivel, but the gruffness in his voice expressed concern well enough.

"I have had plenty of time to think about the way I treated you."

The setting was surreal—a hayloft straight out of a movie set—but the tone of repentance in my stepfather's voice seemed real.

"Look, we're both lucky to have a future. Let's not waste it reliving the past."

"That's the trouble with you Americans. You have no respect for history. There are things that can happen from which no country is exempt." He was beginning to sound like Feydor Marov, but I didn't say so. He stared up at the skylight as he spoke, making it impossible to tell if he was sharing his story with me or the stars.

"My father was Yevgeny Sadekov. I don't remember the last time I said his name aloud. He was a Red commissar in the civil war and then a hero resisting the Nazis. A loyal general. Perhaps he had too many medals on his chest or maybe Stalin was tired of his face, I'll never know. 'If there is no person, then there is no problem'—that was Koba's favorite saying.

"It was 1952 and I was fourteen years old. I came back from

a walk in the country and my sister told me they had taken both him and my mother in a black-raven car. I asked Olga why she herself had been spared and she said she had no idea. For many years I was convinced that she had betrayed us."

I thought of Olga's stricken face as she recalled her brother's past treatment of her and his suspicions, but I held my peace, afraid that if I interrupted him, Nikolai would stem the tide of his revelations.

"The next day I was picked up by two men at the conservatory. Like everyone else, my music teachers turned out to be cowards. They stood around like idiots and watched while the *Cheka* agents pushed me into a car. I was taken to the Home for Children of Enemies of the People, where we were taught that the state was the only parent we would ever need and our naïve notions of love and family were systematically destroyed. My sister Olga never visited me at the Home, not even once. I'm sure she had her reasons."

At this point, it was impossible not to comment. "I went to her house, Nikolai, the day after I flew into Moscow. She said she did try to visit you, that she brought food but was not permitted to see you. She also said she sent you many letters in America, all of them unanswered."

Nikolai picked some straw off his sleeve while he thought about this. "Before I left New York I read all the letters my sister sent that I had left unopened. I decided they were filled with lies to ease her guilt but now it seems I was wrong about that too. How could I have been so stupid?" He was speaking into the wall, his muffled words difficult to hear.

"When we were children she thought I did not appreciate how she looked after me when all she wanted was to be out playing with her friends, how she helped with the sewing my mother took in to pay for my music lessons, how she always made a point of saving the last piece of bread on the table for me. What Olga failed to realize was that her sacrifices made me feel like a leech and a beggar, inferior to her in every way. When our parents were arrested, I was so eager to pass judgment, to find fault with my perfect sister."

He turned to look at me, his eyes red, his lower lip trembling. "I owe Olga a lifetime of apologies," he said. "And there are also many things about which I have been less than honest with you."

He rolled up his sleeve, and there on his forearm was a single tattoo—a hand, with two of the fingers held close together and extended, as if ready to slide into the nearest unsuspecting pocket.

"Your mother thinks these fingers are preparing to pluck the strings of a violin," he said with a sad smile, "but after I escaped from the Home I fell in with a band of thieves. They were the only people who were willing to have me. They trained me first as a pickpocket and then as a train robber. They showed me how to ride in the 'dog box'—a contraption fastened to the undercarriage for transporting tools—with my head so close to the speeding ground I was sure my brain would be bashed in at the first bump in the track. Me and my partner, whose nickname was Tarzan, would stuff ourselves so tightly into the small space that we could barely breathe. We rode for hours this way, and when night fell we would pull ourselves up and enter the railcar to relieve the sleeping passengers of their valuables. Afterward we had to face the true test of our profession and jump from the moving train into the darkness.

"Who knows, I might still be a train thief had I not missed playing music so much. One day Tarzan and I were in Leningrad. We walked past the conservatory and I told him about my training on the violin and my boyhood dream of becoming a conductor. On impulse, Tarzan dragged me inside. We waited outside the practice rooms and the first unfortunate student to take a break had his violin 'liberated.' It was a cheap, beginner's model but to me it sounded like a Stradivari.

"That same afternoon, a policeman spotted us on top of a train and blew his whistle. Tarzan took a flying leap to freedom and I should have followed. But I couldn't bring myself to damage the violin. Instead, I climbed down the ladder, into the arms of the militia. And because they knew I'd escape if I was sent again to the Home, I was incarcerated in Vladimir Central."

"Where you met Feydor's father."

"Yes. Ishkhan Lamsa rescued me. I said something stupid to a cellmate of his, a ferocious Ukrainian known as Wolf. Ishkhan intervened and took me under his wing. He said I reminded him of his own son, although I was ten years older than Feydor at the time. When I told him my father had been an army general, Ishkhan decided I needed a new identity."

"Why was that?"

"Because the only people thieves hated more than stoolies were those of them who broke the code and served in the military." Nikolai shook his head at the absurdity of it all. "The *vory* were strictly forbidden to collaborate with the government."

"Judging from how they dealt with Squint, they still are."

"Don't be an idiot, Jo. The code is just an excuse for eliminating threats to their power."

Insulting as his words were, it was good to know that Nikolai's spirit had not been broken by his recent ordeal. After a while, he settled down and resumed his narrative.

"Ishkhan decided that because I was the youngest thief there and my claim to fame was riding in the dog box under the trains, my nickname would be *Pesik,* Little Dog. He protected me from the worst of his confederates and even had a guitar brought in for me to play. When my cellmates found out that I could compose songs, they began to pay me in cigarettes and food to immortalize their exploits. For them, boredom was the worst enemy, and as long as I kept them entertained I had a chance of staying alive. Ishkhan was the most senior *vor* at Vladimir, and because he vouched for me no one dared challenge my status. When he fell ill and was taken to the infirmary, I thought I was done for. But a few days later he sent for me. He told me we were going to escape and that he would take me home with him. I was overjoyed."

As Nikolai relived the memory, his eyes lit up with excitement at the prospect of freedom. I remembered what he had said to the *vory* assembled in the cell beneath the monastery.

"Was it true, what you claimed at the trial? Did Ishkhan tell you to disappear so that he could sacrifice himself and bequeath the *Obchak* to Feydor?"

"All true. I swear it. He never told me where the *Obchak* was hidden. I was merely a pawn in his game."

"Yeah, I know—it ain't you to blame."

Nikolai's blank look said he'd missed my reference to my favorite Dylan song.

"What happened next?" I prompted.

"When I returned to Moscow, one of my music teachers, Aleksei Platov, took me in. Aleksei secured papers under the fictitious name of Kharpov and sponsored my re-entry into the conservatory. I was so changed by that time that not one of my old teachers recognized me. Platov encouraged my love of conducting and I discovered that when I was in front of an orchestra the past did not exist—it was all about the future— making sure that each note was added to the next one in a way that drove the piece to its climax, to completion. I came to believe that Nikolai Kharpov was who I really was and always would be. Even that night in the elevator, events that should have brought back everything only served to push me further into denying my old self. It was as if everything that transpired was happening to someone who falsely claimed to be me. I see now that I was meant to return here, to Russia, so that I could become whole again."

"Nikolai Sadekov has a nice ring to it," I said.

He stood up and stretched, the intimate moment gone. But the fact remained. The stone that was Nikolai had at last squeezed a story out of itself. I would probably never know why he had waited so long to confide in me. Pride has its own logic.

We shared a comfortable silence in the hayloft for the next few hours, before deciding it was safe to get back on the road.

We stopped at a drug store in Suzdal, where Nikolai bought some bandages and antibiotic cream. He then directed me to a hotel with a parking area well hidden from the street. In spite of the looks the staff gave my stepfather, who needed a bath more than an astronaut on leave from the space station, I was able to book us adjoining rooms.

After Nikolai had fixed up my arm with brisk efficiency, I asked him to translate the letter that Ishkhan had left for Feydor inside the last *Matryoshka*. He read aloud from the fragile, yellowed paper, his voice softening with wonder as the meaning of the words sank in.

My Rybka,

In life we did not have much time together but you must remember always that I loved you. It is time for you to collect your inheritance. It is safely hidden in our spot in "Germany." Give enough to your mother to take care of her old age and then you must leave Tula forever. Live a long life and stay away from thieves.

Your father,
Ishkhan

Nikolai told me that Rybka was an affectionate nickname,

meaning "small fish." This meant that from the moment he read the letter, Marov had known that it was genuine and consequently that Nikolai was innocent. By that time, however, his quest for revenge had boomeranged out of control and already taken down Micah Goldman and Lenny Grimes.

"I'm going to call Ruth and tell her everything," Nikolai announced before disappearing into his room.

In the morning he told me he wanted to visit Olga before we returned to the States.

On the highway en route to Moscow, he finally asked me, "What happened in Tula between you and Feydor?"

"He's dead. As for the rest, you're better off not knowing."

"It is your privilege not to tell me, but if you ever change your mind I would like to know." That's exactly what he said, impossible as it may sound.

The few seconds it took for her to recognize Nikolai seemed to take ten years off Olga's age. Her translucent eyes examined every inch of him, seeing only what a sister can see. She reached out, and I could actually see her sweeping away their past, drawing him into the future they would share. "Kolya," she said softly.

Nikolai stroked her face and then took her hand.

"I'll see you back at the hotel," I said, not sure if either of them had heard me.

The sky had cleared, and as I drove toward downtown I could see the spires of the Kremlin in the distance. I noticed that along with the usual kebab houses and bistros there were coffee houses on almost every block—some of them recognizable chains, others independent. Black tea with sugar was still popular, which meant the country was more caffeinated than ever. A Russian bear with a speeded-up heartbeat—that's the image I'd be taking home.

Larissa had made arrangements for us to spend the night at the Marriott Courtyard and fly out of Sheremetyevo tomorrow. I looked forward to wallowing in some gun-toting American TV.

CHAPTER TWENTY-THREE

"Silas Harding is going to represent you. He's an outstanding attorney and he loves a challenge."

"Is that really necessary?"

"Yes, considering that we'll both be arrested as soon as we land in New York." A reasonable assumption, since Spinelli had APBs out for both of us.

We were flying first class, grateful that we could get tickets to New York at such short notice. The fares were as inflated as a film star's ego, but Nikolai had paid without complaint.

"What about all the new evidence we have?" he asked.

"You know as well as I do that fingerprints on a murder weapon are hard for a D.A. to ignore."

"But Marov confessed in front of witnesses."

"All he confessed to was wanting revenge. And think who those witnesses are—three crime bosses who will never set foot outside of Russia and a family member they'll accuse of perjuring herself on your behalf."

This glum conversation was interrupted by the arrival of a gourmet lunch, which we consumed with the relish of the condemned. Might as well dig into the chocolate cake and go bottoms up on the champagne. All Nikolai had to look forward to was languishing in jail while I made a last-ditch effort to find some hard evidence that would crack the case.

"I do have some leads."

"Why didn't you say so?" The old irritable Nikolai was breaking through. Probably a good thing. His subdued demeanor since our night in the hayloft had me worried.

"I'm saying so now."

"I'll tell you what. Get some results and then we'll talk."

It was dawn when our plane came to a smooth landing on American soil. It felt good to be back on familiar territory. Comforting as it was, this illusion was soon replaced by what looked like an entire platoon of police cars.

As soon as we got off the plane, Spinelli cuffed Nikolai and loaded him into the cage in the back of a squad car.

"Lucky for you that your hotshot lawyer talked my boss into cutting a deal or I'd be taking you in too." He was glowering at me, and I glared right back. Nikolai stared straight ahead. I knew what he was thinking. All those miles traveled and exorbitant expenses paid for naught. Maybe he was right.

Soaking in the bathtub was a luxury I now appreciated more than ever, after the sporadic hot water in Russia. Maybe it was the intensity of recent events or more likely my success at surviving them that made me certain there would be no more flashbacks to last year's attack.

After toweling myself off, I made a list: call my mother, contact Silas Harding about Nikolai's case, heal the breach with Hasim, catch up on some sleep before the jet lag hit.

What to do first? I called Sanyo.

"I'm sorry I didn't stay in better touch. I was pretty busy."

"Me, too. I've got a show coming up at a new gallery. I'll tell Ramón to dig your car out of storage."

We discussed getting together over the weekend. "Call me when you can see straight," he said, the only recognition that I'd returned from a 12,000-mile roundtrip.

After eating my first home-cooked meal in weeks, a tuna melt dripping with cheddar, I reached Silas at his office in Union

Square, where he put in so many hours that his workplace could have been re-zoned as a live-in loft.

"Kharpov has been charged with first-degree murder and denied bail. Flight risk." That's what I loved about Silas. No wasted words.

"I faxed the case notes you sent from Russia to the District Attorney's office and they've agreed to contact Major Desho in Moscow. If he corroborates your story, then they'll consider re-opening the murder investigation."

"Thanks Silas. I knew you'd come through for me." What I didn't say was that I had zero faith that the NYPD would look any further afield than Nikolai. Not without some new evidence.

"Think nothing of it, Jo. It's not every day that an attorney gets a chance to derail the speeding freight train of injustice. By the way, I contacted a friend in the ME's office—if I waited for the D.A. to provide discovery I'd be lucky to get the documents delivered to my grave. She read me the autopsy report on the phone. Micah Goldman had a blood alcohol level of .17 at the time of death."

This didn't sound like the brother that Rebecca described. But how many of us could pass a test on the habits of our family members?

"Silas, we've got to prove that there were three people in that elevator on the night of the murder and that Frank Mitchell killed Micah Goldman and then forced Nikolai to pump a bullet into the body."

"How are we going to do that, when two of the people involved are dead and the third is in jail?"

"I've got an idea."

"Of course you do, dear. Stay in touch."

While we'd been talking, the incoming light on my fax machine had started to blink, and by the time we were done the in-tray was full. I retrieved the cover sheet, a handwritten note:

Welcome home. Hope these help. We found them inside the door panel of Grimes's car. It was signed *HS.*

The Lieutenant had sent me three photos, all of them taken in the Avenue L Car Service parking lot, all of them grainy but with a clear story to tell. The first was a close-up of Micah Goldman, his blurred arm pounding on the hood of a car, Nikolai's face visible through the windscreen on the driver's side. The second was a pull-back of the first, showing the limo in its entirety and Rebecca Goldman with her head sticking out of the back window at an awkward angle, mouth open, obviously yelling at her brother to stop harassing Nikolai.

The third photograph was the one that gave the story a twist. It included a side view of two spectators standing in the doorway of the garage and observing the altercation. One of them was Veton Bardhi, the Avenue L dispatcher, and standing next to him was Frank Mitchell, aka Feydor Marov. At last the breaks were coming my way.

Waiting for the number 3 train I couldn't help but compare the dingy 96th Street station with the relative grandeur of the Moscow Metro. There were no chandeliers or exotic marble walls, but as we rolled into Astor Place, I decided that simple white tiles and colorful mosaics had a lot to say for themselves.

After changing trains twice, I got off at Delancey Street and walked over to Avenue B to pick up the Protégé. The day was a warm one for early November, and sun was glowing over Brooklyn like an angry pumpkin as I drove across the Manhattan Bridge. I headed south on a series of parkways to Rebecca Goldman's place in Bensonhurst. She was back in the U.S., and I was lucky enough to find her in.

Rebecca gave me a warm welcome, said she'd returned without Baranski—that he had a lot of business to take care of in Moscow. I wondered if this included going to jail after the police raided his factory in Ivanovo, but I didn't mention this because I had no way of knowing if he'd been aware of or been involved in the extracurricular activities of his factory personnel. If he had, then Rebecca would hear about it soon enough.

"I felt I owed it to you to tell you in person who it was that killed your brother," I said, overcome by an unexpected feeling of formality. And then, sitting in the cramped living room, over cups of hot mint tea, I told her what had transpired in Russia. When I finished, Rebecca thanked me through her tears. I was moved, but I also knew I had to get down to business.

"Please don't take this the wrong way, but did Micah drink?"

"Not very often. He was what you would call straight-laced. That's why he was so incensed over my working for the escort service, even though I told him there was nothing indecent going on. He had this zeal for religion that made him think of himself as an authority on how to behave. I told him, 'Just because I don't show off my piety like you do, that doesn't mean I'm a whore.' "

Maybe Rebecca's brother had wanted her to live up to his standards because he couldn't do so himself.

"Can you tell me anything about Veton, the dispatcher?"

"Veton Bardhi gives me the creeps and I will never ride in one of his cars again."

I showed her one of the pictures that Hasim had faxed. "Is this a familiar face?" I asked, pointing to Feydor.

"I saw him come into the Avenue L office a few times. He and Veton were friends, I think."

"Thanks, Rebecca. You've been very helpful."

Before I left, I asked her if I could take one of her pictures of Micah with me, and she let me take my pick.

I showed the pictures of Mitchell and Goldman to bartenders at three watering holes—*Dad's Alibi, The Brazen Keg,* and *Jessie's*

Dive—before striking gold while talking to Billie at *The Sport and Spill.* "Yeah, those two came in and put away more than most," she said. "Especially the young one. He was a rowdy drunk. Kept repeating himself, 'He won't feel a thing,' over and over again. That's not something you forget, is it?"

"No," I said, picturing how Marov must have stoked the embers of Micah's resentment until they burned with a constant flame. Imagining Micah pulling out his knife in the elevator to exact his revenge on Nikolai, the surprise on his face when Feydor turned against him. "It isn't."

I had one more stop to make, and it was the most tricky.

Veton was sitting at the same desk where I'd left him but a lot had happened since then.

"No openings. I told you I'd be in touch if anything came up. Pestering people doesn't get you hired."

"Why would I want a job here? I'm neither a fashion knock-off artist or a drug counterfeiter."

Veton sprang out from behind the desk, and we faced off. "Whatever you heard, it's a lie."

"I've got more than words—I've got photographs of hundreds of bottles of Lipitor stored in a basement that I'm sure you rented. I also have in my possession a dress with a Mantle label that I'm sure isn't included in the Baranski inventory. I'll bet you lost some stock when you had to move after Detective Grimes was murdered in the basement. Was it Frank Mitchell who warned you?"

"No! It wasn't him. I mean, no one did." Shocked at his own admission, Veton let go of my arm and stepped back. I pressed my advantage, knowing I only had a few seconds before he threw me out. "On the night Micah Goldman was murdered, Frank Mitchell needed someone to tip him off that Nikolai had returned the limo to the garage and was on his way home. My money's on you."

"What are you, a cop? If you don't have a badge, you'd better get lost!"

"I may be your last hope, Veton. I understand why you're reluctant to rat on Mitchell, but he's dead, and since it's going to come down to you or him, your choice is obvious. Provide the police with vital information in return for leniency, or go to jail as an accessory to first-degree murder."

His posture slackened; I'd clearly gotten through to him. But there was no way he'd admit it. "Do you know what my name means in Albanian? It means lightning. And that's what will strike you if you don't get out of this office!"

Midnight in Sanyo's kitchen, where Sanyo had just treated me to his specialty—baked fish and plantains, spiced with flaming green chiles. I thought of how his good luck charm had helped me make it through the night in a Russian prison. I could get used to this sensation of needing someone, as opposed to simply enjoying their company. If he felt differently, he wasn't saying.

The sex was not as transcendent as on the night we went to the Nuyurican. It was better—gentle and more down to earth, the passion punctuated by spells of laughter at how relieved we both felt, him because I'd come home safely and me because I'd found him alone in his apartment when I sprang my surprise visit.

A delicious aroma pulled me out of sleep the next morning. It was a cup of Cuban coffee that Sanyo delivered along with a goodbye kiss. "I've got to open the stand for lunch. You can take your time getting up."

I glanced at the clock and realized I'd slept for eleven hours.

"Just make sure you lock the door on your way out. I've made you a key."

Casually spoken words that jolted me to full wakefulness. A key. This was huge.

CHAPTER TWENTY-FOUR

On the day Nikolai came home, exactly one week after my return to New York, Ruth called me, her mind apparently as sharp and clear as her voice. "Thank goodness it's all over. He bought me roses, Jo. He's a new man. Please, have dinner with us tomorrow night."

I accepted the invitation, wishing I could share her joy. But there was something I needed to do before I could let go of the Goldman case. Something that had been weighing on my mind since the day I got back from Russia.

I poured a glass of courage from a bottle of Spanish port and called Hasim Saleh.

"Can you get me Detective Mitchell's address? I'd like to talk with Karen Mitchell about what happened to her husband."

"Hold on a minute."

He was back on the line sooner than I expected. "She lives on Central Park West."

Hasim had told me that Mitchell's wife came from a wealthy family, and from the tasteful red tint in her well-nourished hair to the casual elegance of her jeans and silk blouse, she was the kind of woman who impressed you without trying. I consider myself well proportioned, a belief supported by some of Sanyo's recent comments, but seeing myself reflected in the mirror on the mantelpiece next to her refined features—eyebrows sculpted in harmony with cheekbones higher than a Siamese cat's—

made me want to whittle my big bones down to size.

Although I had called ahead, she buzzed me in downstairs with less caution than was healthy for an urban dweller, much less the widow of a police officer. More of a surprise was the fact that she also failed to ask for my ID, and insisted on serving me a glass of iced tea before seating herself in the comfy upholstered chair opposite my own.

"What can I do for you, Ms. Epstein?" Her cerulean blue eyes were not puffy or bloodshot, but they did hold an expression of permanent sadness befitting a widow.

"I was with your husband when he died in Russia."

At that point the handkerchief came out. "Did he suffer?"

The paradox at the heart of my mission was encapsulated in this question, asked in a carefully controlled voice by the wife of a blackmailer and double-murderer.

"I honestly can't say, Mrs. Mitchell. What I can tell you are the words he made me promise to deliver. 'Please tell my wife I love her. She is my treasure, an innocent in all this.' "

"He never talked about his work." It was as if she hadn't heard me, or maybe the non-sequitur was a defense mechanism, a way of delaying her emotions from flooding the room until after I'd left.

"It's too bad he didn't write you a letter." I got up to leave, having fulfilled my promise to Feydor, no more, no less.

On my way to the door, I couldn't help asking, "Didn't you think something was wrong when you didn't hear from him?"

"It's quite simple, really. Frank told me he was in the Bahamas. He said he'd be cruising on his friend's boat, out of cell phone range, and that he'd call me when they were in port."

She was a terrible liar who sounded like a child reciting by rote.

"Mind if I use your bathroom?"

She nodded, and I opened the door off the foyer, assuming it was the guest bathroom. It was a closet, packed with luggage. One of the carry-alls sported a bright blue sticker with red letters, identical to the one the security personnel had attached to my bag at Sheremetyevo.

"I've been meaning to peel that off. It's left over from a trip we took to Moscow last year," Karen Mitchell said.

Looking a bit shook up, she pointed me to the bathroom door. When I came out, she had regained her composure.

"Well if that's all, I have a library fundraiser to go to," she said in her most pleasant finishing school voice. I departed with an unpleasant taste in my mouth. Probably an inevitable result of taking pity on someone like Feydor Marov. I thought about calling Aeroflot and asking if the color of the security stickers changed from year to year. Double-checking is a hard habit to break. But why dig up details on an over-and-done-with case, when I could be sharing a late fall barbecue with a sexy Fijian?

I let myself into Sanyo's apartment around seven o'clock, using my brand-new key. Last night I had reluctantly left him at ten to pull a shift at Scandal's.

He was in the kitchen, cutting up mushrooms, a bowl of marinated chicken on the sideboard. He gave me a quick kiss and a pack of matches. "Light the hibachi, I'm almost ready."

I opened the window in the living room and climbed out on the fire escape. There was a bag of charcoal and a can of lighter fluid on the window ledge, and I reached back inside to grab them, then pulled the plastic sheet that Sanyo used as a rain cover off the grill. In five minutes the coals were red hot.

Barbecuing was one of Sanyo's many passions, and after tasting the results I was an enthusiastic convert. Gnawing on a chicken leg, I checked out his latest creation, a totem pole he was in the process of painting black, green, and orange, as indicated by the three cans of spray paint on the top shelf of the bookcase cattycorner to the window.

Feeling too full to sit around after dinner, I got to work on the dishes. As I looked out the window at the pea patch garden across the street, and dried the plates in time to the Salsa rhythms pouring out of my lover's boom box, I thought what a perfect evening this is. Even washing dishes was a pleasure when you were with someone special. I didn't realize anything was wrong until I felt the knife at my throat.

"You couldn't leave it, had to show her what a decent human being you are, willing to lower yourself to carry messages from a dead criminal."

I twisted around, trying to see through the doorway behind him, not caring about the sudden pain on the side of my neck as the knife bit down, caring only about Sanyo, afraid of what might have already happened.

"I understand perfectly," said Feydor, reaching behind me for a dishtowel to wipe the blood from my neck from his arm. "I feel the same way about my wife."

He pushed me into the living room, where Sanyo was tied to a chair, his mouth taped shut.

"Losing your touch, Epstein? You should have told your boyfriend that good guys are not the only ones to flash a badge."

When he had both us securely trussed to chairs with duct tape, he sat down on the couch to enjoy himself. Not the kind of entertainment one would choose to have during life's last moments, but what choice did we have?

"If you had only waited for one more day, I would have been gone." He held the knife blade in the air, as if signaling a taxi. "A gun would be too noisy. Too bad. A shot to the head is much less painful than having your throat slit."

I wished with all my heart that I had followed my intuition instead of being so eager to close the case book.

Sanyo and I locked eyes and I felt his energy leap across the space between us. He was telling me not to surrender to fear, that I had to keep my head. I tried hard to listen.

"What is that? Barbequed chicken?" Marov walked over to the window and retrieved the hibachi, still smoking, from the fire escape, placing it on the wide sill next to the aloe vera plant. He went into the kitchen, and when I heard the sound of the window being closed I knew what his game plan was.

Just to make sure, Feydor added some lighter fluid and a few more briquettes before shutting the living room window. "So many accidental deaths from carbon monoxide. How careless of people. I'll be back later to untie you and put the finishing touches on the sad scene." He walked out the door without a backward glance.

We didn't have much time, given the heat of the coals and the small space in which we were confined. The act of breathing, praised by poets as the source of *inspiration,* was now a deadly, life-threatening reflex.

Sanyo tried wiggling toward the window, but his chair immediately toppled over, making it impossible for him to move. My chair was next to a bookcase filled with found objects that, if I didn't do something fast, would never become pieces of art. I used my elbow to nudge one of the supporting poles. It would be easy to topple this thing, but why bother when it wasn't tall enough to reach the window and break it when it fell.

My head was starting to ache and dizziness had begun to set in. At levels like the ones we were experiencing, the end could come in minutes. Sanyo was moving his head, trying to catch my eye. He kept shifting his eyes up toward the ceiling. I looked up and saw what he wanted me to do.

I jiggled the bookcase pole again, at first gently and then, as I felt myself losing consciousness, as hard as I could. The spray cans fell from the top shelf. One of them landed on the hibachi, and then I passed out.

Chapter Twenty-Five

I woke in the hospital in a state of mental confusion more profound than I'd ever experienced. A mask was fixed over my mouth with a cord leading to an oxygen tank. My stomach felt like it had been scraped by a rasp.

"You're lucky to be alive." The nurse checked my glucose drip and then took my blood pressure.

"My . . . friend. Is he alright?"

"You mean the one they brought in with you? I think so, but if you want me to, I'll check."

She was gone for a few unbearable minutes. When she came back in the room her reassuring smile restarted my heart.

"I need to call the police. Can you help me?" It took her a while to understand my speech through the mask.

"There's no need, dear. Everything's under control now."

"Call 911 and give me the freakin' phone!" I ripped the mask off my mouth. "Damn it! There's a killer on the loose!" I reached for the phone, but she was too fast for me and pulled the cord out of the wall jack. It was then that it dawned on me that she thought I was mentally unbalanced from all the carbon monoxide in my system.

"I'm a private investigator, not a deranged person. Call Lieutenant Saleh at the 42nd Precinct in the Bronx. He'll vouch for me."

The nurse remained skeptical and refused to make the call until I agreed to take a sedative. By the time she connected me with Hasim, my speech was slurring, and I was having trouble holding the receiver up to my ear. The last thing I remember before dropping off the planet again was his steady voice saying, "Don't worry, Jo. We've got it."

The morning nurse told me, as she hooked me up for the obligatory wheelchair ride out of the hospital, that the spray can that landed on the hot coals had propelled itself out the window like a torpedo and set fire to a grocery store on Avenue C.

CHAPTER TWENTY-SIX

In spite of the weather having changed overnight from mildly friendly to distinctly chilly, I drove the Protégé down Ocean Parkway with the windows wide open. Once you've had CO molecules bind to the hemoglobin in your blood and block the delivery of oxygen to your brain, you can never get enough fresh air.

I parked near Crawford's, an espresso bar that after opening in the front of a furniture store on Kings Highway had become a neighborhood hangout in minutes. After purchasing a fortifying latte, I strolled down East 15th.

Riding up in the elevator, I reflected on how my compassionate decision to tie off Feydor Marov's arm as he lay bleeding on the forest floor had come so close to costing me and Sanyo our lives. Yesterday, while sharing a taxi with him from the hospital to my apartment on the Upper West Side, I had asked Sanyo if he thought I should have acted differently. He smiled in that serious way of his. "You say you're not religious, Jo, but you did what you needed to keep your soul intact."

Now Marov himself would be a candidate for revenge—the state-sanctioned kind involving a needle. Violence—the ultimate descending spiral.

Nikolai answered the door. "She's worked her fingers to the bone, so keep your comments about her cooking to yourself."

It was like the bond we forged in Russia had never existed. Why did this man have such a need to put me at a disadvantage?

Might as well ask why kids go through the terrible twos—the ego must emerge.

Ruth had made salmon cakes, sautéed in enough oil to incinerate a vat of French fries. After dinner, I sat them both down in the kitchen and proceeded to relate, over a bottle of the same wine that Nikolai had been drinking on the night of the elevator shooting, how Veton Bardhi's phone call had made it possible for Frank Mitchell aka Feydor Marov to time his ambush in the elevator with Nikolai's arrival in the building; how Marov had gotten Micah drunk and goaded him on, giving him the knife and suggesting that he use it to frighten Nikolai and defend his sister's honor.

When I got to the part about Marov's attempt to kill both Sanyo and me, Ruth's eyes filled, first with tears and then with hatred.

"Don't worry, Mom. He's not going to hurt anyone anymore. He's in jail, awaiting indictment."

Nikolai sat in silence for a while. "Frank Mitchell was under your nose all along. Why did it take you so long to identify him as Feydor Marov?"

I stared at him in disbelief, getting ready to give him a piece of my mind, but Mom was getting visibly upset—she had read the signs and knew I was about to blow.

"I'll call you next week," I said to her. "Maybe we can take in a movie."

"I'd like that." She sounded like a shadow of her old self, but a contented shadow.

I was putting on my coat when the doorbell rang. It was Sasha, reluctantly admitted by Nikolai. Nervous but determined, he delivered his invitation. "Tatiyana Leontiev, the mezzo-soprano from Kiev who is staying with us, has agreed to perform for a group of our friends, and if you would give us the honor of your company—"

"You should have given us more notice," Nikolai grumbled.

"We'd be delighted," said Ruth.

Sasha looked at her gratefully, as if she'd been the only one to speak. "Please. If you will come with me right now."

Nikolai started to hedge, but Sasha had overcome his own perennial shyness and wasn't taking no for an answer.

"Just give me a minute to freshen up," said Ruth. She exchanged her housedress for a velvet skirt and a loose-fitting caftan, and we followed Sasha downstairs, where Ludmilla waited for us, the door held open.

Nikolai went in first, and I heard the burst of applause and laughter before I saw them surround him—a group of maybe twenty, most with gray or white hair, all of them chattering excitedly in Russian and English.

Sasha's voice rose above the rest. "It was made in Russia by Anatoly Leman. My friend Gregory left it to me when he died last month, and I've been saving it for you."

Nikolai stood motionless, rooted to the spot, until Ludmilla lost patience and pulled his right hand up to make contact with the violin.

"Don't be shy! Play us a tune!" someone shouted.

As the first resonant notes filled the room, I looked around for Ruth. She was still in the hallway, looking befuddled, but seemed to recover when she saw me. I found her a seat in a comfortable chair, upholstered in shiny silver brocade to match the glittering décor around us, and sat on the armrest as we listened to Nikolai making friends with his new instrument. Ludmilla and another pianist, a wisp of a woman visiting from Connecticut, took turns accompanying him, and soon they were joined by Tatiyana, who obligingly sang all the old songs they loved.

I was enjoying the music, which would most likely last until the wee hours, but I had promised Sanyo I'd make an early night of it. When they took a break from playing, I took my leave.

Nikolai walked me to the door. "Don't forget to put all your expenses on the bill, everything. In the end, you did a good job, but I don't want any complaints later that I ripped you off."

It was the best I'd get from him, but as long as he made my mother happy I wasn't going to quarrel with that.

Epilogue

It was seven-thirty and so far there were only two names on the sign-up sheet. Usually all the spots in the slam were spoken for by eight P.M. Then I remembered that the serious talent, the ones who competed in the finals two weeks ago for a place on the team, would be at home tonight, resting up for their upcoming trip to the nationals. Last year I had come close to making the team myself. No one was more surprised than me, and it had been fun to be in the spotlight. Until I lost that last round to Reggie Pinero.

By nine P.M. Linda—who was filling in for Elaine Elias—had chosen the judges and there were seven names on the sign-up sheet. Time to make up my mind. Linda looked disappointed when I told her I had decided to be tonight's sacrificial poet—the one who warms up the crowd and helps the judges figure out what they're doing before things get serious.

After some announcements and a ritualistic reading of the rules, Linda called me to the stage. As I got up from the table I saw Sanyo carrying over our drinks from the bar. He gave me a thumbs-up, accompanied by an encouraging smile.

I placed my voice-activated cassette recorder on the floor in front of me and used the base of the mic stand to pin a copy of the poem to the floor—my insurance against memory loss.

INDIGO

On a cliff high above the sea there lived a weaver
a woman with the patience
to grow the plants
to make the dyes
that colored the wool of her woven skies
the stories in her tapestries poured into your eyes
before you had a chance to think
some came from her years
on smoldering streets
with the smell of rotten oranges and sweet
   tobacco
others were born of lost innocence
and steeped in anger long spent

Lately, staying up nights with candles
and kerosene lamps for company
she felt a strange tugging
as she ran her shuttle
through the strands
of deep green and pale yellow as if
an invisible hand was loosening
what she would tighten
intercepting her designs so they
could not reach her fingers

so one day in late summer
she covered her loom with an old bedspread
walked to the station and boarded a train that
   pulled out and picked up speed
blending the familiar landscape

into a flow of light
she visualized moving into her chest

among the three choices
the conductor gave her
she chose Indigo
"I like the sound of that," she said
and that night the speeding darkness
was full of promise

In the morning
with a sharp intake of breath
she stepped from the train to a platform
painted just the shade of blue-green-black she
   had expected
she loved the sound of her boot heels
tapping on the old planks
under the shade of the mountains
overlooking Indigo
it was a town as blue as fresh chalk on a gritty
   sidewalk
blue as her first silk dress
painted with horses
blue as a bruise
turning slowly to lavender
a color with a scent
captured in a brown bottle
soft lavender worn as a child
billowing over a black patent
leather road running
through a burnt orange field near Main Street

where green money crumples
and passes from fist to pocket
and unsuspecting girls played basketball
their fingernails coated
with silver and red
bright as brake lights sneaking
down the highway
to the place where Indigo ended
and houses gave way to cacti and sky
where all the colors
were burned and purified in miles
of hot sun
covering the trail
with a soft blanket of ebony
shining black as skin in the African twilight

The house grew quiet and I slowed down my delivery as I went for the finish.

and then the moon rose to scour
the pigments from her eyes
replacing them with
banner headlines
scratched in un-listening rock
the force of their gravity
turning her inside out
her body responding
like a sun gone nova
her fingers streaming with colors
and she a whirling wind
a weaver desperate to rejoin

just a few pieces of a world
broken even as it was formed

she spent the night in a hotel
kept awake by footsteps on the rickety porch
lit a candle that flickered to a knock on the door
"come in," she said
to her neighbor from back home
the one with the sheep
that roamed the hillside near her house
she took the soft tangled wool he carried
and pressed it against her face
already thinking of how she would gather
the plants and mix the dyes.

My lowest score was a five, the highest a nine point two, leaving a seven and two eights for a total of twenty-three. A good beginning.

ABOUT THE AUTHOR

Joyce Yarrow has worked as a screenwriter, lounge singer, multimedia performance artist and, most recently, as a member of a world music vocal ensemble that performs in eighteen languages. Her short stories have been widely published, and she is the author of two other works of fiction: *Ask the Dead* and *The Ring of Truth.*

Raised in the southeast Bronx, Ms. Yarrow resides with her husband and son in Seattle.